ZORA
BOOKS HER
Happy Ever After

Taj McCoy

mira

mira™

ISBN-13: 978-0-7783-3352-4

Zora Books Her Happy Ever After

For questions and comments about the quality of this book, please contact us at CustomerService@Harlequin.com.

Mira
22 Adelaide St. West, 41st Floor
Toronto, Ontario M5H 4E3, Canada
BookClubbish.com

Printed in U.S.A.

Praise for *Zora Books Her Happy Ever After*

"...IcCoy expertly crafts a well-balanced love triangle between
...npathetic and passionate characters—and delivers plenty of comic
...ief in the form of Zora's lovable matchmaking grandmother. Readers
...ll delight in cheering on this strong heroine."
                                    —*Publishers Weekly*, starred review

"...beautiful love letter to Washington, D.C., #BlackLove, and cozy
...ookstores.... Taj McCoy serves up heart, humor, and spice that
...mance readers have come to expect [and] an added mystery that's
...re to delight fans."   —Charish Reid, author of *The Write Escape*

"...ooks, humor and two handsome men vying for bookstore-owner
...ra's affections, what more can you want in a story? *Zora Books Her*
...ppy Ever After* is the perfect read!"
                —Catherine Adel West, author of *The Two Lives of Sara*

"...ne love McCoy has for literature, D.C. and Black women winning is as
...thentic as the first editions Zora collects and the two fine Black men
...ng for her heart. Pour yourself a drink and kick your feet up with this
...e because McCoy delivered!"
                            —Lane Clarke, author of *Love Times Infinity*

"...j McCoy delivers a love triangle that romance fans will go gaga for...
...artfelt, hilarious, and deliciously sexy."
                        —Sarah Echavarre Smith, author of *On Location*

"...this mouth-watering and mysterious romance, Taj McCoy champions
...ters, celebrates culture, and honors womanhood...all while tempting
...u with the very best guilty pleasure vibes."
                            —Kai Harris, author of *What the Fireflies Knew*

"...cCoy's snappy dialogue, witty banter, and sizzling love scenes tackle
...icky feat: a convincing love triangle.... Taj McCoy is an author to
...tch!"   —Danielle Jackson, author of *The Accidental Pinup*

"...elightful and perfectly paced. Simply put, this book is magic."
                        —Allison Ashley, author of *Would You Rather*

"...oved Zora's fierce commitment to her community, her family, and her
...nds, but what really sizzled was Zora's chemistry with both men as
... decided which path would lead to her happily ever after. A sexy,
...rming rom-com!"   —Farah Heron, author of *Kamila Knows Best*

Also by Taj McCoy

SAVVY SHELDON FEELS GOOD AS HELL

For Lane, my favorite bibliophile and writing compass.
For chosen family and dream chasers of all ages.

ZORA
BOOKS HER
Happy Ever After

1

"Well, is he attractive? You know I don't want no ugly great-grandbabies."

"Granny!" Zora laughed, pulling books from the stocking cart to arrange on the shelving display for the storefront window. The sun poked through the cloudy morning, threatening to scorch another early September day. Opus Northeast had been open for less than fifteen minutes, and its owner was already rolling her eyes. Silly her for making the mistake of mentioning the man who hit on her as she walked from her parked car into the store. "There's no such thing as an ugly baby."

Granny Marion shook a ruby-red fingernail at her granddaughter. "Now, I know I taught you better than that. Ain't no reason to lie, baby. You know good and well that the li'l girl two doors down from you has one, bless his heart."

Zora stifled a snort as she stacked middle-grade fantasy books next to some young-adult ones. Stories of witches, magic, and other worlds rich in cultural traditions and majesty. Running her fingers over the foiled titles of their hardcover jackets, she pictured her younger self staring into the window in awe, ready to devour each word in the safety of her cozy bedroom fort. Her parents would shake their heads in amusement before turning her loose in the children's section. She'd beg to take home every new story that she hadn't previously spent hours poring over, eventually convincing her parents to allow her a new armful. "That baby is cute. He just has a big head."

"Hmmph. I think the word you're looking for is *oblong*. And why are his eyes so big?" Granny Marion widened her eyes until they bulged behind her wire-rimmed glasses, her taut brown skin hugging high cheekbones and a proud forehead. Her long, salt-and-pepper hair twisted neatly into a bun at the nape of her neck—a nostalgic reminder of her past as a professional dancer turned dance teacher. Every move of her petite frame flowed with grace and intention, even when she ridiculed their neighbor's newest family addition.

"Granny." Zora squeezed out from the window front, smoothing her hands over her shapely figure clad in her usual skinny jeans, camisole and cardigan—today's was hip length and plum colored. She loved a layered look, and her sweater matched her matte lipstick perfectly. "I'm sure he'll grow into his features as he gets older." She leaned down to kiss her grandmother on the cheek. "Remember, I had to grow into my smile—I had that awful headgear the orthodontist made me wear."

For her entire fifth grade year, Zora had been plagued with jeers and jokes about the metal contraption affixed to her upper jaw to help with her overbite. Her only reprieve was when she ate, but even then, her classmates would tease Zora about her protruding front teeth. She'd sit with her closest friends on benches outside to avoid the meanest kids posted up at tables in the cafeteria.

Granny Marion kissed her granddaughter back, eyes sparkling. "Mmm-hmm, I remember. That gear gave you character. But there ain't no headgear to fix a misshapen head, baby."

"Jesus." Zora shook her head, unable to hide her smile. She grabbed Granny's hand, entwining their arms, and led her farther into the store. "So what are your plans for today?"

They walked past rows of bookshelves, display tables full of must-read paperbacks, and the checkout counter to a large corner filled with comfortable furniture for patrons to enjoy their purchases. Four-top tables lit with antique desk lamps were often filled with college students studying or local writers needing a change of venue. Against the farthest wall stood a coffee kiosk operated by a local Black-owned coffee shop and bakery. "I'm going to grab myself a latte and a breakfast bagel before I enjoy today's newspaper."

Granny Marion visited the store daily without fail, only deviating slightly from her routine when the Kerri's Coffee kiosk sold holiday-inspired treats and she craved a holiday spice latte with a splash of eggnog instead of her regular skim latte. From open to close, Granny was often the one constant, greeting patrons, playing with kids, sharing her favorite reads and best cake recipes and reading her morning paper. She set her newspaper down on her favorite plush, high-backed chair in the reading corner, winking at the barista as they neared the coffee kiosk. "Hey there, young man, how you doin' today?"

As they approached, Brian, a shy college sophomore, circled in front of the kiosk to wrap his arms around her. "Good morning, Ms. Marion. I'm doing good. How you doin'?" He waved at Zora. "Hey, Z."

"What up, B?" Zora slapped him five and grabbed her usual from the counter—a raspberry cheese Danish and an oat milk latte. Before she could grill Brian about his upcoming calculus exam, the bell on the front door jingled. She raised her latte in thanks, and left her grandmother to chat. On Zora's way to the front, she picked up a folded paper towel from the floor and chucked it into a waste bin. "What's this doing here?"

Rushing in with several bags in her hands and flushed cheeks was Emma, Zora's best friend and roommate. Her box braids were swept up into a high bun and framed by a colorful head wrap. Big hoop earrings barely skimmed the shoulders of her chambray dress shirt, which was tied at the waist over a colorful pleated skirt. "*Girl*. It's already hot out there—I'm sweating! Now, don't get mad. I know I'm late."

Zora bit into her Danish and chewed, waiting. "I'm not mad." *Ain't nothin' new.*

"It's just that, I don't even know how to tell you this…" She shoved her bags into a cabinet under the checkout counter, clenching and releasing her hands as she shuffled from one foot to the other nervously.

Zora sipped her latte, side-eyeing her friend. Nothing was new about these antics. "Rip the Band-Aid off, Em."

She blew out a breath, grimacing. "I think I lost the inventory tablet. I couldn't find it last night. It wasn't in any of my bags or at home. I am so, so sorry. If we can't find it, I promise I'll pay for a replacement." Emma wrung her hands. "I'm kinda hoping you can do your Zor-lock Holmes thing and help me retrace my steps."

Emma lost everything. Back when they were college roommates, she lost her dorm keys the day she moved in. She lost her car in parking lots, lost her water bottle at yoga, and lost good wigs on multiple occasions when there was no logical reason for them to have been removed in the first place. One time she lost her date, which Zora never let Emma live down. Emma tried organizing differently, or keeping a note on her phone so that she knew where she parked, but then she'd lose her phone. Their freshman year Zora spent all of her free time retracing Emma's steps to find her lost items, eventually printing instructions to call Zora onto adhesive labels to stick onto most of Emma's property for the next time it went missing. They used Emma's number originally, but she lost her phone more than anything else that she owned.

Chewing on a bit of Danish, Zora interlaced her fingers, pushing her palms out in front of her to stretch her arms before shaking them out at her sides. She tilted her head side to side, cracking her neck. "Okay, so you stayed to do inventory last night. What section were you working on?"

"Cookbooks." Emma bit her lip.

Zora pulled her lips into her mouth, pressing them together as she nodded. "What did you eat for dinner?"

"I bought a chicken wrap from Brian, but then I wanted French fries, so I grabbed some duck fat fries from next door." The bistro next door boasted New American cuisine with a hefty price tag.

"Ooo, I love those." *Now I want some.*

"Right? They're perfection." Emma brought her fingertips to her mouth, kissed them and splayed them wide.

"Hmm." Zora sipped her latte thoughtfully. *This is too easy.* "Did you check the bathroom? On top of the paper towel dispenser."

Emma frowned, hugging her arms over her stomach. "Why would I check the bathroom? This isn't like that time I ate those deep fried Oreos..."

Zora giggled. "I promise you, I wasn't thinking of the day you blew up the bathroom. Honestly, I'd rather forget that one. Just go check."

In a huff, her friend turned on her heel, walking back toward the coffee kiosk. "Hey, B! I'll be right back for my coffee." The bathroom door opened. "What the— *How?*" Emma rushed back, tablet in hand, mouth wide open. "How did you know it would be in the bathroom?" She plugged it into a charger hidden behind the counter and grabbed the backup, which was fully charged.

Zora sipped her latte, serving enough suspense to make her friend bounce with anticipation. "You had a chicken wrap and then ordered duck fat fries. You brought the food over to the cookbook section, but you always forget napkins, so you went to the bathroom. You carried the tablet with you, because you were worried you'd lose it. I found a paper towel on the floor next to the cookbook display."

"So much for keeping it safe," Emma muttered, eyeing it like the device betrayed her.

"It's fine, we found the tablet, and now we can keep going through the inventory. Are you still on cookbooks?"

Emma nodded. "One last shelf, and then on to travel."

"Okay, well let's try to get through travel and self-help today? I want us to get through a full inventory sweep so that we can place our next orders and start planning out the short-story contest. We only have a couple of months left."

"You got it. What are you working on today?" Emma leaned against the counter, looking surprised when Brian brought over her cinnamon-topped cappuccino. "You betta stop flirting with me, B!"

He grinned, walking back to the kiosk, as several shoppers wandered into the store.

"I've got social media posts, graphics for event flyers, and I'm trying to nail down this author for a book signing in two weeks." Zora logged in to her workstation, climbing onto her black mesh-back stool at the main checkout desk of the bookstore.

Emma surveyed and greeted the guests, offering a friendly

nod. "You know you could work in your office, Z. Take advantage of the peace and quiet? I can handle this out here while you get through some of that computer work."

"I know you can, but I like it out here." Zora shrugged.

Emma sucked her teeth. "You should be a professional people-watcher, girl."

She chuckled in response. "It's an addiction. I really can't help it!" Zora watched her friend turn toward the cookbooks, but not before giving Granny Marion some sugar. Squeezing the matriarch's hand, Emma plopped a big kiss on her cheek before leaning down to whisper something in her ear. Granny chuckled and they slapped five, as Emma strode to the cookbook display, sat cross-legged on the floor and started reviewing inventory figures on the tablet.

Z exchanged an amused look with her grandmother, who blew a kiss in her direction. Catching it, she touched the tips of her fingers to her cheek. She blew a kiss back and turned her attention to her computer monitor. After pulling up the bookstore's calendar, she made a list of the upcoming events for the next three weeks, putting together digital flyers using templates she'd made previously. She added book covers and author photos to author event flyers, candid photos of regular customers highlighting some of their favorite reads that year, and a photo of Granny Marion reading to a group of children to publicize upcoming story time events. She dropped links to all of the graphics into her social media spreadsheet, where she scheduled out posts weeks in advance, complete with post language, hashtags, author account handles, and registration links. *Such a Capricorn.*

Being organized was how Zora had gotten the business running smoothly so quickly. After her father died, she'd received a generous inheritance that allowed her to purchase Opus Northeast from its previous owner, Ms. Betty. A book-seller for decades, Ms. Betty had decided to retire and move to Arizona to be closer to her grandchildren. Betty had known Zora since adolescence, and she was delighted to sell her store to someone who loved the place just as much as she did. Zora took great pride in updating Opus Northeast in a way that invited the community to come in and stay awhile.

After a couple of hours of events and social media planning, she moved on to email, deleting all of the spam before responding to emails from book distributors, patrons inquiring about upcoming releases not currently available for preorder, and local authors replying to her invitations for in-store author events. Looking down at her desk, she clicked her tongue at herself for leaving her breakfast sitting there as she worked. She had a habit of leaving food sitting next to her for hours as she zoned in on a task only to pick at it once it was cold. She popped the last of her flaky Danish into her mouth, as a new email hit her inbox. "Oh, my God."

"What is it?" Emma asked curiously as she advanced toward the counter, setting a fresh latte in front of Zora.

"He said yes." Her voice was barely above a whisper. She lifted the latte to her lips on autopilot, humming softly as she took in the scent. "Thanks."

Her friend peered over her shoulder. "Is *he* who I think he is?"

Stunned, Zora looked up at Emma, her brows furrowed in confusion. "He said yes?"

"Are you having a stroke? I'm gonna need for you to use your words, sis." Emma waved her hand in front of Z's face.

She couldn't find the words. Her mouth went dry. Helpless, Zora pointed to her computer screen.

Emma leaned forward. "'Dear Ms. Dizon,' blah blah blah. 'I've spoken to Lawrence Michaels, and he would love to have an author event hosted at Opus Northeast! As you may know, he grew up not far from there, and he is excited for an opportunity to read an excerpt from *Trial by Fire*, which is also based in Northeast D.C. Following the reading, he can stay for a brief Q&A and a book signing,' blah blah blah. Wow, are you freaking out right now?"

It was no secret that Zora had been crushing hard for years on bestselling author Lawrence Michaels, whose newest installment of his Langston Butler mystery thriller series was selling like hotcakes, and word on the street was that the first two books in the series were being optioned for film. Aside from being a local star, Lawrence's good looks were undeniable. "I bet he's tall," Zora murmured, grabbing his book from a pile of new releases on the counter behind her. Opening the book to the author photo inside the back cover, she ran her fingertips over the image of his clean-shaven brown skin, a hint of a smile curving at the edge of his closed mouth. A cleft in his chin and strong jaw led down the column of his neck to broad shoulders cloaked in a dark blue blazer. "Wonder if he has dimples."

Emma stared at her friend, pinging her eyes back and forth between Zora and the author photo. "I think you might need to break out the ol' vibrator tonight, girl. This 'hot for author' thing is getting unhealthy. Look at you—you can barely string words together right now. What are you going to do when he gets here? Drool on him?"

Zora swatted her friend away. "I'm fine. It's just... I didn't think he'd actually be willing to come here."

"Why? He's too big and bad for Brookland? He's from here!" Emma shoved her hands onto her hips.

Zora pulled at one of her tight curls, coiling it around her finger. "You know what I mean. Folks like that set their sights higher than modest indie bookstores like this. And he's from Petworth."

"He's from D.C. And he could still be a total douche. Besides, when have you ever cared about someone having too much bravado to fit their big ass head through our doors? He's lucky to be invited, girl. Don't gas that dude up too much." Emma dragged her fingers across her throat, deading the subject. *She really should have gone to law school.*

She struggled to find the words. "I just— I'm surprised is all."

"'Oh, Rexy, you're so sexy.'" Emma quoted one of their favorite movie quotes from their college days—they'd scored a box of her sister's old DVDs and binge-watched everything, but some lines stuck forever. Emma was forever quoting *Empire Records*, *Center Stage*, and *The Cutting Edge*. She curled her fingers into a claw and delicately pawed in Zora's direction as she turned toward the travel section.

Exasperated, she pursed her lips, still tugging at her curls. "I hate you."

"I heard that, heffa."

Zora composed herself enough to get through her emails and to order inventory for upcoming book releases before taking her grandmother home, leaving Emma to close up the store. She helped Granny into the car, placing her purse and a hardcover book on the floor near her feet. Her elder scooped the book into her hands as Zora rounded to the driver's side door.

"My, my, he sure is handsome." Granny Marion surveyed the photo of Lawrence Michaels. "Now, this is as fine a specimen as any to help you give me some more great-grandbabies!"

Zora groaned. "Granny, we've been over this already. I don't have time for babies right now, and I don't even know this man! Don't you want to meet him and make sure that he's actually worth considering for such an important role?"

Granny reached over the center console of Zora's Honda CR-V to pat her on the hand. "Times have changed, baby. Women are so much more independent now, like you. You know some women just go to a sperm bank when they want a child. They don't wait around for no man. At least this way, you know what the guy looks like."

Zora smirked, keeping her eyes on the road. "Are you telling me that I shouldn't even bother dating? I should just find some eligible sperm from a handsome donor?"

Granny patted her thigh gently as if to chide her. "Handsome and intelligent. And from good stock according to that family memoir of his. Now, baby, I'm not the one who always makes dating excuses. You're 'too busy with inventory' or 'you want to create new opportunities for young writers' or 'you need to improve your social media numbers.'" She made air quotes, exhaling a heaving sigh. "You, my dear, are afraid."

Zora sucked in a breath. "What could I possibly be afraid of, Granny? I own my own business, we have strong neighborhood support, and I may be able to duplicate this store in other parts of D.C. I will have time for the partner and the family, but this is my priority right now."

Her elder tsked. "You're thirty-five, baby. You and I both know that you don't have a lot of years left to have your family. It could take decades to build your empire."

"You've been asking me for great-grandbabies since I graduated high school!" Zora braked at a stoplight, turning to her grandmother.

"Which means you've left me waiting for seventeen years." Granny Marion reached over the console again, gripping her hand. "You know Granny won't be here forever, right? I am seventy-two years old, baby. I know I don't look a day over sixty, but I got a few good years left 'fore the Lord takes me home." Her soothing voice took a gentle tone that made it impossible to be mad at her.

Zora squeezed her grandmother's hand. "You don't look a day over fifty-five, and I hate when you say that." She turned onto their street in Mount Rainier, Maryland. After pulling into the long, gravel driveway, Zora turned off the car and faced Granny Marion full on. "You've got a lot of years left, Granny. It's you and me."

The elder shook her head slowly. "Don't get too comfortable. I'm here for a season, baby." Granny turned toward the passenger door, easing it open carefully to avoid hitting her thriving perennials. Swinging her purse over her shoulder, Granny closed the door and rounded the back of the car.

Zora watched the way her grandmother swung her legs out of the car, gingerly placing each foot on the ground, and moved to help her climb the steps to a wide porch sporting red Adirondack chairs. Opening the front door, Granny immediately stepped out of her shoes, placed them on the shoe rack, and sighed happily as she poked her feet into her favorite fuzzy slippers shaped like little booties. She walked through the living room and past the dining room table to the expansive kitchen, with its massive island and leatherback stools. Zora took off her flats and locked the front door, following her grandmother to the kitchen.

"You know, baby, it sure will be nice to see you fill this house with a family. Now, don't get me wrong. I adore Emma, but this is a whole lot of house for two bachelorettes." Decades ago, when Zora's grandfather passed, Granny transferred her interest in the house to Zora, deciding that she was happy to live there but didn't need the benefits of ownership. She renovated her mother-in-law suite and moved into that section of the house when Zora was in high school—she and her parents lived in the main house. Granny rooted around in the refrigerator. "You've got some nice shrimp in here. How about a fresh salad?"

"Salad sounds perfect. I can make that for us," Zora offered, assuming her grandmother would refuse like she always did.

"Nonsense. You've been working hard all day. I just read a couple of picture books and my newspaper. Oh good, you have everything I wanted." Granny pulled out heads of little gem lettuce, raw shrimp, a container of hard-boiled eggs, some fried bacon, and fresh asparagus. She set all of her ingredients on the speckled quartz countertop and began rooting around in cupboards for a skillet and some bowls. "So tell me more about this handsome author you've got coming to the store. Why are you so smitten with him?"

Zora grabbed a bottle of chilled white Rioja from a wine fridge built into the island and poured them each a glass before sitting on a leather stool. "I don't know if *smitten* is the word I would use, Granny. It's just an innocent crush. I don't know a ton about him outside of his books, but there's just something about his writing that I find daring and intelligent. Plus, I like how he portrays Black women in his stories."

Granny grabbed an array of spices from the cabinet and an empty spice jar. Using the palm of her hand instead of measuring spoons, she poured sweet and smoked paprika, cayenne, thyme, garlic powder, white pepper, salt, and onion powder into her hand one at a time, dropping the desired amounts into the jar. "Mmm-hmm. And how does he portray Black women?" After securing the lid to her spice jar, she shook it lightly until the seasonings were adequately blended together. She peeled and deveined large shrimp with deft fingers and a sharp paring knife, rinsing them with water and then blotting them dry with paper towels. In a bowl, she tossed the shrimp lightly in olive oil and then coated them with her blackening spices.

Zora watched her grandmother move around the kitchen comfortably, setting her skillet on the gas stove to sear off the shrimp. "It's in the way that he shows the strength of a Black woman, and he doesn't make them inferior to the men, even the main character. His famed private investigator relies on a Black woman, seen as his partner and equal, who really is the brains of the entire operation. It's just refreshing that she doesn't feel like a sidekick. She always ends up piecing things together for the PI."

"Hmm." The elder used tongs to place the shrimp into her hot pan coated in melted butter, patting dry her rinsed lettuce and tearing the leaves into two wide salad bowls. After turning the shrimp, she moved on to slicing the eggs, shallots, and asparagus. "Avocado?"

"Always."

"So what if he looks nothing like his photo in real life? Would you still like him based on his writing?" Granny Marion pulled the seed from the avocado, peeling off the skin to neatly slice through the flesh. She made quick work of a lemon vinaigrette, setting a bowl in front of Zora before sitting next to her at the island. Grabbing hands, they lowered their heads. "Father, we thank You for this meal and for the blessings You bestow upon us daily. Bless this food, that it may nourish and sustain us, and bless our hearts that we endeavor to be more like You always. In the name of Your Son, amen."

"Amen." Zora's eyes fluttered open to the sight of her grandmother staring at her. "Granny…"

"I'm waiting." Her tone was gentle but firm.

Zora puffed out a breath. "Even if he doesn't look exactly like his photo, yes, I'd like him because of his writing. I mean, I've never interacted with him, so he could be a hot mess or a complete jerk. Who knows?" She mixed the contents of her bowl to try and get all of the ingredients into a single bite.

"So simple, but so delicious. I still don't know why my vinaigrette never tastes like yours."

The elder poked her fork around her bowl, loading it up. "I can tell you why, baby, but you're not going to like the answer. The truth is you worry too much about precision when you should just cook the way you feel. We do this kind of cooking all the time, and you know my best ingredient is love."

"Well, Grandma, I don't know what you're talkin' about. I don't know how to put *love* into my food, but I can use a recipe and follow it to have a consistent outcome."

Granny tilted her head patiently. "You think too much. That's always been your problem. I won't say that I'm holding out hope for you with this author man, because I don't know him from Adam, but I would love to see you start your family. I think that you'll start to see that life is about more than a strict schedule and a task list. Plus—" she took a bite, then pointed her fork in her granddaughter's direction "—I want my great-grandbabies."

"Now, Granny, you know that the reminders don't make this happen any faster. And now you don't want me to do this the traditional way?"

"Traditional meaning what? I have to wait around for you to be open enough to date and be courted and then commit yourself enough to land a husband?" She leaned close to her granddaughter, looking her in the eyes. "You know I could go with you to one of those sperm banks, help you narrow down the field..."

"Granny! What are you talkin' about right now? No! You are not coming with me to a sperm bank!" Zora tossed her head back and laughed. "I mean, yes, I am an independent woman, but I am traditional about some things. I just don't have time to invest in a bunch of guys who aren't going to lead me to what I want in life. Right now, I'm happy managing the bookstore and finding new ways to connect with our community. The man and the kids will come."

"But will I still be around?" Granny stood, wrapping her arms around Zora. Holding her close, she whispered in her ear, "You know that twins and triplets run in our family, right?"

Zora burst out laughing, squeezing her grandmother's arms as they crossed around her neck and shoulders. "What am I going to do with you?"

"Not nothing, baby." Granny Marion smiled, heading toward the back door. She gestured toward the kitchen. "You got this?"

"Absolutely. You know, I think I figured out why you always like to cook at my place." Zora's eyes crinkled at the corners.

Granny smiled, tapping an index finger to her nose. "That's right, no dishes. I'll see you in the morning?"

"Yes, ma'am." She watched her grandmother walk out the back door to the entrance of her own private mother-in-law-style suite—an English basement previously used as a rental property, accessible from the back patio via a stone walkway. Hearing her door shut, Zora heaved a sigh as she cleared away the plates and utensils, rinsing everything off, including the pan from the stove. She loaded the dishwasher before retiring upstairs to her bedroom.

In the spacious master suite, Zora dropped her purse on a tufted velvet bench at the foot of her massive bed. From it, she grabbed her laptop, which she set on the night table to charge. She stretched her bare feet on a fluffy area rug before heading into her bathroom to turn on the water in the standing shower. She eyed her soaking tub with longing but opted for the shower since she planned to tackle more inventory at the bookstore early the next morning. After stripping down, she smoothed her thick, dark curls into a bun, wrapped a scarf around her hair, and donned a shower cap with a decorative African print in royal blue, black, white, and a mustard yellow.

Steam enveloped her as she stepped inside the glass-encased shower; the high-pressure showerhead kneaded hot water into her shoulders. Washing the day from her face and body, Zora sighed happily, grabbing her favorite products from the teak bench she used to shave her legs or sit on when she wanted to steam. Feeling relaxed and exfoliated, she turned off the water and stepped into a soft bath sheet, which she wrapped around herself tightly.

"Zo?" a female voice called from her bedroom door.

"Em? Come on in." Zora dropped her towel and grabbed a silk robe from a hook on her bathroom door, tying it around her waist before walking back into the bedroom. "How was closing, sis?"

Emma scuttled toward the bed in her house slippers. She'd already changed into a soft knit jumpsuit. She climbed onto the bed, tucking her feet underneath her. "Girl, it was fine. Things quieted down around eight o'clock, so I consolidated the clearance display and set out the new releases."

"Perfect." Zora curled one leg onto the bed, letting the other hang over the side. "We stayed fairly busy today."

"I wasn't sure you'd noticed." A glint in her eye. "The way you were pawing that book, you seemed pretty distracted today."

"Not you, too," Zora groaned. "Granny gave me grief the entire drive home."

"To be fair, he does look like a prime specimen to father your children." Emma's wry smile grew until she took a pillow to the face. "Ouch! Careful of my lashes—I drove all the way to Vienna for these."

"You drove to Vienna, Virginia, for lash extensions?"

Emma shrugged, a smug smile curving her lips. "She's that

good." Emma didn't wear a lot of makeup; she focused on taking good care of her skin and was constantly reminding Zora to wear more sunscreen. Lash extensions and monthly pedicures were all she needed—her thick brows arched naturally and her strong cheekbones appled perfectly without any need for contour.

"Damn." Zora propped herself against the pillows, looking across the room to a chaise longue with a pile of books to be read next to a lamp on a side table. Craft books purchased with the intent to figure out where and how to begin a story she'd been plotting out in her head for years. Something she put off for whenever she had some free time, which was never.

Emma leaned back against the upholstered headboard, stretching out her legs as she nudged Zora with her elbow. "Tell me what's on your mind. You've gone all pensive."

She considered lying, but her best friend would see right through it. "We've all been hyping this guy up, and I'm just trying not to be too hopeful. It's all about bringing the shop excellent business, and Lawrence will be a big draw. I don't even know why I'm thinking about him in this context anyway. You know I don't have time to date anyone, but this one—"

"You like him. I know, girl. Listen, I won't gas him up to you, but you have to promise you'll stop drooling on the books. Deal?" Emma raised her brows in anticipation.

Zora stood, crossing the room to her walk-in closet. "Deal." She ran a hand over her headscarf.

"What else is wrong?" Emma's long legs strode across the room in fewer steps.

Zora pursed her lips. "What in the hell am I going to wear?"

Emma stared into Zora's closet, littered with cardigans, work dresses, jeans, and suits. "You're right. We're going to need to do some shopping."

2

Only the rustle of drying leaves tousled by the breezy morning air, and the rumbling of water beginning to boil in Zora's kettle, disturbed the quiet of 6 a.m. When she had the energy, Zora would rise an hour or two early to hit a barre class, ride her Peloton, or read books about the craft of writing. Her love of reading had developed early, back when her family still lived in the Bay Area—Zora's parents built her a cozy reading nook out of an old shed in the backyard and asked family and friends to include an addition to Zora's personal library in any birthday or Christmas gift. Soon, the shed could no longer hold all of Zora's books, so she created her own library system, loaning out copies of her prized titles to her friends and classmates.

At their local public library, she'd been notorious for requesting that the librarians order more copies of new releases she was excited about. She'd volunteered to help organize the libraries at both her middle school and high school, often reaching out to authors via social media to inquire about book donations to local schools. She put MySpace and Facebook to use in high school to create community reading challenges and literacy programs. Zora never shied away from her identity as a bibliophile, and anyone who dared to tease her for it received an immediate clap back.

Losing her mother in high school had only intensified her love for books—she used them to process her feelings and escape from loneliness, especially when they relocated to D.C. to be closer to Granny. She'd dive into different worlds and chase the characters through their discoveries and challenges; her vivid imagination helped her picture everything transpiring on the page. Books helped her grieve and reflect on special memories.

It wasn't until college, at Georgetown, that Zora discovered a love for writing. As she balanced courses for a double major in comparative literature and African American studies, Zora had been required to take an elective course that pushed her to explore and build new worlds, new characters, new conflicts of her own. That one class had her hooked; though her goal at the time had been to eventually become a librarian at the Library of Congress, she'd decided to minor in creative writing. Just in case.

After Georgetown, Zora got a master's in library sciences from the University of Maryland. She initially intended to complete this degree in California, to return to the West Coast sunshine, but Zora had to admit that she'd fallen in love with seasons and atmosphere she only experienced on the East Coast. Then her father's cancer returned, and she was grateful for the opportunity to be close to him—his passing came much quicker than anyone anticipated. The access to museums, the bustle of D.C.—even the chaos of snowy winters—

brought Zora comfort. Plus, there was no way that she could leave Granny Marion.

Zora spent all of her summers and evenings after classes working in Ms. Betty's bookstore, and as Zora prepared to start applying for library jobs, Ms. Betty shared that she wanted an apprentice to eventually take over the bookstore when she retired. Betty made Zora an assistant manager, then manager. Soon, Zora ran the entire day-to-day while Betty spent time traveling to see her grandchildren in Arizona. Zora became the obvious successor of Opus Northeast, and the plans to become a librarian dissolved as she became a bookstore owner—her parents left her a trust for when they passed, which made the store purchase possible.

Zora poured the scalding water into her coffee press to steep and turned to gaze at a large family photo on the wall. Her parents, her half sister, Tessa, ten years older and from her father's previous marriage, and young Z smiled at her. Zora's dad had insisted on professional photos after finishing chemo, and when Zora's mom was killed months later in a car accident, they were grateful to have captured those moments together. Zora was still staring at the photo when Granny crept in the back door.

"Hey, sugar, what are you doing up so early?" Catching her eye, Granny stepped closer to Zora, grasping her hand. "You know, they'd be so proud of you, baby," she whispered gently, her voice catching. She leaned her head against Zora's arm.

Granny was a firm believer that children should never die before their parents—for her it wasn't just terrible luck, it was a crime against nature. Before Zora's mother died, Granny had been an avid traveler; she was active in the community, pushing council members to approve initiatives that promoted equity and inclusion, and ran her own book club with her close girlfriends. She was still taking on clients for private dance lessons. After the crash, though, everything stopped. She'd fallen into a deep depression, and Zora had been the one who'd convinced Granny to seek therapy, agreeing to go together so that they could both be equipped with the tools they needed to manage the waves of grief that still found them on occasion.

After that Granny stopped giving dance lessons for good and while she started to travel again, she didn't stray far as she had before. But she did go back to her book club friends and found solace there. She continued her work pushing local representatives to make decisions that would benefit the community as a whole, and not just those who were constantly looking to redevelop, thereby pushing out Black families. Her newfound purpose was in protecting Tessa, Zora, and the potential legacy of all of her great-grandbabies. So far Tessa had been the only one making progress in that department—Zora's brilliant niece, Safina, was already in her first year of college at GW. Tessa and Safina lived closer to Baltimore with Tessa's husband, Ken, and though the drive was only about forty miles, the distance and work obligations kept them apart more often than not.

Zora squeezed her grandmother's hand. "I think they'd be proud of both of us. I got up early to read one of these craft books. I haven't touched my writing in a while, and I thought this might help me get my creative juices flowing."

"That's right." Granny climbed onto a stool at the kitchen island. "Your own mystery series. You haven't talked about that in a few months."

Z shrugged. "We've been so busy preparing for the writing contest, I haven't had time. Emma is right. I need to go ahead and post a position for some added help."

Zora had been toying with a premise for a mystery series—something that straddled the line between cozy mystery and romantic suspense, somewhere between Kyra Davis and Janet Evanovich—since she took ownership of Opus Northeast, but she wasn't confident enough with her writing to draft more than some initial outlines and character descriptions. She spent hours poring over books on act structures and beat sheets, trying to discern the right way to introduce conflict and stakes into her story while keeping the reader on their toes. She longed to sign up for a writing residency or take an extended vacation as a solo writing retreat, just to allow herself the time and space to really delve into the process, but it felt indulgent when she had a store to run.

Granny considered Zora's response. "You could hire a couple of people. Additional, capable hands would allow you to step back more and give yourself time off when you need it. The store's been doing good business for a few years now, and it can sustain a couple more bodies. Everybody needs mental health days and vacation time now and then, baby. Even you."

Z nodded quietly, grabbing a pair of mugs and pressing down on the filter in her coffee press. She dropped some oat milk and raw sugar into one mug and poured black coffee into the other. "What are you doing up so early?" She set a mug in front of Granny.

Granny smiled at her black coffee. "I woke up and saw the light on, figured it was you. Wanted to check on you."

"Yeah, there's no way Emma would be up." Zora cracked a smile. Emma did not like to have her sleep interrupted unnecessarily. Getting up early to read or work out were unjust abominations that should never be prioritized over sleep. If she had to be up for some critical event, she'd go to bed early to ensure she got eight hours, and no one had better disturb her even a minute before her alarm.

Granny's lips twitched. "Only someone with a death wish would wake that girl early." She refocused her attention. "So how are you feeling?"

Zora eyed her grandmother across the island as she sipped her coffee. "I'm good, Granny... Why?"

The elder's eyes widened as she shrugged. "I just want to make sure you feel healthy and in your prime. In case you meet that author gentleman and things go well."

"Granny," Zora groaned. "Did you ever consider that I might get this whole great-grandbaby thing going faster if you stopped harassing me about it?"

Granny sipped her coffee pensively. "Wouldn't that mean that you were being purposefully defiant? I know I taught you better than that. Harassment where?" She stood and headed toward the back door. "Anyway, you get to that craft book, my darlin'. That book won't read itself!"

Zora bit back a smile as she shook her head. "Yes, ma'am."

"Hi, Lisa, this is Zora Dizon over at Opus Northeast, and I wanted to check in with you to see if you would like to continue your sponsorship of the *D.C. Speakeasy* Young Writers' Contest? As you know, I am now spearheading the contest, and I'm hoping to expand on the foundation of the program that Ms. Betty built, increasing the number of stories published and including all of D.C. public schools—"

"Hello, Zora! Why, yes, Betty was a pillar of our community. We certainly miss her spirited discussions. So I take it that her move is official?" Lisa Mwalimu owned a local wine bar and had befriended Ms. Betty at the start of her business venture. Everyone in Brookland knew Ms. Betty.

"Yes, I miss Ms. Betty, too... Yep, she's in Arizona now, fully retired and enjoying the sunshine with her grandchildren."

"We've loved the changes that you're making, Zora, and events like these drive people into the neighborhood. We'd be happy to support again this year. How about we increase to fifteen hundred dollars?"

Zora's eyes widened. "What a generous donation! Thank you so much for your support. And can we count on your team to participate in our community food bank event as well?"

"Absolutely—it's one of our favorite service events. The entire team will be present. It's in about a month, right?"

"Yes, four Saturdays from now. Excellent! Lisa, thank you so much—this program is such a special opportunity for our young people."

"Anytime, Zora. Stop by soon for some tapas!"

"It has been a while, so I will definitely do that! I look forward to seeing you soon. Okay, you take care. Bye, now."

Emma stood hunched over the counter with her chin resting in her hands. "That sounded promising!"

Zora's smile grew wide. "Lisa is one of our biggest supporters. Not only is she on board, she's doubling her donation!" She slapped Emma five and did a little wiggle dance in her seat.

Lisa was the owner of a string of wine bars in Northeast D.C. and Maryland. She and her late husband had been childhood patrons of Ms. Betty's store, and when Ms. Betty approached them about sponsoring the inaugural *D.C. Speakeasy* Young Writers' Contest, which would allow the winner's creative work to be included in their annual anthology of D.C. talent, the Mwalimus jumped at the chance.

The *D.C. Speakeasy* was a local publication only available in print in the DMV or online. The magazine had started out as a guide to local restaurants and bars, highlighting establishments with hidden lounges accessed with special passwords. The magazine expanded to include arts and culture as it gained a following, eventually collaborating with a publishing imprint in New York to invite local youths to submit their work for potential publication via the Young Writers Program. Initially, the program only included high school entrants from D.C. charter schools, but Zora understood Ms. Betty's vision to grow. Betty kept the program going for three years before her retirement and came back to help for three more years, while Zora gained her sea legs as the bookstore owner, seeing her through the expansion. This year, with Ms. Betty relocated to Arizona, Zora had the reins and was determined to have a successful cycle.

"That's amazing! How many more calls like this do you have to make?" Emma peered over the counter to Zora's checklist.

Z scrunched her nose. "Lisa was just the first." She lifted her checklist to reveal a spreadsheet of contacts underneath. "I have easily fifty more calls to make today. We just want to make sure that we're reaching all of our previous supporters and some new ones."

Emma chewed on her bottom lip. "Well, I'll handle the floor, and you want to switch when you get tired of calling?"

Zora contemplated that for a moment. "You really wouldn't mind?"

"Girl, you really think you want to make fifty phone calls in one day by yourself?" Emma grabbed a pen and marked the list near its midpoint. "Stop when you get here, or you get tired, whichever comes first. Then we'll swap."

Zora leaned back in her chair. "What did I do to deserve you?" she whined.

"You only employ and house me...no biggie." Emma winked. "Plus, I may have borrowed that fly racerback maxi dress and decided it looks better in my closet."

Zora heaved a deep sigh. "We'll see about that."

"I sorta already spilled something on it." Her friend grimaced as she squeezed her thumb and forefinger together. "Just a little."

"Emma!"

"Whatever, Zo, when were you ever going to wear it? You bought it two seasons ago, and it still had the tag on it when I lifted it from captivity."

Zora rolled her eyes. "You better go shopping and put something nice in its place."

Emma sucked her teeth. "Fine. Anyway, tell me when you're ready to swap," she called over her shoulder as she walked away.

3

Patrons arrived hours early on event days, milling about with coffee from the kiosk and buying books for signatures. Emma and Zora stayed late the night before, erecting extra displays of books by Lawrence Michaels and signage directing people to the sitting area. For busy days like this, Kerri sent an additional barista to help Brian at the kiosk, along with extra baked goods and lunch items.

To combat her nerves, Zora nibbled on buttery lemon madeleines with her third latte of the day. Having already checked her makeup three times that afternoon, she sat at the checkout counter reading snippets of Lawrence's book. The faux leather pencil skirt that Emma found for her was surprisingly comfortable, hugging all of her curves just right. Her sleeveless black blouse was tucked into the high waist of her skirt, and her feet rested comfortably in ballet flats after Zora was ridiculed for looking like Bambi learning how to walk in her classic Stuart Weitzman pumps. *Emma never held punches.*

"Excuse me," a deep voice resonated from the other side of the counter, "can you tell me where I can find Ms. Zora Dizon?"

Zora closed the book she was reading to look up and see Lawrence Michaels standing there looking at her. Her heart thudded as she took in his brown skin, long lashes, deep brown eyes, and megawatt smile. *Be cool.* "Oh, hi, Mr. Michaels, I'm so glad that you made it! I'm Zora." Behind the counter, she tried to covertly slip out of her ballet flats and into her cutest high heels, gripping the counter for balance.

"Please, call me Lawrence." He smiled down at Zora, who fluffed her curls under his gaze. If he noticed that she grew four inches behind the counter, he didn't show it. "It's so nice to see a Black-owned independent bookstore in my old neighborhood."

"That's right. You grew up in Petworth, didn't you?"

He looked impressed. "That's right—just down the street. Wow, you really did your research."

She smiled, her lips lacquered a deep bluish-red. "We try to make sure that we have a good understanding of where our authors are coming from when we host an event. We were really excited to learn that you agreed to join us for this. I'm glad you're here."

He tilted his head. "Are you?"

Tension built between them as they stared at each other, his dark eyes boring a hole into her. Tiny hairs rose and prickled on her skin as Zora felt a flush crawl up her chest and neck to her cheeks and ears. "I—I mean, I am a fan of your writing."

Emma appeared. "Hey, Z? I think we're all set to begin. Are you ready to announce?"

She nodded, turning back to Lawrence and smiling brightly. "Ready?"

"Always." His gaze lingered on her for a long moment, the

word vibrating at Zora's core. He gestured toward the seating area. "After you."

Hyperaware of Lawrence's eyes raking over her and settling on her ass as she walked in front of him, Zora ignored the wobble in her ankles and added a little extra zing to her switch. Somewhere off to the side, she heard Emma whisper, "Yesss, bitch!"

Smiling to herself, she stood at the front of the group gathered in a semicircle of chairs and benches. "Good evening! Thank you all for joining us at Opus Northeast. Tonight, I have the great pleasure of introducing one of Petworth's own, author Lawrence Michaels, whose bestselling mysteries have been flying off of the shelves. Central to the series are Langston Butler and his extraordinary partner, Annette, who hunt down the most notorious murderers in the Mid-Atlantic. Prior to the Butler series, Mr. Michaels tugged at our hearts with a beautiful memoir on three generations of community activists in his family. That window into the issues raised and challenged by the Michaels family gave a poignant view of what it means to be Black in D.C., and it was so beautifully portrayed in documentary form this past spring. Please join me in welcoming Lawrence Michaels."

The crowd whooped and applauded, and Zora moved aside to sit on the end of the back row so that she'd be able to get back up to direct patrons to refreshments after the talk. Sitting, she whispered a greeting to the bearded, spectacled man next to her only to receive an icy stare in response. Rebuffed, she turned her attention forward, focusing on Lawrence.

"Good evening," he said, surveying the room.

Three or four people in the audience replied back.

Lawrence shook his head. "Let's try this again. Good evening!" He projected his voice, deep and rumbling enough to make Zora squirm in her seat.

"Good evening!" the crowd projected back, some laughing.

"Thank you so much for coming out tonight. Nothing makes me happier than seeing a successful, Black-owned independent bookstore just a few blocks down the street from where I grew up." He nodded in Zora's direction. "Thank you, Ms. Dizon, for the warm invitation and welcome. Hopefully, this will be the first of many events we can host here at Opus Northeast."

She beamed, her cheeks warming.

"Laying it on thick today," the man next to her muttered.

Zora's head snapped to her left. "Sorry?"

The man glowered at her through his glasses, dark brown eyes piercing through her. He turned back to face forward. "Nothing."

Before them, Lawrence continued. "I didn't dream of being a writer growing up. I was sure that I was going to end up on Wall Street." His smile widened as he straightened the lapels of his blazer. "There's nothing I like more than a sharp tailored suit."

The audience laughed, but the man next to Zora sighed loudly. "Just get on with it," he whispered.

"Sir? Are you okay?" Zora turned again, taking in his crossed arms, pursed lips, and hunched demeanor.

"I'm fine." A muscle in his jaw twitched.

Rolling her eyes, she refocused on Lawrence, who stood comfortably before the crowd. "The Butler series started out as an homage to some of my favorite mysteries. I'm a sucker for puzzles, and creating stories where I can lead the reader in one direction while hiding clues in three others is a challenge I enjoy tackling. And the partnership of Langston Butler and Annette Williams—their friendship, work tensions, and chemistry—is often tested, but perhaps more in this fourth installment in the series than in its predecessors."

The cranky man sighed loudly enough for people in front

of him to turn and glare in his direction. He lifted his hands in apology, crossing his arms.

Zora tried her best to ignore his antics as Lawrence began to read an excerpt from his book. While he read a section where tension between the two main characters ran exceptionally high, Zora realized she was mouthing the parts of dialogue she remembered. Straightening in her seat, from the corner of her eye, she realized the man next to her watched her quietly. "Quite the fan," he quipped.

"If you're *not* a fan, then why are you here? What, are you some disgruntled journalist?" she shot back.

He stared at her silently, blinking hard. The side of his mouth twitched slightly, his expression imperceptible. *What was this guy's problem?*

She shook her head at him. "Hot mess," she muttered.

As Lawrence answered questions about his series, the grumpy man remained quiet. Zora was acutely aware of his proximity; the heat radiating off his body made her temperature rise, and all she wanted was a gust of fresh air.

"What is next for Langston and Annette?" a local book blogger called out.

"Great question." Lawrence smiled wide. "I should have some updates to share next week, so stay tuned—I generally make announcements on my Twitter account."

After Lawrence had answered his last question, she stood to close out the event. "Wow, wasn't that great?" Zora addressed the crowd. Several cheered, while others took photos of the author holding a copy of his book. "Now that the question and answer period has concluded, if you are interested in having Mr. Michaels sign your copy of one of his books, please jump in line. Emma is over there waving and ready to help anyone who may want to snag a copy now to get in on this opportunity. Again, thank you all for coming, and please feel free to help yourself to some refreshments over by the coffee kiosk."

Patrons broke into applause, several sneaking over to buy a copy of Lawrence's latest book from Emma at the checkout counter. Zora directed those ready to line up to have their books signed, while Granny Marion snuck candy to a couple of kids sitting quietly while their parents waited for signatures.

The signing started, and Zora watched as Lawrence spent time with each of her patrons, listening to their stories, asking for the spellings of their names, and personalizing his messages to them on his title sheet. He laughed often, shaking hands and taking selfies with anyone who asked. People left with hands full of books and satisfied smiles on their faces— the mark of a successful event.

Granny Marion caught her eye, and she winked in response. The woman motioned in Lawrence's direction and mouthed the word, "Grandbabies."

Zora could only shake her head and laugh at her grandmother. *She will never give up!*

"Something funny?" The prickly man from before wandered in her direction.

She looked over her shoulder, assuming that his question was meant for someone behind her. "Me?"

Standing, the man towered over her—he had to be at least six foot four. His dark eyes trained on her, his mouth still set in a sour curve. "Yeah, you. Listen, I wanted to apologize if I took away from your ability to enjoy the event. It's just been a long day, and I didn't mean any harm."

A glint in his eye caught Zora's attention, and she looked him over curiously. He was dressed in a polo and slacks, with a jacket on his arm. It was unclear from his attire what kind of work he might do, but something about his eyes read intelligent. Even if he was kind of an asshole. *Maybe it's just his glasses.*

"I figure that you must be going through something to have such a chip on your shoulder. I tried not to hold it against you, and that's why I asked if you were okay. I appreciate your apology." She began to turn away.

"Do you accept it?" he pressed, his dark eyes searching hers.

"Is that a requirement?" Something about this man made her feel like she needed to stand up for herself. Like he was questioning whether she actually deserved the apology he had just offered her.

"No, it's not a requirement, but it would be nice to know that there are no hard feelings." He gestured with his hands that he meant no harm.

Zora considered his point. "Well, there are no hard feelings, and I do accept your apology. I hope that you were able to enjoy something about this event, even if you're having a hard time with other parts of your life."

His gaze unnerved her. It looked like he wanted to say more, but all he did was stare at her. She watched as his eyes trailed down to her mouth, her throat, and farther south, but nothing about the look on his face changed.

Why can't I tell what he's thinking? Everything inside Zora screamed that she should stay away from this man, because there was nothing about him that seemed warm or inviting. But her Spidey senses were triggered by the care with which he watched her.

"Are you going to buy the book? It looks like Lawrence is getting toward the end of the line, if that was something that you wanted to do while you were here," she offered.

The man pulled a copy of the book from his shoulder bag. "I've already got one. I brought it with me."

Huh. "So why are you talkin' to me? Are you shy or something? I can take you over there to meet him if you need some assistance."

The man rolled his eyes. "I'm quite capable, thank you. I don't need it signed."

Zora had enough. "I'm still trying to put together why you bothered to come to this event. Okay, so you have the book, but you don't want to interact with the author, and you didn't seem to like anything that he had to say, so...why are you still here?"

"Maybe I'm enjoying your company." He looked down at her, and something about his face softened. He licked his lips, stretching his fingers at his sides.

Unsure what to make of this guy, she put on her judicious store owner hat. "I don't know that either of us are being very good company this evening. But again, thank you for coming to the event. We are trying to build our events calendar up, so we will definitely be having more like this in the very near future. If you're a big reader, maybe there will be another author that you care to engage with more, and you can sign up for our newsletter and updates from the website." She gave a tight smile and started to walk away, but she stopped short as Lawrence advanced.

"Oh, Zora, I'd like to introduce you to one of my oldest friends." Finished with signings, he clapped the cranky guy on the back. "Reid Hughes, this is Zora Dizon. She owns this place."

Reid nodded at her, his face clouded over once more. "I figured that part out. It's a cool spot."

Zora sucked in a breath, mentally counting to keep her cool. "Thank you. And what do you do?"

"I'm a literary arts teacher," he replied, watching her closely. "So to answer your question from earlier, no, I'm not a disgruntled journalist."

"Just disgruntled, then," she replied coolly. Turning her attention back to Lawrence, she flashed a quick smile. "I'm really glad that you were able to join us tonight."

Lawrence shot a curious glance at his friend. "Thank you for having me." His voice was as smooth as velvet. "Listen, I hope I'm not being too forward, but would you be interested in going for a drink with me?"

She looked up at him, surprised, but could think of nothing that would wipe the smug scowl off Reid's face faster. "I'd love to. Let me get my purse." She turned to look at Reid but was unable to decipher his expression. His dark eyes moved from her to his friend.

"I thought that you wanted to work on our project together tonight, Lawrence? You know that's why I'm here." The frustration in Reid's voice rang crystal clear. "I canceled a tutoring session to be here for this, man. I can't turn away my students for your stuff if you're not going to follow through."

Lawrence smiled that smile you give in front of mixed company—the one where his curved lips were plastered in place but his eyes threatened violence if the other didn't behave appropriately. "Come on, man. We can always get started on that tomorrow, but tonight I have a chance to take out a beautiful woman. You know I appreciate you for coming all the way out here, though."

Zora turned on her heel and stepped toward a couple of patrons to thank them for coming, taking the opportunity to give the men some privacy. Though she was unable to hear the rest of their conversation, Reid was visibly upset. *I wonder what his issue is.* As Zora reached the back office, Emma and Granny Marion immediately swarmed her. "Whoa, what's going on?"

"Did I just hear you agree to a date with your author crush?" Emma's hushed voice neared sonic levels, her hands clenched into hopeful fists. "Are you actually making time for a date?"

"Now, don't get too excited. It's just drinks."

"But that's more than you've done in almost a year! Are you finally getting back on the horse?" She squealed.

"Now, Emma, don't get too riled up," Granny Marion warned. "We both know that the store is Zora's top priority, and so we shouldn't get our hopes up too high." She leaned close to her granddaughter. "But I will tell you that man is finer in person, and I would be proud of my great-grandchildren. He sure would make some cute babies."

Zora groaned, unable to take much more of them talking about her like she wasn't there. "It's just drinks," she whined.

"Come on, baby girl, we all know that drinks can lead to a whole lot more." Emma smirked.

Granny raised her hands, fingers crossed. "One can hope!"

Zora had enough. "Can y'all help me? I mean what am I going to do? My feet are killing me!"

"Should have worn those flats." Granny shrugged.

"Thank you, that is extremely helpful right now. But he's already seen me in the heels."

"Never let a man dictate your footwear." Emma shook her finger. "You and I both know that you can't walk in those heels anymore—hell, you barely could earlier. Change into your flats, refresh your lipstick, and get back out there."

Zora fluffed her hair. "Okay, you're right." She sighed relief as she removed her high heels. Stretching her toes, she shuffled her feet into her ballet flats from before—Emma had moved them to the office before the signing. "This feels so much better."

Emma grinned. "You know we're going to wait up, right?"

Zora ticked her tongue. "Now, you know that's really not necessary. I can update you on all of this tomorrow."

Granny smiled. "Now, where is the fun in that?"

"I swear, the two of you are co-conspirators. Always plotting against me," she muttered.

Emma and Granny pointed index fingers at each other and leaned closer, tapping the pads of their fingers together—their silly version of a high five.

Zora rolled her eyes. "I guess I'll see y'all later."

"Take your time with this one." Her grandmother waved. "He looks like he's got stamina."

Emma's jaw dropped as her head jerked in Granny's direction. "Okay, Granny! I see you!"

Her lips curved into a sweet smile, and she winked coyly. "I'm old, baby. I ain't dead."

4

Lawrence held the door as Zora stepped outside, taking in the clean scent of his cologne. "Thank you." She smiled. She pulled her blazer a little tighter around her; the late-summer air cooled off once the sun set. "It feels good out here."

"So do you want to tell me what happened back there?" Lawrence eyed her curiously as they walked to a Spanish tapas bar two blocks down—one of Lisa's establishments. He slowed his long-legged stride to match Zora's. "With Reid?"

What did he say about me? "Oh, it's nothing. He just seemed like he was in a foul mood. Is he always that grumpy?"

He laughed heartily. "Ah, Reid, the curmudgeon. Honestly, I blame it on his students. He teaches a lot of kids, and I would be grumpy after trying to manage that all day. He's just tired and overworked."

"I guess that's fair. Do you write full-time or are you balancing another job?"

Lawrence shook his head. "It's become full-time at this point, but it wasn't always that way. I did some business consulting on the side, and I helped out with a family business, but now that writing has really taken off for me, it's become my main work and source of income."

"That's so cool! I have had dreams of someday writing a novel since college, but my love for reading is far more established," she laughed. "Since I was a kid, my favorite trips with my parents and my grandmother were to libraries and bookstores. There's nothing that I like more than picking up a brand-new book, with that new book smell, and diving into a completely different time and place." She became more animated the way she always did, talking about books, gesturing with her hands. "I've slowly been building up a collection of first editions, and even though there's a huge push to move reading to digital, I just love handling the pages of a printed book—running my fingers over an embossed cover, the foil details and seeing the details of the inside covers. Like yours, with the sketches of Langston and Annette searching for clues—you simply don't get those details in digital copy."

Lawrence observed her as she talked and gestured, his smile widening as her excitement grew. "That's a great way to describe it. It's funny, but because of all of my deadlines, I don't have a lot of time to read. Of course, I try to do my part, and I get early looks at books by other writers who have asked for me to blurb. Most of the time I focus my attention specifically in my genre, because it's considered 'market research.'" He used finger quotes. "But I always find that I would rather be within the pages of my own books."

"Is that because you feel really close to your characters? I really like the way that you describe them and their relationship to each other." Zora bit her lip, willing herself to calm down, hoping that her genuine interest didn't make her sound like she was an ass-kissing groupie. *Is it creepy to tell someone you've read all of their published work?*

He nodded thoughtfully, stealing a glance at her from the corner of his eye. "I would say my characters and I have a strong bond. What is it you like about their relationship?"

Zora paused for a moment to think about how to articulate what she wanted to say, still reeling that she even had this opportunity to speak with him so openly about his work. "I think it's really awesome that you have such a strong Black female character in the forefront of your book. I mean, yes, Langston is the main character and the one who facilitates the solving of these horrendous crimes, but she brings in all of this logic and reasoning, and I love how she is able to weigh in and not be minimized. Was that intentional?"

He mulled it over, his expression matching her enthusiasm. "You know, I've always had very strong women in my life. I never really thought about her in that light before, to be honest. She is his partner, and she should be able to come up with similar conclusions as him, otherwise what's the point of her being there?"

Zora pressed. "But the way that you describe her, and the way that you have her almost as a person that he needs more than she needs him, I find that dynamic really fascinating."

He pursed his lips, brows wrinkling slightly. "So are you saying that you see her more as the primary investigator?"

She pumped the brakes. "No, not at all. Langston is central to the story—his growth over the course of the series is super clear. But she is the constant. He relies on her, needs her, and it's cool to see that role reversal. Female characters are so often cast as reliant on a man, or irrelevant without one, that your take is just refreshing."

They stepped into the tapas bar, taking seats at a high-top table. Lawrence frowned. "I've never heard that take before. Interesting." He pulled off his blazer, tugging at the sleeves.

Zora placed a hand on his firm arm, quickly removing it as though the heat emanating from it shocked her. "I hope that I'm not overstepping."

"Not at all. I'm enjoying this." His smile returned, stealing her breath away.

A cheerful server stopped at their table, asking for their order.

"Are you hungry?" Lawrence asked, eyeing the menu.

"Starving," she admitted. "It's been a long day, and I love this place. Do you mind if I order a few tapas to share?"

"If this is a regular spot for you, please do." He gestured in her direction.

She rattled off a few of the house specials and ordered a dirty gin martini.

Lawrence's lips twitched with the hint of a smile. "That sounds delicious. I'll have the pink peppercorn and blood orange gin and tonic, please." The server grabbed the menus and stepped away. "Your perspective is refreshing." He leaned forward.

"Really? I would think that people would point it out to you all the time. But I suppose you probably have a larger male readership?"

His smile widened. "I guess so. You are unusual, Zora."

"Is unusual a good thing? I would hate to be completely putting my foot in my mouth when it comes to you and your writing. I promise you that I don't mean you any disrespect or criticism. I have been a fan of your work because of how these characters interact, so it's really interesting to get your perspective."

"Makes sense." He nodded. "But enough about me and my book. I want to hear about you."

She lifted her shoulders. "What do you want to know?"

"Are you a local? What made you decide that you wanted to own a bookstore? And more importantly, are you single?"

The directness of the last question caught her off guard. "Er, yes, I'm single. I was born in the Bay Area, but my mom and grandmother are from Brookland, and we came back when my dad was diagnosed with cancer. We moved into my grandmother's house to cut costs with all of the medical bills. My mom ended up passing away when I was in high school, and my dad died a few years ago." Zora slowed when Lawrence's expression softened. She typically rushed through this part of her story—if she stopped to think on it for too long, she'd cry. She wasn't ashamed of her feelings, but Zora never wanted people to feel sorry for her or treat her differently.

"I'm so sorry," he whispered quietly, his dark eyes searching hers. The sincerity in his gaze unnerved her.

Zora blinked and looked down at the table, her fingers fidgeting in her lap. "Thank you. Anyway, I went to college and grad school here, and I decided I didn't want to leave. I've always loved books, and I thought I was on my way to becoming a librarian, but my parents left me enough for me to invest in my own shop just as Ms. Betty was considering retirement. It's been a lot of work building it up to what it is now, but it's been so rewarding to feel like we've become a part of the community."

"What a blessing. Were your parents academics?" He leaned forward on both of his elbows.

A flutter in her stomach at his proximity made the corners of her mouth curve. She shook her head. "My mom was a lawyer, and my dad owned a Filipino restaurant in Oakland. His cooking is actually how he convinced my mom that he was the one."

Lawrence piqued an eyebrow. "Did you inherit any of those skills?"

"I get by, but my grandmother's cooking is everything. What about your parents? Aside from what's in your family memoir, of course."

"So you read that, too?" His mouth twitched again.

Zora's face heated up. "Like I said, I'm a fan of your writing. It's very…vivid."

"Thank you. I will say working for myself has been extremely freeing."

She nodded. "Right? I feel so lucky to be able to say that I love my job."

"Me, too." He smiled. "We can never go back now."

She grinned. "So true! I wouldn't know what to do with myself if I couldn't have my store."

He moved his hand over hers, the warmth sending a tingle down her spine. "Let's hope we never have to find out."

The server returned with their cocktails and a bowl of marinated olives and Marcona almonds. Zora raised her glass. "I'll drink to that."

Tapping his glass against hers, Lawrence's mouth curved. His thick lips parted slowly. "Cheers."

They looked at each other over the rims of their glasses, and heat spread to Zora's belly. Exhaling a quick breath, she steered her mind away from his lips.

"Mmm, nice cocktail. Since this is close to work, do you come here a lot after you close? Where do you normally go out?"

A rhythmic song began to play as scents of saffron and seafood wafted up from the kitchen. "Honestly, I'm a little embarrassed. I don't get out much at all. I love this restaurant, but I order a lot of takeout. I usually carry the food back to the bookstore because it consumes so much of my days. It can be a lot of work, but I—I love my store. That's my top priority right now."

"I got that. I don't go out all that often, either, unless it has to do with a reading or speaking engagement somewhere. As a matter of fact, I'm supposed to be speaking to one of Reid's creative writing classes in the next week or so." He slowed. "Now that I think about it, I might have a conflict, and I'll need to check with him about that." He winced slightly and typed a note into his cell phone.

Back to Reid, Lawrence's loser sidekick. Zora pictured a younger, charismatic and popular Lawrence, and Reid as a brooding loner. "That's so nice of you to go and speak to a bunch of kids. I'm assuming this is a high school?"

Lawrence took another sip of his drink and nodded. "Yes, he teaches high school juniors and seniors. I know he teaches classes on creative writing, English literature, and different things, but if I'm honest I haven't paid as close attention as I should."

She sipped her drink, toying with the cocktail pick of green olives. "So this will be the first time that you're speaking to one of his classes?"

"Probably the first of many." He smiled.

"So how long have you two known each other? You seem so different." The gin started to loosen her shoulders, and she nibbled on an almond.

"We've known each other a really long time. We went to college together and were roommates in our freshman year. I probably would have failed out if it weren't for him. He is such a strong academic, and at the time that was not my focus." Lawrence shook his head as if to relieve himself of a memory.

"So he does have some redeeming qualities, then," she joked wryly.

"Oh, come on. He's a great guy. Sometimes he just needs a minute to warm up to people. Or, maybe, people need time to warm up to him. Clearly, he didn't make a great first impression today." He laughed.

The food arrived, and they handed each other dishes of steaming hot food, putting different tapas onto their own individual plates. Zora had ordered grilled pulpo, albondigas, and a small pan of paella. The scents of saffron and smoked paprika hung in the air much to her delight, and she smiled over at Lawrence. "You're really going to enjoy this."

"I have no doubt," he said, watching her as she took in all

of the steamy aromas. "Everything smells amazing. Where should I start?"

Mastering her nerve, Zora grabbed Lawrence's fork. "I'll make you the perfect bite," she said. He watched as she sliced the tender octopus. She scooped a forkful of paella, spearing the piece of octopus at the end, and slid the bite through a lemony emulsion. She handed the fork over to him, careful not to drop a single grain of rice. "There."

He gingerly took the fork from her, fingertips grazing her hand, and she sucked in a breath. "Thank you," he whispered, "this looks delicious." Taking a bite, his eyes widened and then closed, senses homing in on the flavors and textures he experienced. "Wow."

Zora made herself a similar bite and hummed softly as the combination hit her tongue. "So good."

"Do you know that you do a little dance when you eat something you like?" Lawrence's smile grew wide. "That may have been the cutest thing I've seen in a while."

After swallowing her food, Zora licked her lips and blinked in his direction. "You think I'm cute?"

"You're a lot more than that, Ms. Dizon."

His steady gaze colored her cheeks, and a heat that she hadn't felt in a long time churned in her belly and moved south. Maintaining eye contact, she lifted her glass and clinked it against his. "I'll drink to that."

Zora closed the front door quietly, relieved to find the main floor dark. After dropping her shoes on a shoe rack, she tiptoed up the stairs, almost making it to her bedroom when the hall light turned on.

"So how did it go?" Emma appeared in sweats.

"What are you still doing up? It was such a long day!" She'd hoped to have more time to digest the date before talking about it.

"We've been over here trying to figure out who that other guy was and which one would be a better match for you." Emma's hair was wrapped in a headscarf, and she used the tip of a rattail comb to scratch her scalp.

"What other guy?" Zora scrunched her brows together. "Oh, you mean his friend, Reid? He was such an asshole!"

"He was so handsome!" her grandmother exclaimed, popping her head out of Emma's room.

"Granny! What are you doing up here?"

"I was here with Emma making some observations about how the event went today."

Zora followed them down the hall to Emma's room, plopping down on the floor. "Well, I would love to hear what these observations about the event are."

"*Well*, we would love to hear about how your little date went," Emma replied. "Let's start there." Granny perched on the padded window seat, hugging a decorative pillow.

Zora shrugged. "It was nice. He was a perfect gentleman—super charming—but he was also attentive and funny, and I really got the impression that he's interested in dating me."

"What gave you that impression?"

"He asked me flat out if I was single. Pretty early on in the conversation, actually. It caught me off guard, but it was nice to know that he was looking at me as more than just a book-seller to take for a drink as a thank-you."

Emma side-eyed Zora. "You didn't actually think that that's why he asked you to go out, did you? Girl, we really need to work on your perception when it comes to men approaching you."

Over the years Zora had flubbed opportunities to flirt back with attractive single men because she didn't recognize the signs. She just thought they were being nice to her. "I just don't really know what to expect, especially from him. I mean, he was the author for our event today, and now I have a date with him this weekend!"

"You do?" they exclaimed in unison.

"I do." She nodded.

"So what's the date?" Emma rested her chin in her hands. "Is he taking you somewhere fun?"

"Actually, he invited me over to his place. He said he really enjoys cooking and would like to make something for me." She shrugged, tugging at a curl.

Emma and Granny exchanged a glance.

"I swear, it's like you two have a hive mentality. What was that look?"

Emma shrugged. "When was the last time that you had a man cooking for you? I mean, this sounds like quite a momentous occasion, but…"

"But what?" She threw up her hands in frustration. "What's wrong?"

"How do you know it's not some elaborate attempt at Netflix and chill?"

"Are you serious?" The thought had never occurred to Zora.

"Don't tell me you've never met the types. They make excuses about getting reservations or having a long wait, so staying in is better and blah blah blah. Especially here in D.C. Half of the people that try to talk to me don't want to go anywhere in public. It's like they're afraid of sunlight. Either they are socially awkward and don't want to interact with others or they're in other situationships and don't want to get caught."

"Where are you meeting these folks?" Zora laughed so hard she snorted.

"Girl, listen. And Granny—" she gestured "—you may want to cover your ears." She lowered her voice. "One time I met this guy through a friend. Crazy chemistry. He was all sexy and beardy. Chile, I blame myself, because the first time we got together, I was making some Old Bay wings and planned to watch some new movie on Netflix. I invited him over to join me, but I should have known full well that he was coming over with motives. Talkin' 'bout he wanted to give me a massage."

"Was the massage any good?"

"And then some, girl! That's how I ended up naked. But after that he never wanted to be outside the confines of the house. Six months and we never went on an actual date. Fool had me dickmatized." Emma sucked her teeth.

Zora cackled. "I guess so. To last in that holding pattern for six months, he had to be dropping a hammer."

Granny Marion covered her smile with the back of her hand. "Oh my."

Emma facepalmed. "I'm so sorry, Granny. I know that was a whole lot. I promise I'm not always that fast." She grimaced at Zora, who snatched a decorative pillow from the bay window to cover her face, unable to control her laughter.

She wheezed. "She really is that fast, Granny, but she doesn't want you to think poorly of her."

"Y'all act like I didn't have a life before your grandaddy. Long as you're being safe about it, you better live it up while you can, baby." She lifted her index finger toward Emma, who lifted her own in response for their teeny five.

"I know that's right!" Emma grinned.

"I'm curious what you thought of the other young man. Reid, was it?" Granny mentioned as the energy in the room calmed. "He was very handsome."

"He was such a jerk! The whole time that Lawrence was speaking, he was muttering different things under his breath, he just had all these snide remarks and he was so rude to me when I tried to get him to stop. And after all of that, I come to find out that they're best friends. Who acts like that at an event for their best friend, which affects their livelihood?" Zora asked hotly.

Emma nodded, tapping her finger against pursed lips. "Fair, but did you *see* him?"

"Obviously, I must have missed something, because I couldn't see past his attitude." She thought for a minute. "I mean, he was tall..."

"Girl, that man was fine." Emma's unblinking gaze made Zora's lips curve into a half smile.

"Damn fine," Granny agreed.

Emma turned to look at Granny with wide eyes and hiked her thumb in the elder's direction. "What she said."

"Well, I can't see how anybody is fine when they have such an ugly attitude. It just makes me more curious about the nature of their friendship. At one point I asked him why he bothered to show up if he wasn't there to enjoy the reading."

"Oop! What was his response?" Emma leaned closer.

"He didn't have one. He just kind of stared at me."

"Well, I'm sure if you start dating Lawrence, you're going to see him again. So I need you to choose definitively which one you want, because I'm coming for the other one. It really doesn't matter which one, because both of those men are damn fine on the Granny Marion scale," Emma assured her.

"Mmm-hmm." Granny nodded. "Maybe Reid was just having an off day."

Zora raised a brow. "What is it that you're seeing in that guy, Granny?"

Her grandmother shrugged with a tight-lipped smile. "I'm not sure yet, baby. Time will tell."

5

The next morning Zora arrived at the store early to make sure that everything was in order following the book event. Tired from all the event excitement, Granny decided that she would catch a ride with Emma into the store later.

As Zora parked, Brian locked up his bicycle on a rack outside the store. "Good morning, B! How's school going?"

"Hey, Z. It's okay. I've got a test coming up in biology, and I really need it to go well." His brows pinched; Brian had circles under his eyes. *He's probably doing all-nighters in the library again.* Brian had dreams of becoming a pediatric surgeon.

Zora squeezed his shoulder. "You've got this. You've been studying your tail off—I see your books are out most of the time that you're here."

"Yeah, I think it's just nerves. I need my bio grades to be strong for med school."

Zora unlocked the front door, flipping the open sign out toward the street, while Brian carried a sandwich board display with chalkboard drawings of the day's menu and book specials onto the sidewalk to entice passersby. When he came back into the store, Zora walked with him over to the coffee kiosk. "You're going to be fine—you're putting in a lot of hard work, so the important thing is to go in there and stay confident. You know the answers—you just need to avoid second-guessing yourself."

Brian nodded, an easy grin stretching across his face. "Yeah, that's true. Thanks, Z. Want a latte?"

"Yes, please!" She poked her head into her office to drop her purse and keys on the desk.

First thing in the morning, she liked to walk through the space to make sure that everything was as it should be—that the display tables were fully stocked, that any trash or leftover coffee cups from the event had been disposed of, that the sitting area didn't have any spills or smudges on the furniture. Zora wasn't a neat freak at home, but her business was something else entirely.

Running her own bookstore had been a dream that she didn't think would come true until she'd put in a decade of work with Ms. Betty and other booksellers and gained experience to feel confident that she could manage her own business. The loss of her parents had been one gut punch after another, but her parents had agreed far in advance that if anything happened to them, they wanted their only daughter to realize her dreams. It was bittersweet that she only had the bookstore now because she'd lost them. Zora ran her fingers over a framed memorial photo of her parents' smiling faces, who seemingly greeted customers as they entered the store.

Early days at the bookstore had been hard—she didn't have personal connections to publishers the way Ms. Betty did; didn't know how she was supposed to build an inventory that would keep her regular patrons happy; didn't want to keep bothering Ms. Betty while she basked in retirement. As if the universe heard her struggle, Zora stumbled upon a local book festival and immediately befriended other Black indie booksellers in the region, who took her under their wings and explained the ins and outs of how to manage cycles of book releases and to create buzz around the books she wanted to sell. The store slowly grew, and Ms. Betty's one small storefront expanded into Zora's being able to purchase the space next door after her second year of business. Now, entering its fourth year with Zora as owner, the store felt more established and more a part of her own vision. A local institution she knew her parents would've been proud of.

"Here's a latte and a Danish for you, Z." Brian handed her a hot cup and a fresh cheese Danish, its buttery, laminated layers still warm.

"You're too good to me, B! Now, go study before we get our morning rush." She shooed him away, grinning. Looking around the store once more, satisfied with the state of the displays and stock, she strode to the checkout counter to work on event-promo and new-release orders.

"Hello, Zora," a deep voice grumbled behind her.

She stood at the checkout counter with Sam, a regular patron who was researching ancient artifacts—like the Baghdad battery—for a historical fiction project she planned on writing. After decades of work as an archaeologist, Sam had hung up her tools and transitioned into drafting novels of historical mysteries with searing romances and death-defying action sequences. Sam thanked Zora for the pile of books she'd amassed on her current subject, and Zora smiled before turning toward a brooding Reid.

"How are you today? Welcome back to Opus Northeast." Her manners nudged her to offer a hand in greeting, but the scowl on his face wiped the polite impulse from her mind. Her bright smile for Sam turned to a tight-lipped purse.

He ignored the pleasantries. "I am searching for some writing craft books. Three in particular." He held out a list, his penmanship a spidery cursive on unlined paper. He blinked at her expectantly through his wire frames.

Zora took the list from him, her fingertips brushing his hand gently. As she perused the list, she noticed Reid rub a finger over the spot that her hand had touched. "Bit of a germaphobe, are we?" The singsongy, playful tone in her voice hopefully masked her annoyance. She couldn't see what good qualities Lawrence saw in Reid that made him worthy of being a best friend. "These are definitely titles I typically carry. Let me make sure that they're currently in stock."

He nodded, standing in place like an uncomfortable statue, looking like he wished he was anywhere other than in Zora's store. *Clearly, he's not one for small talk.*

Zora blew out a breath, hoping she could find these books quickly and he would leave. Her fingertips flew over the keyboard of her workstation computer as she searched the titles one at a time, marking the number currently available on Reid's list as she went. She felt his eyes on her, and Zora's face warmed as she imagined him scrutinizing the amount of time it took her to complete her search.

"Here." She handed the list back to him, gesturing toward a wall dedicated to craft books. "We have at least three copies of each of these in stock, and there are some others in the section that you might also enjoy. Are these for personal use? I remember Lawrence mentioning that you're a teacher."

"They're for my students."

She ignored the abrupt response, maintaining her professional warmth. "Great. Well, we do offer a discount for classroom materials, so feel free to pick out what you'd like, and I'll be sure to apply the teacher rate when I ring you up."

He looked at her, a pinch between his brows, his full lips in a straight line framed by a well-groomed beard. Much like the other day, he was in jeans and a polo shirt, a leather satchel slung over his shoulder. He looked like he worked at some sort of prep school—his wire-rimmed glasses framing his deep brown eyes and dark, curling lashes. Zora couldn't tell if he wanted to say something or if he just hated her in general, but the citrusy scent of his cologne had tricked her into lingering longer than she meant to.

She blinked. "Right, I'll just leave you to it." She turned back toward the register.

"Thanks," he replied gruffly, turning to look at the selection on the wall.

Zora glanced at him over her shoulder, then rolled her eyes as she sat behind the counter and opened the bookstore's general email inbox. "You're welcome," she muttered under her breath.

Less than a minute later, Emma and Granny blew into the store in a flurry—Emma running late per usual, and Granny rushing over to give Zora some sugar. After kissing her cheek, Granny squeezed Zora's hand in greeting. "You'll never guess what we did this morning, baby."

Knowing Emma, nothing I'd approve of. "What's that, Granny?"

"We made appointments to go get tattoos!"

"You what?" Zora exclaimed.

"That's very progressive of you." Reid appeared next to Granny; his large hand gripped five texts on writing techniques. "Would this be your first one?"

Granny winked at him. "A lady never tells."

Reid's mouth seemed to curve upward the slightest bit on one side, and Zora wondered whether that was as close as he came to smiling. The rest of his face looked like the movement pained him, so maybe the expression was more of a grimace.

"Find what you needed?" Zora held out her hands to ring up the books for Reid.

"I did." He handed them over, his dark eyes boring into hers.

She paused, waiting to see if he had anything more to say. When he continued to stare back at her, she averted her eyes to the register's computer screen. "Okay. That'll be $48.50 with the teacher's discount applied."

He pulled a card from his wallet, which Zora accepted, wary of touching him this time.

"Do your students have a big writing assignment coming up?" Zora chatted as she ran his card.

"Yes," he replied curtly.

She pulled the receipt from the register, providing Reid with a pen so that he could sign for the purchase. Once he did, she placed a duplicate into a monogrammed bag made from recycled paper and handed it to him. "Well, good luck with that," she said brightly, willing him to leave.

He nodded and turned away. As he passed Granny, he nodded again. "Ma'am."

"Bye, now!" Granny finger-waved at him sweetly.

As the bell on the closing door tinkled, Emma swept over to the counter. "So what do you think?"

"Of what?" Zora glanced blankly between her best friend and her grandmother.

"Isn't he hot?"

Exasperated, she protested. "That man is tepid at best."

"I don't know." Granny fanned herself. "I thought he was charming."

Zora threw up her hands. "Because he called you *ma'am*?"

"Didn't you see him smile at me?"

"Was that a smile or did his face twitch?"

Granny waved away her granddaughter. "You're so feisty whenever he's around. Excellent chemistry," she whispered to Emma, who nodded conspiratorially.

Rolling her eyes, Zora turned back to her work. "We're going to need to get your eyes checked. There was no spark between us. He got grossed out when I accidentally touched him—it's like he was rubbing off my cooties."

"How old are we, five?" Emma tilted her head in amusement.

"The guy hates me. Besides, I'm dating his best friend."

Emma and Granny looked at each other and then leaned toward Zora. "So?" they asked in unison.

Zora heaved a deep sigh. "Okay, you two and your hive mentality need to go somewhere. I have work to do."

"He was so tall," Granny said to Emma, ignoring her granddaughter.

"Wasn't he? What do you think, maybe six foot four?" Emma responded in a hushed tone.

"Give or take an inch. I bet he's got a generous package, too." Marion waggled her brows.

Emma bit her lip as Zora gasped. "Granny!"

"What? Didn't you see those hands? I bet he can palm a basketball. Or a melon." She reached out her hands like claws and pretended to squeeze two large spheres. "Or melons..."

"Someone wake me up from this nightmare," Zora muttered. "Ouch! Did you just pinch me?"

Emma shrugged. "Just making sure you're awake."

6

The rest of the week breezed by, and before Zora knew it, Saturday had arrived. With zero time to shop, she enlisted Emma's styling talents to help her choose an outfit for her date with Lawrence.

"Uh, Z? When was the last time that you went shopping without me? I can't exactly pull a look out of my ass here." Emma fingered the clothes hanging in Zora's closet, pushing hanger upon hanger clad in colorful cardigans aside to see whether any treasures lay hidden behind them. "We need to step up your wardrobe, babe."

"I have plenty of options in here! Look at this!" Zora nudged past Emma to snag a couple of fit-and-flare dresses from their hangers. The jewel-toned green and purple dresses were identical to each other, complete with a faux wrap cut and pockets at the hip. "I could wear one of these and then put a cardigan over it."

Emma snatched the dresses from Zora and hung them back

in the closet. "Sis. You're not even going out, nor is this a business meeting, so why waste a wrap dress? Hmm…wait." She rummaged around farther in the packed closet, pulling out Zora's favorite pair of distressed jeans, a soft white T-shirt, and a lightweight duster coat with a bright African print of reds and yellows. "Wear this with some poppin' red lipstick and your wide gold hoops."

Zora stared at the three pieces of clothing, puzzled. "Why have I never thought to put these together? This is cute!"

"Sure is! And you're gonna let me borrow that coat." She pursed her lips, throwing Z a knowing glance. "I'm going out with some other friends, and I've been trying to get this girl's attention. She wears stuff like this." Emma's interests varied with her mood, and her social butterfly–esque extroversion attracted some of the most beautiful people Zora had ever seen.

Zora grinned. "Oh, girl, you know I buy one in every color when I find stuff I like." Zora dug into her closet and furnished a second duster coat with a similar pattern in orange and blue.

Emma's jaw dropped as she clutched the garment to her chest. "You may never see this again." Emma was a size or two smaller, but her generous bust would fill out any additional space. She often borrowed Zora's clothes, which was mildly irritating since there was no reciprocation.

Zora held the hanger away from her friend. "I know where you live, heffa," she warned. Though a smile touched her lips, it didn't reach her widened eyes.

"You make the same look your mama did back when we were kids," Emma laughed.

Zora grinned. "It felt like her expression dared me to do something that I wasn't supposed to do, but I always knew better than to try her when she made that face."

"Well, we all knew better than to try her—teeth would click. What time is your date?"

"I've got about an hour before I need to head out. He lives maybe fifteen minutes from here."

"Baby, you up there?" Granny called from downstairs. "You almost ready?"

Zora made her way down the stairs with Emma close behind her. "Hey, Granny." She kissed her on the cheek. "I'm about to get dressed right now."

Emma fluffed Zora's curls. "How are you going to wear your hair?"

"You think down, or I was thinking pulled back from my face."

"Baby hair?"

"Light baby hair." She smoothed her index fingers over the edges of her temples.

Emma nodded. "Let's see it. We'll hang out down here." They tried to spare Granny the trip up the stairs whenever possible, though often she insisted. Emma turned Granny toward the ink-blue sofa for girl talk while Zora got ready.

Upstairs Zora headed into her bathroom, butterflies in her stomach. She pulled her hair back from her face with a cloth headband to do her makeup, her high cheekbones protruding from deep brown skin. She applied primer to her moisturized face, filling in little gaps in her brows with a pencil before brushing gel on them to set. Her wide-set eyes had hooded lids and thick lashes that needed little more than a sweep of mascara. Opting for a fresh face, she applied light makeup, dusting a bit of blush on the apples of her cheeks, and finishing with a quick spritz of setting spray with SPF or Emma would throw a fit.

She used a boar brush to pull her hair back into a high ponytail. Dipping an edge brush in gel to set the baby hairs at her temples, she curved the brush, creating swoops reaching toward her hairline and looping sideburns into tiny curls.

After a spritz of strong-holding hairspray, she pulled off her robe and moved toward the bedroom through a spritz of Jo Malone's Nectarine Blossom & Honey. There was no expectation of action on this first real date, but Zora still pulled some sexy black underwear over her generous curves. *Just in case.*

From her closet, she pulled out a pair of nude block-heel sandals. The thick heel made it easier for Zora to walk—she would not make the same mistake she'd made at the event—and she loved how the thin straps showed off her fresh pedicure. She tossed her red lip stain, cell phone, and a small bifold wallet into a leather clutch that matched the yellows in her jacket, then tiptoed down the stairs.

Granny and Emma sat in the L of the sofa with bowed heads, whispering conspiratorially. As Emma raised her head, she let out a low whistle, snapping her fingers. "You so fine, girl!"

Granny nodded her approval. "Your hair looks pretty like that, my love."

"Y'all don't think the earrings are too much?" Zora patted her hair, turning her head to the side.

"Not at all. Plus, they go perfectly with your red lip and that jacket. It really does fit you perfectly," Emma assured her.

Zora's lips tugged at the corners. "You've got to love a man who can appreciate some curves." She smoothed her fingers over her midsection and hips.

"*Every* man appreciates some cushion, now," Granny quipped.

Emma's eyes widened and slid to give her elder a once-over.

"Yes, ma'am." Zora grinned, kissing her grandmother lightly on the cheek.

"Y'all have a good time, baby."

"See y'all later!" Zora slid on her sandals and waved goodbye. Her GPS led her straight to Lawrence's house in a pretty neighborhood. Big houses with large overhanging trees. The distance between homes indicated the priciness of the location. Comparatively, the sides of her home were less than twenty feet from her neighbors.

Lawrence's corner property featured a U-shaped driveway and steps leading up to a wraparound porch that extended through to the back of the house—a rarity in D.C. Gas lanterns framed either side of the massive front door, which was painted a matte black to match the shutters. The second level's Juliet balcony faced the street, while massive red maple trees towered on either side of the house like sentries; the canopy of a scarlet oak barely starting to change its colors peeked over the roof of the house.

Zora checked her lipstick in the rearview mirror, blowing a kiss to her reflection before stepping out into the early-evening air. The early-fall humidity was tempered by a warm breeze that tickled the exposed nape of her neck above her jacket collar. As she crossed the street, she spotted Reid heading down the driveway in her direction, the same scowl on his face as before.

"I didn't expect to see you again so soon."

The brusqueness of his tone caught Zora off guard. "Uh, I'm sorry to disappoint?"

Reid held up a hand, squeezing his eyes shut for a second. "I'm sorry, that came out wrong." The corner of his mouth curved upward as his glasses glinted in the sunlight. His deep brown features were framed by a recent shape up—his beard also recently trimmed. *Is he attempting to smile at me?* "How are you, Zora?"

Her eyes narrowed at his attempt at civility, but she refused to be petty in her response. "I'm well, how are you?"

He nodded, pursing his lips. "I'm okay. Just finished a business meeting with Lawrence. I didn't realize that he was nudging me out the door because he was expecting company."

Zora frowned. "Does he cook a lot for himself?"

"Cook?" Reid's brows sprang to his hairline.

"He's making us dinner tonight. Or, at least, that's what he said…" Zora watched his face closely, confused by the disconnect. *Maybe he's bored with this conversation.*

"You know what? He was starting to put some food together. I'm sorry. I've been a little distracted lately."

"It's cool. I hope that your class found those writing craft books helpful?"

"Yes, they were excited to have some new material to tear into. Literary vultures." His lips curved briefly at his joke attempt. "So you've come over for dinner, then?"

"Yeah, he said he's cooking for me." Zora nodded.

Reid raised an eyebrow. Zora didn't know what that meant, but she was afraid to ask. Small talk with this man was like pulling teeth.

When he didn't speak, she continued to fill the silence. "So what were you and Lawrence working on today?"

He shrugged. "Just going over his schedule to highlight upcoming events across his social media, planning some additions to his website and a giveaway campaign to increase buzz around his next book."

"How did you get into social media work?"

Reid stood still for a moment with a frown on his face, almost like he was working out a difficult math problem. "Uh, you know. It's nothing too difficult. Just helping out a friend."

"Well, still, that's really nice of you to help Lawrence like that. I'm sure your students keep you plenty busy."

He shifted uncomfortably. "Yeah, well, it's complicated. You know, your food might be getting cold…"

"You're right. I'd better get inside." She waved quickly as she stepped toward the house, making an effort to have a friendly ending to their encounter.

"Yeah, I'd better go. Take care." Without a smile or a wave, he turned gruffly toward the street, and Zora made her way up the stairs to the porch.

As she reached for the doorbell, the door swung open, and Lawrence peeked out. "Ah, you made it!"

"Oh yeah, hey!" She extended her arms to hug him lightly. "Sorry. I ran into Reid in the driveway, and we started talking about books for his students."

"Well, I hope he was on better behavior than before." He stood back in a fitted pullover sweater in navy blue, the collar flipped upward and zipped down toward his chest. His jeans looked freshly pressed, his feet clad in black socks.

"Oh yes," Zora laughed, "he was actually a lot more talkative this time. I think he's warming up." She slipped out of her shoes, stretching out her toes on the lacquered hardwood floors.

"Oh yeah? You look beautiful, by the way." He reached for her hand and watched her turn.

She blushed. "Thank you. Yeah, well, it was really me talking and him more listening and processing."

"Right." He ushered Zora farther into the house, his hand moving to the small of her back. "I love the print." He tugged at the sleeve of her jacket. "Did you get that during travels, or is that from here?"

"There are some great boutiques in the Northeast that I love. My friends and I try not to spend all of our money, but it's a struggle." She flashed a smile at him, hoping her lipstick hadn't migrated to her teeth.

If it had, Lawrence hadn't seemed to notice. His smile radiated warmth, and he hadn't taken his eyes off her. "Well, I hope you brought your appetite. Let me give you a tour." They walked through the living room and a formal dining area to an open kitchen.

"Wow, this is such a beautiful home. Have you lived here long?" Framed family photos adorned console tables and open wall space, displaying generations of Lawrence's family in candid moments and posing for special events.

"Yeah, this is actually my family home. I was raised here, and my parents have since retired in Florida. They love the heat." He gestured toward a photo sitting on the wet bar of his parents on a boat—his dad proudly presenting a large fish for the camera as his mom gave her best Vanna White pose.

"That's awesome." Zora leaned closer to take in the details.

"Where are your parents?" He turned and looked at her.

Zora looked down at her hands. "Oh, they passed away."

"I'm sorry. You did tell me that." He covered his eyes with his hand.

"No need to apologize—I don't expect you to remember everything about me after one meeting." She eyed the kitchen counters with plates already loaded up. "Wow, so you already cooked and cleaned up the entire kitchen."

"Well, that was an important detail, so I really do apologize. And, yes, I find that it's best to clean as you go." Lawrence laughed. His kitchen was spotless—granite countertops sparkled and there wasn't one fingerprint on the stainless steel appliances.

Zora marveled that there wasn't one pot on the stove or in the sink. *It looks like no one ever uses this place—I wonder if he has a housekeeper.* "So what did you make?" She peered at the plates, wondering how he made two perfect portions— she was never able to cook anything without having a day or two of leftovers. "Everything looks and smells delicious. Your kitchen is immaculate!"

"Thank you." He smiled confidently. He gestured toward the plates on the kitchen island. "We have braised short ribs over mashed potatoes and some spinach sautéed with garlic and olive oil. Later, we've got a beautiful, rich chocolate cake from my favorite bakery, which pairs well with this red that I have for us tonight." He tossed a kitchen towel onto his shoulder.

"Well, I can't wait to enjoy this! Thank you so much for cooking." Something about the presentation of the food felt familiar, and Zora's Spidey senses tingled in the pit of her stomach.

"It's my pleasure. Come on." He led her to the table, carrying dishes in both hands. "Actually, would you grab the silverware? It's in that drawer there."

"Sure." She grabbed the silverware and napkins, following behind him.

He set down the plates and pulled out her chair. "My lady."

Warmth kissed Zora's cheeks. "Thank you. Wow, all of the women in your family seemed to have taught you right."

He grinned. "They'd still say I get a little fresh from time to time."

"A little fresh isn't so bad." She looked up at him, her eyes crinkling at the corners.

"Is that right?" Lawrence leaned forward slowly, his eyes dropping to Zora's mouth. He kissed her lightly on the lips, licking his own as he pulled back. "Sorry. I've been wanting to do that since you came in the door. If I'm being honest, since we went for tapas."

"No need to apologize. That was nice." She smiled at him, surprised at the heat building in her stomach. She arched upward to kiss him once more.

Lawrence smiled against her lips. "Well." He sat. "Please enjoy." He gestured to their meal.

Zora leaned forward over her plate, bowing her head slightly with her eyes closed. When she opened her eyes, she noticed Lawrence watching her. "I'm sorry. I should have invited you to pray with me."

"Oh." He waved his hand. "That's okay. I'm more spiritual than religious."

"I see. Well, everything you cooked looks amazing!" She placed a napkin in her lap. "This looks like something I'd order from my favorite restaurant all the time."

"Really? What's your favorite restaurant?"

She sliced a piece of short rib as Lawrence took his first bite. "It's called Cafe Francisco's—this great place in Brookland not far from the bookstore. They make great short ribs, but my favorite thing on their menu is their braised lamb shank." Zora took her first bite; the braised meat melted on her tongue. "Wow, you're a great cook!" She smiled at him.

He watched her take her next bite, his expression indecipherable.

"What are you thinking?" she asked, shielding her mouth with her hand, worried she'd dropped sauce on her blouse.

"Watching you enjoy the first bite." He smiled. "Sorry. I hope that wasn't weird. It's just that, when we went for tapas, I could tell you were a foodie. Watching you experience your first bite is like watching a gift be unwrapped on Christmas."

Zora smiled thoughtfully. "It's true. I am definitely a foodie. I took an opportunity after college to do some traveling and really just to explore culture and connect with people and try all of the food."

"Wow, where did you go?" He took a bite.

"I went first to visit family in the Philippines. From there, I visited a college friend in Singapore, and a good friend's family is in Thailand, and they let me stay with them for a couple weeks, and then from there I went to Spain and Italy."

"That sounds like an amazing trip. Wow," he gushed, "is there somewhere that you want to go that you haven't been yet?"

"Hmm… Honestly, I would like to spend a significant

amount of time in Africa. I have friends from Ethiopia and Zambia and Namibia, and I would love to go and just immerse myself in the cultures. I've been to South Africa and to Egypt and Morocco, and I want to keep exploring."

"When do you find the time to do all of this traveling?" Muscles along the side of his cleanly shaven face flexed as he chewed.

"It's not easy," she admitted. "Especially because I like to put my business first. But usually around the holidays I will take a few weeks and just go somewhere. Now that my parents are gone, I don't feel as tied down. My grandmother lives with me, but we spend almost every day together, so she tells me it's her chance to miss me."

"That's sweet. Was she that nice lady at the bookstore that was welcoming people and getting them into line?"

Zora nodded. "She's my heart. You mentioned having a lot of women in your family. Are you close to them, too?"

Lawrence smiled, dabbing his lips with a napkin. Zora took the opportunity to glance at his mouth, his thick lower lip curving lazily. "I am," he said. "I was raised by a single mom and have three sisters."

"Wow, three! Are you the oldest?"

"The youngest."

"Ah. That must mean you have four protectors," Zora teased.

"It's more like I have four bossy, opinionated women who tell me what I should be doing and when I should be doing it." He laughed, rubbing the back of his neck.

"Do they often try to meddle with your love life?" Zora smirked, playfully winking at him.

"All. The. Time." He grinned. "But I would have it no other way. When I don't listen to them, that's when I really have a hard time."

"Do they know you're on a date right now?" Zora sipped her wine, wondering how deep the meddling was when it came to Lawrence's family. She'd dated her share of mama's boys, and she wasn't eager to go down that road again.

He placed his hand on hers. "I let them know when they need to know. You don't have to worry. It's not some wild Oedipus situation here." He laughed.

The warmth of his hand crept up her arm and sent a shiver down her spine. He squeezed her fingers, the tension sending heat between her legs. "Well, I wasn't thinking *that*," she lied.

"Are you ready for dessert?" His eyes danced around her face. "More wine?"

"Just a drop more wine, please. This meal was delicious, but now I'm a little full." She moved her glass closer to Lawrence, so that he could pour.

He stood, refilling both of their glasses, and gestured toward the living room. "Well, here, why don't we go get comfortable in the other room?" He carried their glasses toward the sofa, placing them on marble coasters.

She sat next to him, running her fingers over the buttery leather upholstery. "Thank you for such a lovely meal."

"Thank you for being such a lovely date." His arm rested on the back of the sofa, and he slid it around her shoulders to bring her closer. "I'd be lying if I said I wasn't distracted most of dinner."

Zora turned to look into his eyes. "What was on your mind?"

Lawrence ran his thumb over her bottom lip. "This." Cradling her chin with his thumb and forefinger, he pressed his lips against hers slowly.

Zora's eyes closed, and she took in his scent as she reciprocated, parting her lips slightly for a second kiss before pulling back. "I'd be lying if I said that hadn't crossed my mind." She smiled. "What is your plan for the rest of the weekend?"

"I'm working on my next book. It's due soon." He gestured toward his office, which opened to the living room via French doors. A huge curving monitor sat on an L-shaped desk with an oversize leather chair behind it.

She shook her head. "It never stops, does it?"

"It's a lot of work, but I like the pace. What about you? What have you got going on this weekend?"

"Just the store—the usual." She checked her watch, surprised that so much time had passed in what felt like the blink of an eye. "I hate to have to skip dessert, but I should actually get going. Emma and I have a big day of inventory planned for tomorrow."

He pulled her close, one arm still around her shoulders as the other wrapped around her waist. "Well, no cake tonight then, but I still want dessert." He kissed her sweetly until her lips parted, his tongue immediately finding hers as the kiss became more urgent and heated. When he released Zora for air, he pressed his lips against her temple.

"You have quite the sweet tooth." She grinned at him.

"I've always been a big fan of chocolate."

7

"Hey, Z, Lane's all done signing the preorders." Emma crooked her thumb toward a visiting author who'd stopped by to sign copies of her upcoming release.

"Great, thank you! How did that feel, Lane?" Zora stepped from behind the checkout counter to walk her out. "On Tuesday you'll officially be a published author!"

"I still don't believe it," she admitted, her bubbly laughter tinkling brightly as her gold-rimmed cat-eye glasses caught the sunshine streaming in through the windows. Lane's curls bounced as she walked, creating their own rhythmic dance as she navigated the store, her petite frame barely visible over the book displays. With her sweet voice and youthful appearance, one would never guess she was a sapphic romance writer of one of the steamiest debuts Zora had read in a while.

"Well, I loved the characters, and the steam level was spicy! It's going to be so easy to recommend this book to our romance readers. Give us a call in a week or two. We'll have another shipment if you'd like to come back and sign some more."

"I will. Thank you, Zora!" She waved as she exited.

Returning to the checkout counter, Zora wheeled a cart of signed books closer to her chair. "She has a lot of preorders, girl." Both levels of the cart were packed with books, folded invoices neatly placed inside like bookmarks. From a drawer, she pulled a roll of "signed copy" stickers to affix to the front covers.

"Mmm-hmm, that girl is like a prodigy. She writes in young adult and adult romance. She's already got four more books under contract and she's barely pushing twenty-nine!" Emma sat at the other end, putting discount stickers on a stack of self-care and wellness books for National Wellness Week. "But enough about her. You want to talk about your date? I tried to wait up, but you must have snuck by me."

"It's easy to do when you're laid out, snoring, on the couch!" Zora poked Emma's thigh.

Emma slapped her hand away. "Girl, I don't snore. I got caught up watching old episodes of *Living Single*. I didn't think that show would be so soothing! Anyway, how'd it go? You've been quiet this morning." Emma pulled her braids from behind her shoulders to rest on one side of her neck, eyeing her friend.

"Hmm…" Zora grunted, placing stickers on the signed books.

"Will you spit it out already?"

"There's something that I'm just trying to figure out."

"Like what? Was his house dirty?"

"God, no. The place was immaculate. Big. So clean that it didn't look like he lived there."

"So what's the problem, chick? He got bitches tied up in the basement?"

"Shut up, Em," Zora cackled. "It just felt like things didn't add up. Like he was fronting."

"But how? Walk me through it." Emma gestured toward the space between them for Zora to paint a picture.

"So first, I ran into Reid, and I swear, speaking to that man is like watching paint dry."

Emma snickered. "He's still fine, though."

"Whatever. We talked for a minute about his work and then he left. When I got inside, Lawrence had already made our plates and there were no dishes in the sink, no pots and pans on the stove. Everything was already plated. It was just weird, because he said he was cooking dinner, but the house was so clean that either he magically balances cooking and cleaning at the same time, or he lied and ordered food in."

"What kind of food was it?"

"It was braised short ribs with garlic spinach. It was really good, but it reminded me of—"

"Cafe Francisco's." Emma finished her sentence, her eyes narrowing.

"Yeah." Zora bit her lip, staring at her friend.

"Okay, I admit it, that does sound a little weird, but are you really going to Zor-lock your date?"

"I'm just trying to think of what reason he would have to lie." Zora bit her lip, wanting to believe that she was over-thinking things, but her Spidey senses still tingled.

Emma rolled her eyes with exasperation. "Maybe he was just trying to impress you and couldn't think of a better way. Let's not jump to the worst possible conclusion, girl, okay?"

"So maybe he lied, but it was a good lie? How does that even make sense?" Zora threw up her hands in frustration.

Emma wasn't even looking at her. "Um, Z? I think you have a visitor…"

"Hi. Is it a bad time?" Reid stood on the other side of the counter, staring at Zora expectantly.

"Reid. I'm so sorry. I didn't hear you come in!" Zora stood, placing her hands on the counter. "What are you doing here?"

He glanced at Emma, who stood to give them privacy.

"I'll go get some coffee. Want another latte, Z?" Emma called over her shoulder.

"Please?" Zora called, returning her attention to their surprise guest. "Sorry about that. How are you?"

"I'm good, thanks." Dressed in jeans and a black sweater that hugged the muscles in his arms, Reid shoved his hands into his pockets, a tight smile on his spectacled face. He looked down at the counter, his smooth, dark skin glowing no doubt from the humid autumn air. "I, uh, came to ask you for a favor."

"Me?" She frowned. *What could he possibly want from me?*

For the first time since they met, Reid's face broke into a full smile. "Yeah, I teach writing and literature classes at a local magnet school."

"You teach at Langston Hughes?" Zora interrupted, impressed. "That's a really good school. My niece went there."

"Yeah, I've been there for almost ten years."

"Really? Do you know Safina?"

"Safina was one of my star students. She's your niece?" Reid's smile grew wider, which surprised Zora.

"Yeah, small world. That's my girl."

Reid nodded. "She's a joy." He paused to clear his throat. "Anyway, um, Lawrence had agreed to speak to my class about writing professionally and different avenues that writers take to be published. He just told me that he's not going to be able to make it after all, but he suggested that you might be a good replacement, given your profession." He shifted from one foot to the other, his hands as restless as his feet. When Zora looked at his wringing hands, he shoved them into his pockets.

"Me?" Zora asked, a little shocked. "Are you sure? I mean, I do know of other local authors who might be a better source for you. Not sure that kids would want to hear from a bookstore owner. I'm sure it's a lot sexier to hear from someone who has books optioned for film or who knows some really cool famous people. I'm just in a little book bubble." She gestured to the confines of her store.

Reid stepped closer, taking his hands out of his pockets and resting them on the counter. "But that's why you're perfect. You are on the receiving end of all of these forms of creativity, right? Graphic novels and cookbooks and poetry and nonfiction and fantasy and romance. You come into contact with the authors and illustrators behind all of these works, and you get to have conversations with the people behind them. So not only do you know how the sausage is made, you're an integral part in helping connect these folks with the community. That's what we're about at Langston."

From the corner of her eye, Zora saw Emma standing by Granny's chair, a coffee in her hand. She and Granny craned their necks to watch her conversation with Reid. Emma held her hands about a foot apart and mouthed the word "sausage." Zora sucked in a breath and returned her attention to Reid, willing herself not to laugh.

Reid looked in their direction. "I probably should have called," he chuckled, gravel in the baritone of his voice.

The sound of his laugh stirred something deep in Zora. As he turned to look down at her, she noticed the curl in the lashes framing his dark eyes through the lenses of his glasses. She squeezed her thighs together as he continued to rest his large hands on the counter, just a foot from her own.

"Oh, it's totally fine. Don't mind them." Zora gestured over her shoulder. "But about your class, if you think that I could be a good substitute for Lawrence, I'm happy to help."

Reid raised his hands in victory. "Thank you. You are really helping me out."

"One question." Zora held up a finger.

"What is it?" He hovered over the counter, resting his lengthy fingers on its edge as if the keys to a piano were beneath them.

He smelled of amber and sandalwood; Zora's nose picked up faint traces of vanilla.

"When is the event?"

"Wow," he laughed, rolling his eyes at himself. "That would be sort of an important detail, right? It's this Thursday at one o'clock. Is that okay?"

"Sure. I'll add it to our calendar now. Emma runs the store in my absence." Emma and Granny continued to stare unabashedly. Zora hid a smile as she entered the talk into her calendar.

"Great. Well, here, type your number into my phone, and I'll text you more of the logistics."

Zora accepted his phone, her eyes trained on him. "I don't have to do a slideshow or anything, do I?"

"Only if you want all of them to fall asleep," Reid laughed.

Zora grinned. "Fair. I'll come up with something."

Reid watched her closely. "I know you will." His lip curled slightly as he smiled down at her.

Tension hung in the air between them, so electric that the hairs on the back of Zora's neck rose. She entered her number into the phone, carefully handing it back to him.

Reid nodded his thanks. "I have to catch Lawrence before he heads to the airport, but I'll text you later?"

"Sure."

He waved as he turned toward the door.

Zora turned to find Emma and Granny Marion standing directly behind her. Emma handed her a hot latte. "Now do you see what we're talking about? That dude is fine."

"Did he look like that this whole time? How did I miss that?" Zora shook her head. "I swear D.C. men are fine as *hell*." Whether suited and professional or laid-back and casual, the swag of Black men in D.C. was beyond sexy to Zora—Black men proud to wear their hair naturally, to grow out and groom their beards, who walked into the room dripping with confidence and flirting with ease.

Emma harrumphed. "And too bad they know it."

Over the years, Zora and Emma traded war stories of trying to date men in D.C., only to find that the ratio of single Black men to single Black women pretty much gave men every reason to extend their bachelorhood as long as possible. Dating multiple people was so prevalent in D.C. that, at one point, Zora found herself dating a man who was dating four other women, and she only found out because they ran into an angry ex who put him on blast while they shared a romantic dinner.

Granny patted Zora's hand. "Do me a favor, sugar."

"Anything, Granny." She leaned forward to give her a kiss on the cheek.

The woman's soft voice imparted gentle instruction. "Next time speak up, baby, so Emma and I don't have to strain our ears so much when we eavesdrop. My hearing ain't what it used to be, so let your voice carry a little further for me."

Zora shook her head with amusement. "Yes, ma'am."

Emma was staying late to close the store that night, and Granny went to visit with a friend from church for dinner, so Zora stretched out on her ink-blue sofa with a glass of wine, luxuriating in the solitude after a long day helping customers. Then her phone buzzed.

Reid: Hey, Zora, I hope that I didn't disrupt things too much earlier. (This is Reid, by the way)

Zora: Hey! No worries, thank you for inviting me to speak to your class. NGL, I'm a little nervous.

Reid: You, nervous? I don't believe that for a second.

Zora: It's different speaking in front of kids. No mercy!

Reid: LOL you ain't neva lied! But really, my class is full of budding writers. They'll love hearing about the authors you've met, the kinds of works that you choose to sell at your bookstore, how authors make it onto the New York Times' bestseller lists...

Zora bit her lip, still reeling that she and the cranky man from the book event were texting and somehow via text he seemed funny and approachable. During the event all of his huffing and snark made her miss his handsome features—she couldn't see past his attitude. Now all she could picture were those deep brown eyes and curly lashes fixed on her; thoughts she shouldn't have about the best friend of a man she had just started dating.

Zora: Is there a dress code?

Reid: For students, yes. For adults, I'm sure whatever you choose will be appropriate. You looked nice at the store. Both times. And that African print jacket was fire.

A warmth built in Zora's chest, but she exhaled it out as thoughts of Lawrence crossed her mind. Assuming that Lawrence was right and that Reid had redeeming qualities, she justified feeding her growing curiosity with that rather than her epiphany of attraction.

Zora: What made you want to become a teacher?

Reid: Loaded question, haha. I've been a bibliophile forever, and writing came naturally to me. I always wanted to give back to my community, so I focused on creative writing and literature in college and grad school, got my teaching credential.

Zora: So you're a writer? Is that how you and Lawrence became close?

Zora watched the ellipses start and stop on the screen of her phone several times.

Reid: I am. L and I were college roommates, and we took a couple of writing classes together. He went the publishing route, and I chose teaching.

Zora: Do you aspire to be published some day?

She pictured him standing in front of a crowd, waiting to hear about his book, his brooding exterior breaking to reveal a wide smile with a thick lower lip she just wanted to—
Her phone pinged, breaking her concentration.

Reid: I've been thinking about that a lot lately, to be honest.

Z: Is that a yes? ☺

R: LOL, it's complicated. I want to, but I have some other projects that could pose conflicts.

Z: If you didn't have those projects, what would you write?

R: Is this an interview?

Zora blushed, but she ached for the answer.

Z: Sorry, I didn't realize that I was asking so many questions. We didn't exactly get a chance to really get to know each other when we first met, so I guess I'm just… I don't know.

R: It's all good. I'd like to write a murder mystery series.

Z: Interesting. Did Lawrence inspire that?

R: You could say that, but I think it's my turn to ask some questions…

Zora bit her lip, wondering what he would want to know. Sipping her wine, she closed her eyes, trying to remember the scent of his cologne. A vision of his rich umber eyes, the color of melted dark chocolate, flashed beneath her eyelids and she gasped, fluttering her eyes back open in time for the next message.

R: What made you decide to open your own bookstore?

Z: I love books. Always have, and my parents left me the seed money to open my store when they passed.

R: Wow, I'm so sorry to hear that. I lost my father last year, and I am so glad to have my mom still with me.

Z: I'm glad for you too. It's such a blessing. I've still got my granny, who reminds me endlessly that I won't have her forever.

R: Ah, are you getting pressure to hurry up and have babies? My mom hits me and my brothers with that almost daily.

"You, too!" Zora squealed, pulling herself up to a seated position on the couch.

Z: How do you respond to it? It's literally all the time! And I know she means well, but I have things to do! What would I look like popping out babies right now?

R: Well, if I'm honest, I think you'd be beautiful pregnant. And I haven't figured out what to say to my mom that will get her to stop pressing. I don't think she will until she gets her way.

Zora stared at her phone. *Does he think I'm beautiful?* She stretched forward to grab the open bottle of wine from the coffee table and filled her glass far beyond the standard pour.

Texting with Reid felt like talking with an old friend who she'd known for a long time. It was nothing like when they first met at the bookstore.

Z: So do you eventually want to be a full-time writer?

R: I just think it's going to be a while before I can get there.

Z: Can I see something that you've written?

R: Maybe... I'm a little shy about sharing my work.

Zora bit her lip, trying to think of some quippy come-back that would convince him to let her read it when Emma walked in the door.

"Hey, girl. What's that look on your face? Are you texting with Lawrence?"

"Actually," Zora said innocently, "I've been texting with Reid."

"Oh really?" Emma drew out the word suspiciously.

"Yeah, you know we were talking about his event at school

that's coming up. And then we just started to get to know each other. He's actually… He seems like he's a cool guy."

"Well, fine as he is, it would be a waste if he wasn't."

"True."

"So what you thinkin', girl, you gon' get with Reid now?" Emma sat down on the chaise of the sofa.

"Uh, I don't know about all that." Zora tensed up. She'd be lying if she said she hadn't wondered whether Reid's kissing skills were on par with Lawrence's—just the thought sent flutters from the pit of her stomach to the juncture of her thighs.

"Well, why not?"

"I mean, they are best friends, Em."

"Yeah, but what does that have to do with you?" Emma's eyebrow rose as she looked at her friend.

"Girl, how does that make me look in these streets?"

"What are you talkin' about? Nobody's going to judge you—you're a single woman dating. If you're dating, people assume that you're seeing more than one person. Besides, what man in D.C. is only dating one woman?"

"Well, I just don't know how I feel about it. Lawrence and I have another date this week, and I know we're not in a committed relationship or anything, but it's just weird that they know each other. I mean, best friends?"

"Okay, girl, I can see that you're getting all pouncey." Emma eyed her carefully.

"I'm not getting pouncey. I just want—" She looked at her best friend, who waited patiently for her response as she considered completely jumping ship and avoiding both men. Zora had a track record of making a mad dash from anything that looked remotely complicated, even if the good outweighed the bad. "You're right. I'm getting pouncey."

"Mmm-hmm."

8

At the bookstore the next day things were quiet, and Zora couldn't help replaying the text conversation she had with Reid and wondering how things would be on her date with Lawrence that night. She grabbed a legal pad from under the checkout counter to make a list of pros and cons of dating each of the guys, but she honestly didn't know enough about either of them to rule one out.

"Let's see," she sighed, mumbling to herself as she wrote.

Reid
Handsome
Incredible skin
Beautiful eyes
I'd kill for his lashes...
Intelligent
Cares about his people
Seems down to earth and chill
We enjoy some of the same books and music

Hmm…
Teaches
Loves to write
I think he's probably a good writer.

She tapped her lips with the cap of her pen, averting her thoughts from one friend to the other, but quickly detoured back to Reid.

Tall

"He's definitely winning in the tall department." She bit her lip. "Okay, now Lawrence," she said, regrouping.

Lawrence
Intelligent
Handsome
Flirty
Charismatic
Charming
A bit of an ego, though…
Well dressed
Maybe a little bougie
Incredible family history of activism and advocacy
Excellent writer

Zora looked at the lists she'd made, realizing it was more of a pros list than pros and cons. Especially for Reid. But she definitely had questions about both of these guys. She moved to another line and started writing again.
Why does Reid have a wall up?
Why is he afraid to share his writing?
Is he hiding something?

And Lawrence...

What are his ambitions?

Or does he already have it all and there's nowhere to grow from here?

What would it be like to date someone who had no more goals left to achieve?

Questions for both of them:

Why does Lawrence need Reid to do social media work? Couldn't he hire some college student to do that?

If I choose one of them, what would we build together?

Zora tore the list from her pad of paper, folding it carefully and stuffing it into the pocket of her cardigan. She tapped the toe of one of her ankle boots on the footrest of her stool.

"Hey, girl." Emma had been working in the back office, ordering a supply of new releases. On her way to the checkout counter, she grabbed coffees from Brian and Zora's favorite lemon madeleines. "What are you doing up here? You look like you're lost in thought."

"I am, honestly. Just thinking more about what you said, and these two guys, and I don't really know what I'm doing," she laughed, tilting her head to one side to stretch her neck.

"But you don't have to know anything right now. I know I was giving you a hard time last night, but nothing's happened with Reid. He hasn't asked you out or anything yet, right?" She stared expectantly as her tone shifted to a lower register. "Right?"

"No, he hasn't asked me out. I feel this chemistry, though, and I get the sense that he does, too. I've been playing over our little conversation in my head, and you know, at one point he sort of called me beautiful."

"Wait, so he's making a play?" Emma's eyebrows shot up.

"No, he didn't actually say *you're beautiful* like that. We were joking around about meddling family members that want you to have babies and do all the things. I said something about getting pregnant, and he said that I would be beautiful pregnant."

"I see," her friend deadpanned. "So we just jumped past all the dating and went straight to babies. Like, how does that even happen with a complete stranger who showed his whole ass not more than a week ago?"

Zora laughed. "Okay, you have a point, and I don't know how it got there. We just fell into this easy conversation." She shrugged. "What am I even doing? I think now that I don't have blinders on about the cranky guy at the bookstore signing, I'm seeing Reid in a completely different light, and I don't know what's drawing me to him, but there's something there."

"Well, let's get past the kids' event before you start jumping this man, okay? Don't forget that you're supposed to speak to his class in a couple of days. Let's not make it awkward just yet. Besides, don't you have a date with Lawrence?"

"Yeah, I do. He hasn't given me many details, though, outside of 'dress for a romantic dinner,' so I guess he wants it to be a surprise. I don't know what he's thought up or why." Zora pictured Lawrence taking her to a candlelit dinner or a show at the Kennedy Center—Ledisi had been in town singing a tribute to Nina Simone, and tickets sold out so fast that the center begged her to return for encore performances.

"Well, I think that you should—"

"I should what?"

"I think you should put stickers on this cart of books right here to feel like you're doing something productive. Then, if you continue to think about these guys, why don't you make a list?" Emma watched a flush creep over Zora's face. "You've already made a list, haven't you? Jesus, girl, what is this, a sixth grade crush?"

"Why can't it be an adult crush?" she stammered. "You

just suggested making a list, but me doing it on my own is a childhood scenario?"

"Well, that depends. Did you doodle on your list? Let's see it," Emma demanded. "Give it here."

The crimson in Zora's cheeks deepened as she held up the piece of paper with hearts and flowers with looping stems drawn in the margins. "Oh, my God, I'm twelve years old."

"I have to say, if nothing else, I'm glad that you're actually thinking about men. You know, you've been so focused on this store that you really haven't given yourself this outlet in a long time." Emma pulled her braids away from her face, wrapping them into a high bun.

"Yeah, you're right. I just, you know, this store is like my baby, and I just—"

"What did we say about babies?" Granny Marion walked up to the checkout counter.

"Hey, Granny, I just referred to the bookstore as my baby. Don't get excited." She grinned, leaning forward to press her cheek against her grandmother's.

"I see. Well, what about the real kind?" Marion grinned optimistically.

"Zora seems like she could be smitten with both of these guys," Emma interjected.

"I mean, that's a little premature," Zora said. "If it came to that, I'd have to choose one or the other—I don't even want to attempt to date two guys who happen to be best friends."

"But what does their friendship have to do with you?" Granny asked.

"That's what I said!" Emma exclaimed.

"They're grown men, Zora. Let them vie for your attention and we'll see which one is worthy of you."

"We don't need anyone vying for anything, Granny," Zora muttered. "As of right now, I'm dating one, and the other is just a fascination. I'll let you know when there's a reason to consider the both of them."

"Well, you're the one with this list here." Emma waved the paper around.

"Let's see!" Zora's grandmother whooped and extended her hand to receive the lists. "Mmm-hmm."

"What do you think, Granny? Do you have a favorite so far?"

"You know, I actually have some really pleasant feelings about both of these gentlemen. They're both handsome, they both seem intelligent, and your list confirms these things for me. Neither one of them seems to have a major mean streak as of yet, right?"

"No, ma'am, I haven't seen that, but it's still very early. One of them hasn't even asked me out yet. There's plenty of time for red flags."

"Then let's continue to update this list?" She tapped her finger against it, handing it back to her granddaughter.

"Yeah, that's what we'll do." Zora placed the folded list in a drawer under the checkout counter. "Right, well, I guess I'd better get back to it. I have more potential sponsors to follow up with before our community engagement event. It's important that we have more donor support. We're behind in terms of where we were at this point last year, and I don't want to give Ms. Betty any misgivings about letting me take over the contest."

Emma waved her concerns away. "Ms. Betty is sitting by a pool with one of her godawful hats and enjoying a drink with a little umbrella. She ain't thinkin' about this place. Besides, we'll get it done."

Zora nodded. "You're right. I'll get on these calls. The list will have to wait."

"Thank you." Emma sang her reply. "I'm gonna go straighten up the monthly feature displays."

"You know your granny has one priority when it comes to

these men or another, should someone else catch your eye."
A gleam sparkled in Marion's eye.

There's only one thing that she could mean. "And what's that?"
Zora played along.

"Pick the one that will give me my great-grandbabies."
The elder's eyes were so doe-like and hopeful that Zora burst
into laughter.

"Our priorities are going to align one of these days, Granny,
I promise."

Zora's grandmother smiled sweetly. "I'll wear you down
eventually."

Lawrence picked Zora up in a tailored blue suit and a starched
white dress shirt with dress shoes the color of cognac. Zora
wore an off-the-shoulder chiffon top neatly tucked into a high-
waisted pencil skirt that hugged all of her curves. Worried that
Lawrence would want to stroll the waterfront after dinner,
she'd worn her block-heeled sandals so that he didn't have to
help her walk. He'd picked her up in his Audi coupe, and was
clearly eager to drive through Rock Creek Park to show off
his car's agility on the curving roads.

Zora paid less attention to the car and focused instead on
the nature outside. She watched people running on the paths
and families riding their bikes together. The hundreds of trees
changing to their fall oranges and reds. "It's so beautiful out
here. Have you ever run through the park?" She turned.

He smiled at her. "Once or twice. I drive through it all
the time, though. I love catching it on days like today, when
there's no traffic and I can really enjoy the ride."

She turned back to look out the window. "Looks like it
was the perfect day to grab a blanket and sit outside enjoying
the sunshine and the view."

"Oh, I think you'll like my plans even better. I'm taking you to one of my favorite restaurants in town."

Zora smiled out the window. *How predictable.*

When they arrived at their destination, Lawrence pulled open the door of a quaint French bistro adjacent to the Georgetown waterfront.

"Thank you." She smiled.

As they stepped inside, the maitre d' greeted them enthusiastically. "Lawrence, it's great to see you again!"

The men embraced, clapping each other on the back, and Lawrence turned to his date. "Matthieu, I'd like to introduce you to Zora. She owns an independent bookstore in Brookland."

"Enchanté, Zora." Matthieu's accent in the dimly lit dining room made his cupping of her hand to draw it to his lips that much more romantic.

"Le plaisir est pour moi." She watched the man's eyes light up.

He continued to hold Zora's hand in his. "We will have to continue this conversation after we've gotten you settled." He gestured toward the dining area, leading the way to a curved booth draped in a deep crimson velvet.

Votive candles flickered at the center of the table. They entered the booth from either side, sitting close to each other toward the center of the curve. Matthieu set menus on the table along with a wine list before turning his attention to customers waving him down from another table. Lawrence turned toward her, resting one hand on the table. "So how has your week been?"

"It's been busy." She nodded. "We had a couple of authors come in to sign our inventory of their books, I've got the *D.C. Speakeasy* event to prepare for and we're starting to get some events together for the rest of the fall—you know, kids' events for Halloween. Oh, and Emma and I ordered a big inventory to do this thing where we place little recommendation cards for books that make great gifts. We've done that for two years, and it's really helped our holiday sales."

"Oh, wow, that's interesting. Those are nice personal touches." He nodded approvingly.

"Yeah, and I'm also preparing for that talk with Reid's class."

"Yes, that was the thing I was mentioning on our date the other day. I realized that I had a conflict, and I should have brought it up to you before I said anything to Reid."

"That would have been nice," she admitted, her lips curving playfully.

He grinned back, leaning a little closer to her. The warmth and proximity of his body made her aware of how close his hand was to her thigh. "I just thought you were perfect for it. Obviously, I think the students would probably most like to hear from an author who can tell students exactly what they did from concept to publication, but with you owning a bookstore, you can probably touch on most of that."

Zora agreed airily. "True, I'm very familiar with the business."

"I'm glad you were available to do it."

"Do you ever get nervous speaking in front of people?" Zora looked at Lawrence, who surveyed her face.

"No, I've done it for so long it just kind of comes naturally to me." Their server arrived and asked for their drink orders.

They agreed to wine pairings throughout their meal. The baguette had a perfectly crisp crust and soft insides that practically melted in Zora's mouth with salted butter. They shared an order of escargot and a frisée salad before their entrees of moules-frites for Zora and steak au poivre for Lawrence. "I love this place," he gushed, buttering a slice of baguette.

"Thank you for bringing me here. I love French food, and I'm glad to see you again so soon." She touched his arm gently as he popped a torn piece of bread into his mouth.

His jaw flexed as he chewed. When he'd finished, he tapped

her thigh with the tip of his finger. "Me, too. I had a good time when you came over on Saturday."

She leaned against his arm. "Yeah, I'm still so impressed that you decided to cook for me on our first date."

"Was that our first date, or was drinks our first date?" Lawrence laughed, using one hand to gesture between two distinct moments. The back of the other rested against the outside of her skirt.

"Did drinks count? I thought that was just supposed to be a thank-you for the event," she said, smiling brightly.

"No, I think you're right." His knuckles grazed her leg, making her shiver. He looked at her intently, their connection broken only when the server arrived to deliver their meal.

Zora used her fork to scoop mussels out of their shells. She dipped her fries and the crusty bread in the rich broth of white wine, shallots, garlic, salt, and black pepper. "This is so good!" She placed a plump mussel on a piece of bread she'd dipped, closing her eyes as she steered the bite to her mouth. "Mmm!" She wiggled in her seat.

"There's that little dance again." Lawrence grinned.

"If we continue to eat like this, you're going to have to get used to it." Zora rocked side to side.

"I guess we're going to have to keep eating like this, then." His smile broadened and he winked.

Zora nudged him with her shoulder. "I guess so. So how are things coming along? Are you working on your next book or your promo tour? What does everything look like now with your new release?"

"Oh." He waved his hand like it wasn't a big deal. "My publicist keeps me on a pretty tight schedule. I have different events either via podcast or in person at least a few times a week. I'm in the process of editing the next book in the series and then I meet with Reid pretty regularly for our project."

"What is your project exactly? You said he does your social media?"

"Yeah, so anytime I have a conversation with my agent, publicist, or marketing team, I will...uh—" he stalled like he was searching for the words "—I'll bring him in on some of those meetings or just update him so that he can create a plan for my social media accounts."

"Oh, interesting. So you promote across Twitter and Instagram?"

"You know, I—uh—definitely on the website and there's occasional updates to Twitter when there's book news. I don't do a lot of Instagram promotion. I look at it, but I don't take a lot of candid photos."

"Well, I'm sure that there are others who do. We took photos at the book signing. Would you like those?"

"Oh, sure, that would definitely be something that Reid can use later on."

"So are you a plotter or do you pants your projects? I'm always curious about authors and their writing processes." She popped a French fry into her mouth—its crunchy, garlicky outside giving way to a soft, warm center.

Lawrence seemed to think about the question for a moment. "Do you write, too? You sure know a lot about the process," he laughed.

"It's on my bucket list for someday. I don't think I have enough time to hone my craft at the moment."

"But if you could, what would you want to write?"

"I love contemporary romance and romantic comedies, and I also have a thing for cozy mysteries, so I'd like to try to cross these," she shared. Zora fell in love with genre romance in high school—marveling in the creativity that it took to take predictable tropes and spin them into deliciously different versions of escape and happily-ever-afters. She loved the way those stories always made her feel happy and hopeful.

Lawrence laughed but sobered when he saw that Zora was serious. "Sorry, I thought you were joking."

Zora frowned, caught off guard. "What's wrong with romance?"

"Nothing, of course." He moved closer to her. "Nothing at all. I just figured maybe you'd go for something more like literary fiction or maybe nonfiction. Something more complex."

She stared at him. *Chauvinist much?* "I mean, I wouldn't mind doing either of those, too, but to think that romance isn't complex surprises me. Have you actually read romance before?" She leaned back to look at him.

"Not with any frequency," he admitted. "I'm sorry. I didn't mean to pick on the genre in its entirety. I just feel like those stories are so predictable."

"I mean, predictable in the sense that there should be a happily-ever-after, maybe, but there's still plenty of space for nuance and unexpected outcomes. And as a bookstore owner, I can tell you that I move more romance than any other genre."

"Touché. I guess I never thought about it that way."

He seemed to take in what she was saying, but Zora eyed him, unsure whether he was just appeasing. She sipped her wine, shaking off the shade. "So back to my question—plotter or pantser?"

"I'm definitely a plotter. I can't imagine trying to write a book by the seat of my pants without a plan. I just like the structure of having the story kind of all put together so that I understand the direction that I'm going. Of course, I take creative liberties—I might take some detours along the way and readjust, but I definitely have to plan it out."

"You know, if you're ever looking for beta readers, I'd be more than happy to take a sneak peek at a scene or two. As a longtime fan and all."

"Is that right?" He snagged a fry from her plate and bit into it, a boyish playfulness on his face.

"Mmm-hmm." She smiled, holding her glass by its stem.

He watched her as she sipped her wine, leaning close enough to plant a kiss on her temple. "How would you feel about a stroll by the water after dinner?"

"I thought you might ask that. That's why I wore these shoes."

"Those are your walking shoes?" he teased.

"Not quite, but I know I won't fall in these," she giggled.

"Don't tell me you're a klutz like Reid!" He roared with laughter.

"He's a klutz?"

Dusk at the waterfront meant hungry ducks seeking the leftovers of restaurant patrons, and mosquitoes nibbling on the ankles of sweet-blooded children. As they strolled, looking out at the water, Lawrence wrapped his hand around Zora's to keep her steady. "So how did Reid get into social media marketing?" she asked, still trying to connect the dots on things she didn't fully understand. "I thought he focused his studies on writing and literature."

"Oh, are you two getting to know each other?" He looked down at her.

"A bit." She shrugged. "We talked the other day because he was giving me more details about the school event."

"Right." She wasn't sure what she saw in his face. It didn't read jealousy, but there was a layer of concern in his voice. *Better change the subject.* "I imagine sometimes you have to take a break and refill your cup. Are you big on travel?"

"Yeah, I definitely vacation and take time to myself. I'm a big fan of getting new stamps in my passport."

"Ooo, anywhere fun planned before the end of the year?"

"I'll be headed to the UK just before Thanksgiving. Ever been to London?"

She shook her head. "I wish. Definitely on my bucket list, though. So many places to visit, so little time." They reached an area of the waterfront that was quiet and unoccupied.

"Speaking of time… What are your plans for tonight?" He stopped walking, pulling her around to face him.

"Why, what are the options right now?" She smiled at him, enjoying the feeling of his body pressed against hers, his arms around her waist. One hand trailed lower in a move to cup her ass, and he grumbled playfully when she lifted his hand back to her waist.

"Well, you could come back to my place." He leaned forward, kissing her gently. As he pulled away, he surveyed her face. "Come stay the night?" He kissed her again, this time more deeply. His tongue glided smoothly against the front of her teeth before she tilted her head to reciprocate.

Lawrence's hands moved from Zora's waist to cup her face as she stopped for a breath. His kisses tasted of dark chocolate and dessert wine, and she wanted more. She opened her mouth to accept his invitation before remembering her schedule for the next day. *Damn!* "I'd really love to, but I can't tonight. I've got to get ready for the thing at Reid's school tomorrow. Rain check?"

He kissed her again, trailing his lips across her cheek to her hairline. "Count on it," he whispered into her ear. Releasing all of her but her hand, he shook his head and laughed. "I can't believe I'm being curbed by my own plans."

She giggled at the thought. "You fly out in the morning?"

He nodded. "Down to Atlanta for some book events."

"Lucky Atlanta."

He kissed her hand, and they continued strolling down the waterfront in comfortable silence. Lawrence held Zora's hand to his chest with one hand while holding her waist with the other.

9

Zora sat on the floor in the picture book section of the store, typing counts into the inventory tablet.

"Hey, girl." Emma walked up behind her. "You're moving pretty quickly through this section."

"Yeah, I want to get through chapter books before lunch." Zora's eyes remained on the screen, and she scrunched her nose when the numbers didn't match the amount of product on the shelf.

"Well, you know what we want to hear before lunch," Granny's voice sounded from behind her.

"Hey, Granny." Zora stood, wrapping her arms around her grandmother.

"We want to hear all about your date before you head out to talk to Reid's class."

Zora looked down at her tablet again but relented. "Let's go sit down over by Granny's chair." It was a quiet morning;

only a few customers had come into the store. The seating area was entirely empty.

"Brian, baby, can you bring us our usuals?" Granny called toward the coffee kiosk.

"Yes, Miss Marion," he answered politely.

"So tell me, baby. How was your date?" She settled into her high-backed chair.

"It was nice!"

Emma winced. "That bad?"

"No! It wasn't bad. I just…" Zora's voice trailed off as Brian approached with drinks and a parchment wrapped around madeleines. "Brian, you're amazing. Thank you."

"Anytime, Z," he replied shyly. "Here you go, Miss Marion."

"Thank you, baby." She slipped a twenty-dollar bill from her pocket. "This is for you. Come on and give me some sugar."

Brian laughed, kissing Granny on the cheek. "You know you don't have to do that."

"Yes, but I want to. Go on and take it, my love."

He kissed Granny again. "Thank you, Miss Marion."

"You're welcome, baby."

Brian retreated to the coffee kiosk.

Zora sipped her latte thoughtfully, aware that she had two pairs of eyes trained on her. "So let's start off with the good things. He picked me up on time, he took me to his favorite restaurant in D.C.—this cute French place by the waterfront."

"Okay…" Emma waited for the other shoe to drop.

"Dinner was amazing. I would definitely go back to that place."

"Right," Granny coaxed.

"It just felt like the conversation was flat. I might as well have been interviewing him for an exposé on his writing. It doesn't feel like he's trying to get to know me, either."

"So he didn't ask you anything?"

"He did, but his questions felt thin. I'm over here trying to really get to know him, asking about his craft and his process, showing real interest. He seems most interested in sleeping with me."

"Whoa, how did that interest manifest itself at dinner?" Emma frowned, poking out her lips, as she tried to connect the dots.

"We went for a walk after dinner, just to enjoy the air and the water. He kissed me a few times when no one else was around."

"Whole tongue or just the tip?" Emma leaned forward.

"Emma!" Zora burst out laughing. "I'm sorry, Granny. That sounded horrible."

"I'd like to know the answer. Spill, baby." Granny rested her elbow on the arm of her chair, rubbing her thumb against her middle and forefinger.

Zora covered her face with her hand. "Whole tongue."

"Ooo, yes." Emma snapped her fingers. "So he's clearly interested. Are you worried that he's only interested in *that*?"

"Kind of, I guess. What if he's just into smashing his fans?"

Granny leaned forward. "Baby, there's nothing wrong with being smashed once in a while," her silky voice assured her.

Emma pressed her lips together, her eyes wide as she turned to observe her elder. Her face might as well have been the bulging eyes emoji.

"You should allow yourself that from time to time, baby. It keeps you young."

Zora's cheeks burned as she shot a look to her best friend, who looked like she might burst into tears from holding in her laughter. "Yes, Granny. I just— I'm not sure what's going on. I feel a little stiff around him."

"Are you attracted to him?" Emma tilted her head.

"I am… Maybe I built him up in my head too much, based on what I'd read about him. Or maybe I was just off my game. It doesn't make sense."

Emma and Granny exchanged a knowing look.

"What?" Zora exclaimed incredulously. "What are y'all seeing that I'm not?"

"Baby, this is what you always do. Whenever there's a man in your life, even if you're just dating him, you find all of the good things about him—his intelligence, successes, achievements—and you hype him up so much in your head that when you actually spend time with him, it's a disappointment. He's let you down.

"This particular man is accomplished, he is published, and you were so enamored with his persona before you even met him that it's problematic. And, yes, he's attractive, and I'm sure he's a good man, but you're expecting the ideal that you pictured for weeks. Years, even. You made him bigger than what he really is, and now what you're seeing in real life is a letdown because he's human."

Zora sat with that for a minute. "You know, I never really thought about it that way."

"Well, think about that last guy. He was in politics, had a great job, worked for a senator, and eventually wanted to be one himself. I think in your mind, you thought he was going to be the next Barack Obama," Emma interjected.

She laughed a little. "I didn't think he was going to be *Barack*. I just thought he had a lot of potential."

"But you aren't dating potential," she said gently. "You're dating a human being who has flaws, who makes mistakes, who can't possibly live up to the perfection that's in your head."

"So what do I do with that now? Have I already ruined it—is it too late?"

"No! I think what you need to do is to seriously go out with that man with an open mind, and truly get to know him, not just his writing. Stop being a fan, and date the man. No what-ifs, no questions, just get to know him. You don't have to marry him. You don't have to sleep with him. You don't have to do anything you don't want to do. See who he is as a person before you feel let down, because you always walk away from these really good guys and you never know if you're missing 'the one.'"

"I don't even know if I'm ready for 'the one,'" Zora admitted. "And even the thought of both of these guys being into me is overwhelming. I'm throwing myself off, you know."

"Z, Reid hasn't even asked you out, and you're doing him a favor by speaking to his class. He's been talking to you to get to know you, because you're going to be speaking to his students. Until he says something different, this is only due diligence. Maybe he is interested but if he hasn't said it flat out, I wouldn't put more stock into that. Stop thinking that all these fairy tales you sell are going to happen in real life."

"Well, damn." Zora took her coffee and went back to the picture books to finish her round of inventory. Lifting up a book titled *Dream Big, Little One* and turning it toward the seating area where Granny and Emma remained, she called out, "I guess I should stop using this as my guide?"

Emma snickered. "You can dream all you want, honey, but then you have to wake up and join the real world."

Zora feigned a pout and put the book back on its shelf, admiring the artwork by Vashti Harrison. As she sat on the floor, her phone pinged.

Reid: We're really looking forward to seeing you this afternoon!

Zora looked up at the colorful covers facing her, their contents full of vivid magic and wonder. "No more fantasies," she whispered to herself.

★ ★ ★

"It's been a while since we've walked somewhere for lunch, Granny. I'm glad we're doing this." Zora strolled out of the bookstore, Granny's arm looped through hers.

"Me, too, baby. I just thought we should go out for a change. You're always working so hard and ordering in. Sometimes you need to take a beat and just be in the moment."

"I know you're right, but it's hard sometimes. I get so focused on work that I forget about the little things."

"Mmm-hmm. Your mama was the same way, rest her soul. She'd be staying late at the firm 'til all hours of the night, but she'd feel terrible because she had to sacrifice being present at your recitals and sports games. I want you to think about what it costs to work those extra hours in terms of your personal life, your health, and your happiness."

"Yes, ma'am." They didn't have far to walk—they headed next door for burgers and duck fat fries, promising to bring the same back for Emma, who covered the store during the lunch rush.

After placing their orders, they sat at a booth by the window, enjoying the sunshine. "This is exactly what I was hoping for today, baby. Beautiful weather, a good lunch, and you're gonna talk to and inspire some children today. Doin' good. Doin' the Lord's work." Marion nodded with pride.

"It's gonna be a lot of fun, Granny. I'm excited to meet the students." Zora nodded.

"So I had a motive in bringing you to lunch today." She leaned forward mischievously.

"What is that?" Zora held on to the base of her glass of lemonade, its cool condensation gathering on the cardboard coaster.

"I want to tell you a story, baby." Granny sipped her Arnold Palmer.

"Okay." Zora leaned forward.

"When I was a young lady—a pretty young thang—I had my share of gentleman callers trying to win my affection while I was studying for my degree." Granny attended Howard University in the 1960s, where she studied to become a high school English teacher.

"Oh, this is about to be juicy." Zora sipped her lemonade. "You met Granddaddy in college, didn't you?"

"I sure did, but not before I met several other eligible bachelors. You know, your granddaddy wasn't the only man that proposed to me."

Zora sputtered. It was as if someone pulled the needle off the record currently in play. "Say what now?"

"In college I got to know a gentleman named Joseph. He was handsome and intelligent. He was pre-med and really driven to become a medical doctor. He wanted specifically to work with children, and there weren't many people who could carry a tune the way that he did." Granny smiled, picturing a memory. "I was in my second year and Joseph took me out to the movies. We," she started slowly, "we fell in love. Simple as that. He was funny, he was generous, he was a God-fearing man, and I loved him.

"Then he had to go. He decided to join the military. He didn't necessarily believe in the war, but he thought he could get good medical training while helping out there. And before he could even enlist, he was drafted. I never saw him again." Marion looked down at the table.

"Did he die?" Zora whispered.

"He was injured—" Granny nodded slowly "—but he lived. While he was recovering, he fell in love with a nurse and married her. Told me in a letter. I never heard from him again." She looked down at her hands, folded on the table. The lines around her mouth dug deeper as she pursed her lips. "I believed that he was the love of my life."

"So when did you meet Granddaddy?"

"Senior year." Granny smiled. "I was a mess over Joseph all of my third year, but my studies kept me busy, and I'd been volunteering at a local shelter. One of the other volunteers was your granddad. And he was sweet, and smart, and funny. So kind. He didn't have the aspirations to be a doctor, but he had street smarts." She nodded. "And I loved him. That love was different than with Joseph, but it was *love*, baby. That love grew over the years, and it's something that I cherish every single day."

Stunned by these revelations, Zora shook her head. "If you'd known these two men at the same time, what would you have done?" she asked incredulously.

"To be honest, if that had been the case, I'm not quite sure," Granny admitted, interlacing her fingers. "I think I would have been a doctor's wife. At that time Joseph is probably who I would have chosen. But now, after all these years, I know that I landed exactly where I was supposed to be. Any other choice would not have given me you."

Zora reached across the table and grabbed her grandmother's hand. Before either of them could speak, a server brought their food. They snacked on fries while she refilled their drinks.

"So about that question," Granny started.

Zora took a bite of her burger, covering her mouth as she spoke. "What about it?"

"Are you thinking that you're going to have to make a choice between these two young men?"

"Honestly, I don't know, but I think that I have been doing exactly what you said and creating some fantasy in my head where both these men are super into me and I am gonna have to choose. It's probably never going to come to that, but I keep thinking about it. They're both good guys, honorable guys, who seem worthy of my time, and how am I gonna do that? How do I choose?"

"You'll feel it. You'll know the difference."

"But you just said it's possible to love two men."

"And it is. You can love people for different reasons. You'll be able to see who you would want to father your children, or who you would want to dance all your dances with, or who you'd want to be stuck on a deserted island with. Think about who you'll never run out of things to talk about with. That's the one."

Zora nodded, taking a bite of another fry. "Mmm, these are so good." The thick-cut fries were perfectly golden and crisp on the outside, and a salty savoriness—almost a rich, buttery quality—made them addictive as she chewed through the crunchy exterior to the soft, piping-hot center.

Granny smiled. "The best for the best, baby."

10

As Zora pulled into the parking lot, Reid stood outside the school entrance. He walked toward her once she'd gotten out of the car. "I'm so glad you could make it."

They smiled at each other, and Reid went in for an awkward hug—the kind where his arm came around her shoulder, but their torsos didn't touch at all—a distant embrace. "Oh," she laughed, pressing the palm of one hand against his back. "I'm excited and a little nervous." She noticed that he was wearing cologne—something citrusy clung to her senses.

They turned to walk up the stairs leading into the building. "What we can do is start with introductions and a couple of questions to get you going. At the very end, you can definitely bring up the contest."

She nodded. "That sounds good." She stopped at the top of the stairs and turned. "Hey, would you mind taking a picture of me? I want to send it to my niece. She'll be so jazzed to see me here."

Reid's lips twitched. "Of course." He accepted Zora's phone and snapped a couple of pictures of her, moving the phone higher and lower.

Zora grinned. "Okay, angles. I see you."

He smiled back, handing over her phone. "I think I got a couple of good ones."

The glass doors into the building opened into a lobby and reception area for the principal's office. Farther down, rows of lockers on either side led to classrooms and other corridors, each door with a window into a brightly lit class full of students. They walked down the halls and Zora felt a wash of memories from her last time in the building, when Safina graduated. "Feels like this place has had some renovations?" she asked.

"Yeah, last year. We received a really generous anonymous donation, so the principal decided to update some things in the building—new labs, fixtures, new paint. It's much improved." He gestured toward the walls. "It seems like we get announcements for something being replaced almost every month."

D.C. housed over one hundred charter schools like this one—independent but publicly funded schools that were free to attend and free to innovate without being a part of the D.C. public school system. These schools used a lottery system to select the students that would enroll, and attendance was often hugely beneficial, as the standardized test scores in some wards drastically outperformed those of the local public schools. Langston Hughes, a charter school specifically focused on creative arts, was located in a predominantly Black neighborhood and its matriculants were reflective of their location.

"It's really nice."

They reached the door to his classroom, and Reid turned to her and smiled. The sounds of students laughing and pages in books turning carried into the hallway. "You ready?"

Butterflies dashed about inside her chest. "I think so?" she laughed nervously.

He grinned, squeezing her shoulder. "Just rip the Band-Aid off. You'll be great."

She tried to ignore the warmth of his touch and shook off her jitters. There was something about his cologne that she found soothing. "Okay, let's do it."

Reid pulled open the classroom door, allowing Zora to step inside before him. Twenty-two sets of teenage eyes turned to look at her standing at the front of the room in the orange-and-blue printed duster that Emma had borrowed, which she coupled with black jeans and a matching tank. Reid strode in and planted himself beside her, his demeanor warming as he faced his students. "Okay, class, let's get started. Today, as you know, we have a special guest with us. This is Zora Dizon. She owns Opus Northeast, which is an independent bookstore in Brookland."

"Oh, I've been there!" one student exclaimed. "That store is dope."

A couple of students laughed, sneaking looks at their classmate.

Zora smiled broadly. "Thank you!"

Reid continued, the corners of his mouth curving upward in amusement. "As I was saying, Ms. Zora owns a bookstore. She works with authors every single day. She hosts book signings at her store, she helps to market books, she works with publishers, and orders books to sell. She is right in the midst of everything. She knows literary agents and book editors, and she even knows the author who was going to be speaking today, so I want you to give her your undivided attention."

The students nodded in response, their eyes wide and hungry for information. Each student had a pencil in their hand and notepaper in front of them. Zora took in their faces—a classroom full of Black and brown students anxious to learn made her heart jump in her chest. *You'd never see this on the news.*

"Wow," Zora started, "thank you for that introduction. So how many of you are going to be writers?"

Every student raised their hand in response, and one coughed to get Zora's attention. "Excuse me, miss?"

"Yes, what's your name?" Zora smiled in response.

"MacKenzie." Her smooth brown skin shone in the fluorescent lights as she flipped her silky pressed hair behind her back.

"What would you like to share, MacKenzie?"

"We're already writers." The young girl, who couldn't have been older than fifteen, gestured to her classmates with a confidence Zora wished she'd had at that age.

"Oh! Well, that's even better, because that means that soon, your work will be sold in my bookstore. One of the things I love more than anything is to highlight neighborhood authors and show off their work. Is anyone here working on a specific project that they'd like to share?"

Another girl raised her hand. "I'm working on my first novel."

"Wow, that's fantastic! What genre is your novel in?"

"It's a young-adult novel." She rested an elbow on her desk, blushing as her classmates turned to look at her.

"Is it fantasy, or contemporary?"

"It's a fantasy about Black kids in the neighborhood who wake up with magical powers."

"That sounds like a page turner! Anyone else?" Zora moved around the room slowly.

A young man raised his hand, his slender fingers long enough to palm a basketball. "I'm trying to put together a novel idea right now about being a young Black man in a diverse city who still feels afraid to go outside. Afraid that we're at risk—that we're being hunted."

Several students snapped their fingers. Reid grinned from his desk, his arms folded across his chest.

"That book is timely." Zora nodded. "We'll be ready for it. What about you?" She pointed to a girl who had been trying to make herself smaller behind her desk. "What are you working on?"

"I write poetry," she said softly. "I don't share it often—it's really personal, but Mr. Reid has seen some of my work."

"It's really good," he added proudly. His student beamed.

"So how many people in this room have been published?" Zora moved toward the center of the room, walking between the desks, turning this way and that to take in the eager faces.

Five or six hands shot up.

"Tell me about it."

One girl spoke up. "I won a contest and was published in an anthology."

Another guy spoke. "I wrote a couple of op-eds that landed in the *Washington Post*."

Another girl. "I self-published a collection of poetry."

A guy. "I cowrote a story with my friend." He gestured to the kid next to him. "We submitted it in a contest, and we just heard yesterday that it's going to be in an anthology, too."

Students in the class cheered and snapped.

"So I'm already amongst a community of authors," Zora surmised.

"Not all of us are published." A young man rested his chin on his arms.

"All of you are writing. You're all working toward the goal—so in my eyes, you're authors! Published or not, if you're on that road, you're an author. Don't let anyone tell you differently. This is such an exciting thing to see projects sprouting from so many students of color! Do you know how limited books with Black characters were when Mr. Reid and I were kids?"

He nodded in agreement, looking from Zora to his students.

"I am inspired by each of you, and I'm here today to talk to you all about publishing, different avenues to get there, literary agents, all the things." She perched on the end of Reid's desk. "And so let's open it up to questions."

Reid sat and watched as Zora was peppered with questions from all around the room. Zora could feel the excitement and openness to learning—the energy was contagious. The students took notes feverishly, hands shooting up as soon as a question was answered.

"You know, I have been thinking about writing for a long time, and you all have inspired me." She grinned. "But beyond my own aspirations, I want to continue to motivate you forward. A part of the reason I'm here with you all today is to impart a challenge. I understand that you all just turned in short stories as an assignment for this class?" The students nodded. "So your teacher, Mr. Hughes, is going to give you feedback on your short stories, and I challenge each of you to work on improving your stories to the very best they can be, because I'm holding a short-story contest. Do you want to guess what the prize is?" Her eyes roamed around the room for guesses.

Murmurs began around the room, and one student raised her hand. "Publication?"

"Yes, but that's not all." She rubbed her hands together mischievously.

"Bragging rights?"

Zora looked around the room and put her hands on her hips. "Obviously." The students laughed at her neck roll. "The winner will be published in this year's *D.C. Speakeasy's 'Young Writers Anthology,'* which is a collection of short stories by local writers. But there's also a cash prize of five hundred dollars!"

The students gasped, and one smacked his hand against his desk and pointed to all of his classmates slowly. "Y'all ain't ready!"

Zora giggled. "I love the confidence." She leaned in conspiratorially, meeting the eyes of students all around the classroom. "So here's what you have to do. You're going to work on improving your short stories for two weeks, and then you're going to email them to my bookstore. Will you help me pass these out?" She handed Reid a stack of handouts. "On this flyer, all of the contest information is listed. Now, this is a broader contest, so there will be other contestants from other schools around D.C., but I'm rooting for y'all. Who's going to win this contest?"

Every hand in the room shot up.

Zora followed Reid to a local coffee shop after the bell rang and the class had dispersed.

"You have to let me buy you a coffee to thank you," he'd said.

Zora had blushed. "Sure, thank you." She felt his gaze on her as her cheeks colored, but he remained silent.

When they got inside, they ordered their drinks and settled into a couple of leather armchairs in a comfy corner. The barista brought them their brown sugar oat milk lattes in wide ceramic mugs.

"That was amazing, Zora—this talk went far better than I expected, and I'm so glad that you brought the kids into the *Speakeasy* writing challenge. My students left inspired, and it sounds like maybe you did, too. You mentioned that you've been wanting to write something—is it book shaped?" Reid eyed her intently.

"I'm…still figuring it out? I was thinking about trying my hand at romance." She braced herself for another reaction like Lawrence's.

"Oh, that's cool." He nodded. "Such a big industry."

Huh. That's it? "I love happily-ever-afters. I've been reading a bunch of craft books, and I have a story idea, but I haven't actually sat down to try drafting it out." She blew into her mug softly.

Reid watched her, his eyes lowering to her mouth briefly. "Writing a novel is a big commitment, but there's no rush. Just take your time with it."

"Thanks, I think I needed that." She smiled. "So how often do you have visitors come to your classes?"

He shrugged. "Usually two or three times per semester. It depends on who we can schedule and what's in the curriculum. If we can't bring in speakers, I like to take them to open mic nights to listen to spoken word or book events to meet authors who look like them."

"Hence why you wanted them to meet Lawrence. It's too bad that he couldn't be there."

Reid blinked. "Yeah, his schedule gets pretty busy." His tone lowered to a mumble.

Zora cocked her head to one side, her eyes narrowing. "So this has happened before?"

"Ah." He ran his hand over his beard, his teeth clenched into a grimace. "See, what had happened was…"

Zora giggled. "You don't have to make excuses for him, you know. He's grown."

"Come on, you know a stand-up dude is always gonna have his boy's back. Bro code." He ran his hand over his hair, his thick curls tight and well-kept.

"Is what he did really that terrible that you have to hide it?" Zora watched the gears turn in Reid's mind as he weighed his options.

He cracked a smile. "You're really not going to let this go, are you?"

"Of course not! Clearly, you cover for him regularly."

His smile widened. "I've known him half my life," he laughed. "It's second nature for me to cover for my boy, even if he's not doing anything wrong."

"Well, if he's not doing anything wrong, then why are you covering for him?"

"I—I feel like you're a detective over here." He pretended to hold up a magnifying glass.

She giggled. "I have moments…"

"Is that right?"

"Yeah, I have a knack for figuring out puzzles and solving a mystery before we get to the end of the book or movie. My best friend calls me Zor-lock."

"Zor-lock Holmes? That's funny. So you're investigating Lawrence? Is that what's happening right now?" He swung his index finger back and forth between them.

She pressed her lips together to stifle her smile. "Don't change the subject. You are going to tell me why he canceled on your class and if this has happened before."

"Ahhh." He exhaled deeply from his lungs, sighing audibly. "Okay, fine. Yes, he's had to cancel on the class before—this would be the third time, actually. You know, he's a busy author—he's wanted all over the country to talk and do book events, speak at conferences, et cetera. When something comes up, especially if it's a paid event, he's going to choose that over coming to talk to the class." He sipped his latte thoughtfully.

"So he's never spoken at your school?"

Reid shook his head. "He will. It's just—he's so busy right now. Things will calm down and then he'll make time."

"If he's canceled three times, how are you so sure?"

Reid lifted his hands and shrugged. "He shows up when he needs to. I will say, each time he's had to cancel, he's given me great suggestions for people who could stand in, including yourself. You have my students so excited, and I just really want to thank you for everything that you're doing. This contest is a big one and every student is planning to submit something—a couple of them are submitting multiple stories."

"Well, it's one of the small ways that I feel like I can give back to the community, and I have a friend at a publishing house that I made through the previous owner of my store. Each year Sheila puts together anthologies of really great short stories by folks in the D.C. community, and she lets my contest, which Ms. Betty created, select one of the contributors for the year's anthology. Sheila and I serve as the judges, along with a rep from *D.C. Speakeasy* and DJ Trev from the DCMV Live Radio station." Zora leaned closer and whispered, "And tell your students that everyone is limited to one entry."

He laughed. "Noted. And that's so cool to be making those kinds of connections on behalf of others. I know that doesn't necessarily bring you anything—"

"Oh, but it does! You know, it brings more people to the bookstore, since the contest winners are announced there. Leading up to the event, we do a service event to bring people in the neighborhood together with some of our sponsors. It helps to build community there, and people come back each year. That helps me. It may not be directly correlated to a specific amount of money or to other tangible gains, but it works out in our favor over time."

"Wow," he breathed. His hands rested on the arms of the chair, but he leaned forward slightly, taking in every word. "You are D.C. through and through."

"Indeed." She sipped her latte. "Can I ask you something?"

"Of course." He sat back in his chair. "Anything."

"You know, Lawrence and I were out at drinks the other night, and honestly, I thought that maybe I'd put my foot in my mouth."

"How?" He leaned in slightly, eyebrows furrowing.

"Well, I was talking about the relationship between Langston and Annette, and how refreshing I found it that Annette wasn't treated like a sidekick in the story—she was given a central role and it was never hidden that she often was the one who actually found the final clue or riddled out the puzzle to solve the crime. I just found that interesting about how much of a team Langston and Annette were, rather than just the leader and sidekick dynamic. Even though it's his office, it's clear that he's not the entire brains of the operation. Do you think there's something to that?"

"Some meaning behind their dynamic?"

"Yeah." Zora bit her lip.

He considered the question. "I would say there was an intentional decision to have a forward-thinking team that isn't about giving credit just to a man when women—especially Black women—really are the backbone of society and often have the answers we need to move forward."

"Wow, that's just what I was thinking! It's so weird that you two have such different answers to that."

Something about Reid's face closed off. "Right, well… It was a long day. I'm sure that Lawrence was tired from having talked to everyone."

"Hmm, you're probably right." She leaned toward him. "So tell me about your writing goals. You said you wanted to write a mystery. I want to hear more about it." She sat back in her chair, resting her head in her hand.

"I do. I think I want it to have kind of a thriller aspect to it. I'm really into all-Black casts and Chocolate City and bringing our stories—our culture—alive without trivializing or capitalizing on the pain of our community."

Zora snapped her fingers. "Yes! They don't call D.C. Chocolate City for nothing! I feel that. So where are you in the process? Are you already drafting or still kind of processing or plotting it out?"

He shrugged. "I've been too busy to work on it, honestly. This business with Lawrence and all the social media takes up a lot of my time, and my students eat up the rest."

"Is your family here in the DMV?"

Reid nodded. "My mom lives in Maryland, just north of Takoma Park, and my dad lived in Baltimore—that's where he was born and raised and buried. Everyone's close."

"That's nice."

"And it's just you and your granny?"

Zora nodded slowly. "It's been just us for some years now, and Emma lives with us, too. I have a house over in Mount Rainier."

"Nice area."

"I love it there. I used to have a cute little condo over in Brookland, but I sold it when I took ownership of the family house. My granny lives in the in-law suite, and then Emma and I have the main house."

"That's cool. It's nice to have people around you that care about you, but also to feel like you still have some freedom."

She waved her hand. "Oh yeah, nobody's policing me. More than anything, they're trying to get me to go out more."

"You don't normally go out?" Reid looked at her in surprise.

Zora watched as Reid's eyes pored over her face, landing on her lips. "Not often." She wasn't sure that she was reading the vibe between them correctly, but heat began to build in her stomach. "I put a lot of time into my store. It's still early days—I only took over a few years ago, and we're still growing and learning. I have a lot of goals around that business and what I'd like it to be for the community. I put in a lot of hours and don't put much into dating right now."

"Wow, so is Lawrence the first guy in a while?" He watched

her closely, his wire-rimmed glasses reflecting light from the chandelier overhead.

"Yeah, and I did have a little author crush, I admit it. But Granny and Emma want me to play the field until I find the right one to commit to." She shrugged, laughing at the idea that she had enough time to date more than one person.

"That's good advice." He nodded slowly.

"Is it?" She scrunched up her nose. "I feel like that's the D.C. way, because there's so many people here who seem to be in multiple situationships—"

Reid guffawed. "That's funny. And yes, I know what you mean, but at the same time why put all your eggs in one basket, so to speak? Until you find the right one, it makes sense to kind of get to know who's out there."

"Is that what you do?" Zora bit her lip waiting for the answer, her eyebrow risen.

"When I take time to date, yeah, that's what I do. I don't want to focus my attention on one person unless I know it's real, so I typically will…" His voice trailed off.

"Typically will, what? Are you one of those dudes that has a whole roster?"

Reid laughed deeply, a throaty chuckle that curled Zora's toes. "I wouldn't say a roster. One or two is enough to get to know at a time. Otherwise, it's just playing around."

"Fair."

As they finished their coffees, Zora excused herself to the restroom. After locking the door, she washed her hands and stared into the mirror. "What are you doing, Z? This is a bad idea. They're friends—best friends. Flirting with this man can only end in catastrophe."

Looking at the ceiling, her thought process clicked to the opposite setting. *But he smells so good, and that voice, and that smile…why does he have to be so sexy?* Zora touched up her lip gloss and fluffed her hair, drawing her shoulders back and down her spine to release the tension there. "Pull it together, girl."

When she returned to the table, Reid stood. "So you ready to take off?"

Something in his tone said he wasn't, but she nodded anyway. "Yeah, it's probably best to start heading home. Emma's closing up tonight."

"Okay, I'll walk you out."

The balmy evening air clung to Zora's skin. "I'm glad I didn't wear a heavier jacket—it's still warm out!"

"Yeah, it's taking forever for it to feel like fall."

"It makes me kind of sad. Fall is my favorite season," she admitted.

"Mine, too."

Standing at the back of her car, Zora leaned against the trunk. "This has been really interesting."

"What has?"

"Honestly, I thought you hated me at the beginning when I met you," she laughed.

"I was just in a bad mood. I'm sorry. That wasn't about you." He held a hand to his chest as if making a pledge.

Zora nodded. "Well, thank you. I appreciate that."

Reid stood next to her, leaning his elbow against the trunk. "If I'm being honest, I'm more mad that Lawrence asked you out first." He turned to look at her for a long moment. His shoulders dropped as Zora burst out laughing.

"You didn't really seem like you had any intention of asking me out that day. You were so annoyed." Her laugh subsided to a relaxed smile.

"Yeah, I admit I was in rare form that day, but under other circumstances, I could guarantee you it would have happened." He looked at her intensely.

"And now it's too late," Zora finished, but the question hung in her eyes.

"It's not too late," he whispered. Reid leaned down, placing a hand on her shoulder, as his lips met hers. He kissed her gently once, twice and on the third time deepened the kiss to run the tip of his tongue across her front teeth. His lips were full, almost juicy—the last remnants of brown sugar still sweet on his tongue.

Zora's eyes remained closed even after he pulled away. "Wow."

"I've wanted to do that since you sat down next to me at your bookstore," he whispered.

"Well, why stop now?" Zora wrapped one hand around the back of his neck and pulled him closer, relishing the softness of his lips, the strength of his arms, and the scent of his cologne.

11

As Zora drove home, all she could focus on was the car in the rearview mirror—the one following her. Reid. They'd only just stepped away from each other's presence for a few moments, and she couldn't think straight.

Her cheeks were flushed. She licked her lips just so she could taste him again. "What am I doing? What am I doing?" she muttered under her breath.

She pictured Granny Marion and Emma urging her to go with the flow—to be in the present and enjoy herself—but she couldn't help the pangs of guilt that stabbed at her insides. "What am I gonna do?" she whispered.

As she reached her neighborhood, she decided to let go of her own anxiety. Just for one night. *Let's try it their way.* She pulled into her driveway and Reid parked on the street in front of her house. His sleek black coupe was almost identical to that of her neighbor's down the street.

She watched him take in the neighborhood as he stepped

out of his car. The rows of neat two- and three-story homes with wraparound porches and massive maple trees.

Zora could tell that Emma and Granny were home. Granny's lights were on, indicating she had already retired to her space for the evening. Zora prayed they wouldn't cross paths with Emma, who had no behavior in scenarios like this.

"Hey," he whispered in her ear as he got close.

"Hey." She looked up at him, ready to drink in another kiss. "Come on." She took his hand and led him up the porch. Inside the front door, she kicked off her shoes. He pulled his off, carrying them in the crook of his arm. In the living room, Emma was passed out, snoring on the couch. Once that girl fell asleep, nothing would wake her until morning. Her alarm sounded like a foghorn.

"So predictable," Zora whispered, shaking her head. She held a finger to her lips and winked at Reid, beckoning for him to follow her up the stairs. Hidden in her room with the door closed, Reid dropped his shoes and Zora fell forward into his chest. His hands cupping her face as he guided her lips toward his.

"I could spend all night kissing you."

"Is that so?" she whispered teasingly. "Takes a lot of restraint to stop at kissing."

"Well, there's a lot of ways to kiss, and I would put my very best effort forth." With that, he placed tiny kisses along her jawline, tilting her head with his hand to expose more of her throat. Soft kisses. The tip of his tongue flicked against her skin before his thick lips pressed against her throbbing artery. "I can feel your heartbeat quickening."

Zora's eyes fell shut. "Yes, well, keep doing things like that and it's bound to quicken. So we're sticking to kissing, is that right?"

"We can take it as slow as you want. All I want to do is kiss you tonight, if that's okay?" His low voice rumbled, sending vibrations from her belly to an ache between her legs.

She nodded as he pulled the jacket down from her shoulders, releasing her arms from its sleeves.

"I just want to kiss you," he repeated. His tongue languished over hers, brushing down its center so lightly that her tongue curled, his soft beard tickling her skin.

She moaned against his mouth, not remembering any kiss that compared to this one. He sucked on her lower lip, his hands reaching toward her waist. He untucked her blouse from her jeans, slowly pulling the fabric up over her head, exposing a black bra.

"You're so beautiful, Z," he whispered, nipping at her shoulder, pulling one strap down to trail kisses across her collarbone. "So beautiful."

His kisses made her shiver and crave more. *I can't believe we're doing this… What are we doing?* His lips grazed a sensitive spot below her ear and she forgot her thoughts completely as she pulled him closer. Zora tugged off his jacket and unbuttoned his shirt, exposing a white T-shirt. "So many layers," she teased. Carefully, she removed his glasses with both hands, setting them on her dresser. She lifted his shirt at a glacial speed, marveling at the ripples in his stomach and his muscular chest. "You're all muscle."

The corner of his mouth curved slightly. His hands moved across her stomach, grabbing at her flesh, unbuttoning her jeans. He pulled them down, over her hips, kneeling as he exposed her thighs. "And you are a goddess." He ran his fingertips down her thigh, cupping the back of her calf. "Your skin is so soft." He kissed just above her knee.

She steadied herself by placing a hand on his shoulder and watched his face as he concentrated on her. The way he focused on her, soaking in every angle of her that he could, took her breath away. She stepped out of one leg of her jeans, and he leaned forward to kiss the inside of one of her thighs before he stood to look her in the eye. "I want to kiss every inch of you. Will you let me do that, Zora?" he asked softly, his brown eyes imploring her to give him access to her body. He ran his hands from her sides down to her hips and then rested them at the small of her back, stroking her skin gently.

Devoid of any lingering questions or guilt, or any thoughts at all that didn't involve Reid wearing nothing but a smile, she bit her lip and nodded. "Yes."

He lifted her chin with an index finger, leaning forward as her lips parted. He teased her lips with the tip of his tongue and nipped at her bottom lip before pressing his lips against hers. The kiss started out slow, his tongue languishing over hers until she pulled him closer. She angled her head, deepening the kiss, cradling his face in her hands. He wrapped his arms around her, grabbing her ass and guiding her backward toward the bed until her legs pressed against the duvet.

As his mouth traced her jawline and lapped at her throat, he tugged at the fasteners at the back of her bra. Once unhooked, he peeled it off her skin slowly, as if he was unwrapping a present. "So fucking sexy," he whispered. "Lie back for me."

She ached for him, hoping that these kisses would extinguish the heat building between her thighs, wishing that she'd asked for more than kisses to quell the pulsating fire. Zora lay back on the bed, propped up on her elbows, as Reid removed his pants. His swollen erection apparent in his boxers, Zora squeezed her thighs together as her pulse quickened.

Reid climbed onto the bed, his knees creating space between Zora's legs, nudging them wider. His hips meeting hers, Zora's eyes widened at the firmness against her, and she wondered if he could feel the moisture through the thin material of her cheeky panties. As he rested his body atop hers, he took her hands in his, interlacing their fingers and bringing them up above her head, forcing her to lie back. He kissed her hard, grinding against her until her moan reached his mouth.

"I can't stop kissing you," he whispered.

"I don't want you to stop," she replied breathlessly.

He sucked on her bottom lip. "Good." Leaving her hands above her head, Reid pushed onto his hands, dipping his head to run his tongue along her collarbone and down her sternum. Running his fingers over the swell of her breast, he cupped it, capturing her nipple in his mouth and sucking until he felt its tip tighten with arousal. Zora closed her eyes to focus on the sparks of pleasure overloading her senses. As Reid moved to her other breast, Zora ran her fingers over the first, catching its peak between her fingers.

Reid ventured lower, and her breath shallowed. His beard tickled as he nipped at her, his tongue exploring every bit of her flesh, her body trembling with want.

"Lower," she instructed, her voice breathy and faint.

He looked into her eyes when his mouth and hands reached the waistband of her underwear. She nodded, and he hooked his fingers under the material, tugging it off as she lifted herself up. She watched as Reid playfully bit the inside of her thigh before placing a wet kiss on the same spot. She widened her legs, and he positioned his arms beneath her thighs, allowing her legs to rest on his shoulders.

With his tongue, Reid parted her folds and anchored his mouth to her clit, licking and sucking the sensitive bud until she cried out. Her hips bucked against him, but he continued until she arched closer to the pinnacle. Her legs began to shake and he slowed his movements; the width of his tongue brushed against her gently like a paintbrush on a canvas until the trembling of her thighs calmed, and then he brought her back to the brink, this time allowing her to climax.

She cried out, tangling her fingers into his curls as he worked at her core, guiding her through wave upon wave of orgasm until she fell back against the mattress completely winded. "My God," she breathed, her eyes squeezed shut. "That was the best kiss I've ever received. Ten out of ten." She lifted her hands, stretching out all of her fingers before promptly dropping them down again.

Reid hoisted himself up next to her on the bed, a smile on his face. He wiped the moisture from his beard. "I can beat that score."

Zora giggled, giddy at the thought of him exceeding what he'd just done. "I'd need to mentally prepare for that."

He pulled her close, nuzzling her neck. "Take all the time you need."

"Good morning, beautiful," a voice murmured against the back of her neck, as fingertips grazed her belly. "My God, your skin is so soft, Z."

The vibration of his voice tickled her skin, as Zora opened her eyes. "Mmm, good morning."

The sun peeked in through gaps in the curtains, light bouncing in bursts across the bed. Buried under the soft duvet, Reid nuzzled against her, his beard soft. As little spoon, Zora could feel Reid's morning wood harden as she stretched and wiggled against him. She gasped, obscene images flashing across her mind, having neglected her physical needs for some time. True to his promise, Reid stuck to kissing, but Zora's body begged for more.

She turned onto her back, suddenly aware that she hadn't wrapped her hair before they'd fallen asleep. Reaching upward, her hand met Reid's, which had already begun to play in her curls. As her fingertips met his, he caressed her hand, holding it gently. She turned her face toward his. "Hi."

"Hey." He dipped his head to plant a kiss on her lips. "Did you sleep okay?"

Her face softened. "I'm not going to lie, that was some of the best sleep I've had in a long time." She turned onto her side to face him, and he moved his hand to rest on her hip, his thumb caressing her gently.

He leaned in to share a secret, his eyes crinkling at the corners. "You snored a little."

Zora's eyes widened, and she covered her mouth. "I am so sorry! It's only when I'm really tired."

"Don't worry. I thought it was cute."

"Did it keep you up?" She wiped the sleep from the corners of her eyes.

"No, not at all. I wake up pretty early most days—my internal clock won't let me sleep in."

"I know that feeling. Busy day today?"

He slid his hand from her hip to her back, resting his arm comfortably over her side. He drew light, lazy circles on her collarbone with the pads of his fingers. "I have a project for Lawrence that I'll be working on between classes and for the evening. What about you?"

Lawrence. Shit. Zora had all but forgotten the man existed. She nodded. "We're hosting a book event tonight—it's a panel of local authors who each have books releasing this month, so I'm anticipating a big turnout."

"Your bookstore stays busy."

"Someday, you'll have your own book event there. Have you thought about that?"

Reid blinked and his fingers stopped moving against her skin. "No," he answered slowly. "I guess I...hadn't thought that far ahead."

Something in him changed. Zora couldn't tell what it was, but his smile grew tighter. He pressed his lips together as if to hold something in, and he moved his arm to rest on his side. *Maybe the thought of his own books being out in the world made him anxious.*

He propped his head up on the elbow of his other arm, and Zora could tell his mind was moving quickly. "I should probably head home and get ready for school. Is it okay if I call you tonight, once I get done with work?"

Zora searched his eyes for clues, wondering if she'd said something that rubbed him the wrong way, but his eyes remained steady. "Are you sure you don't have a couple more minutes?" she asked slowly, walking her fingers across his chest, tracing her nails down his torso.

He grunted, his eyes closed to take in the sensation. "What is it that you plan to do with those minutes, Ms. Dizon?"

"Well, Mr. Hughes, we did an awful lot of kissing last night." She grazed the line where his abdomen curved away from his hip.

"We did... God, you're good at that." His breath was jagged. "You are a woman of many talents." He twitched as her nails gently raked his skin.

She scooted closer, continuing to rake her nails against his skin ever so slightly in delicious torment. "You were very generous with your kisses."

His lips curved. "I pride myself on being a giver," he said, squeezing her ass. "If you lie back, I can provide further demonstration along with a commentary on the benefits of generosity."

Before he could nudge her backward, she placed a firm hand on his shoulder, pushing him onto his back instead. "I look forward to your demonstration, sir, but first, I'd like to share a bit of my expertise on the subject. You see, I'm extremely proficient myself."

He bit his lip, sucking in a breath as she kissed his chest, her warm lips and tongue meandering down his abdomen. "I am always impressed by the thoughtful techniques of other well-versed individuals such as yourself," he whispered.

Zora looked up at him, a sly grin stretching across her face. "I look forward to your closing remarks, Mr. Hughes."

12

"Good morning!" Zora breezed into the bookstore, smiling, carrying a box of Emma's favorite breakfast food. It was Emma's day to open, and Zora used that to her advantage to sneak Reid out of the house undetected. "I brought donuts and cupcakes!"

Emma sat at the checkout counter answering bookstore emails, but at Zora's tone, the smooth skin between her brows pinched into a frown. "Um, thanks..."

Zora stopped short. "What's wrong? Did you already eat breakfast? If so, we can set them out for customers." She set the box of eight specialty treats down on the counter, lifting the lid slowly to entice her friend. Emma always ran straight to the chocolate donuts with sprinkles and the key-lime-pie-filled cupcakes, so half of the boxes were her flavors; the rest varied from strawberry cheesecake to peanut butter fudge to tres leches.

Emma sat her elbow on the counter, cradling her chin in

her hand. Her fingers pressed against her lips as she stared into the box and back at Z. "I'm seeing something here. Something is…different."

"Oh, well, I haven't worn a dress to work in a while, I guess," she laughed, doing a little spin. Her leopard-print wrap dress whirled out around her.

Emma used her middle finger to scratch down the part line between her braids until her eyes widened in epiphany. "You fast little floozy! Who got them drawers?" She pointed a finger at Zora, who hunched over in immediate embarrassment at her friend's exclamation.

"Jesus, Em, do you have to be that loud?" she whispered, taking inventory of how many people were within earshot of their conversation.

Emma huffed a whisper through gritted teeth. "Who got them drawers, heffa?"

"Did someone say *drawers*?" Granny sidled up to the counter. "Ooo, cupcakes!" She reached for the tres leches.

Zora's face burned, not only because the conversation was happening, but because there were customers ear hustling in the cookbook section. Every time she looked in their direction, she made full eye contact that made her want to curl up into a ball and combust. Just *poof*! "No one said *drawers*, Granny. Right, Emma? Nope, she said *flaws*."

Granny looked at Emma and back at Zora, her pursed lips and unblinking stare indicating that she wasn't buying it. "Mmmkay, baby. You'll tell me when you're ready." She held up her cupcake and turned back toward her chair. "Thanks for the sweets."

At Granny's exit, Emma burst into hard, silent laughter followed by tears streaming down her cheeks. "You are going to hell for lying to your granny! You know she hears perfectly fine."

"I don't want to field questions about potential baby daddies right now when it didn't go down like that."

Emma raised a brow. "But it did go down?"

"We both did."

Em sucked in a breath, bringing a hand to her chest. "Ooo, you nasty! Wait, were y'all at the house?"

Zora bit her lip. "Maybe."

Her mouth dropped open. "I thought I heard a man's voice this morning! And y'all were getting freaky? I am so confused by what's happening between you two. What about Lawrence?"

Zora waved her hand to quiet her friend as Brian brought her a latte. "Thank you, B. You good?"

Brian knew enough about Zora and Emma to stay out of their business. He kept his head down, getting in some study time in between customers. He nodded shyly. "I'm good, Z. Good morning. Do you need another cappuccino, Emma?"

"Yes, baby. Thank you!" She winked in his direction.

Brian waved and retreated to his kiosk.

Emma scrunched her nose. "How does that coffee shop make any money when they fill us up with free coffee all day?"

Zora arched her brow. "Free? Girl, I maintain a tab for employees and Granny. That coffee is not free."

Her mouth fell open. "You've been paying for my coffee and food this whole time? Why didn't you tell me?"

She shrugged. "You work long hours. Least I can do is get you coffee and some pastries or lunch here and there."

"Here and there—it's literally five or six days a week!"

"We here at Opus Northeast like to foster a collaborative environment with high energy and morale," Zora squeaked out in a nasal, high-pitched voice, like a ticket agent on an airport loudspeaker.

Brian returned with Emma's cappuccino, grinning wide

when she pulled ten bucks from her pocket and handed it to him. "Add this to your tips, baby."

"Thanks, Em!"

Granny called to B, who immediately turned in her direction, and Emma turned back to Zora and leaned forward, cupping her drink. "Okay, sis. I need details. How did y'all go from the school to the bedroom?"

Zora grinned. "Well, there was a stop along the way. As a thank-you, Reid took me for coffee, and we just talked and got to know each other. It's amazing how different he is from how he acted at Lawrence's book event."

"Meaning he's a normal human being?" Em deadpanned.

"Okay, fair. His behavior was inexcusable that night—I think that we can both agree on that. I mean, I thought the man hated Lawrence and me and I had no idea what I could have done for him to act like that."

"Right...yet somehow, we've turned a red flag into a sleepover? Help me understand, sis," Emma chuckled and reached out a hand. "He's fine, don't get me wrong. I know your well has been dry for a minute, so I'm not judging you for wanting to fill your cup. I just want to connect all the freaky dots that landed y'all in bed." She leaned forward mischievously, the glint in her eyes equivalent to her own pair of horns sprouting above her browbones.

"Jesus, you're practically giddy. Remind me why I put up with you again?"

"Who can resist this face?" She looked up to the heavens, batting her lashes for effect.

"Ugh." Zora rolled her eyes.

"Come on, chick, spill. I have inventory to get through. How was his class?"

Zora's face lit up. "They were amazing! I can't believe that he gets to teach so many talented, intelligent Black kids. It was so refreshing to be in a room full of budding creatives who were really chomping at the bit to have their next story published. They're all so excited to participate in the contest, and I am pretty confident that it's going to be a really tight competition this year.

"And really, I think that's where it started. Watching Reid in his element, as he managed his class, it was really sexy. He's intelligent and funny, and he naturally relates to these kids in a way that they respect."

"That's cool. We need more teachers like that, who meet kids where they are."

"Exactly! He's relating to them successfully, so it's like these kids have nothing left to do but show off their talents. Such a great vibe in the classroom."

"So where did we go from there?" Emma sipped her cappuccino.

Zora pointed to her cup, smiling. "Right, so then coffee. We sat at this cute little coffee shop right near his campus and talked for a couple of hours. We talked about family, work, and writing. He wants to be a novelist, too."

"Like Lawrence?"

"Yes and no. Not unlike Lawrence, I think. I bet it's hard to want to write in a similar genre to your best friend, who's already killing it. And does that change the dynamic of your friendship and business dealings?"

Emma thought it over. "I mean, it shouldn't. Anyone who is secure in their friendship shouldn't have an issue, right? We wouldn't have any issues."

"True." Zora poked out her lips, thinking. "I'd be your biggest cheerleader. And I can't tell if that's why Reid seems hesitant. He just says he's too busy because of his students and the work he does for Lawrence."

"But how much time does social media really take for one

person? It's not like he's doing marketing for some giant corporation. A few hours a week should be plenty if he's planning ahead and scheduling his posts."

"You think there's more to the story that he's not telling me?"

She shrugged. "Could be. He sounds too intelligent to be bogged down by social media posts about book events and speaking appearances."

Zora's shoulders dropped. "You're right." Maybe he was worried about Lawrence's feelings, or maybe he really didn't have time, but his excuse was thin.

"Zor-lock it out, sis," Emma encouraged. "But in the meantime, I need to know how y'all made it from the coffee shop to your bedroom."

"We drove." Zora stared ruefully at her best friend.

"Bitch. You know you're going to give me these details, right?" Emma rested her chin on her elbows.

Zora rolled her eyes, hating that they were discussing this in public, but leaned closer to the counter. "So as we left the coffee shop, he walked me to my car and kissed me."

"Good kisser?"

"Excellent kisser. No excess spittle or face-eating attempts. Not like that one guy—"

"Let's not even speak of it." Emma held up a hand.

"Right. So he kissed me, and then I kissed him, and then he was following me back to the house, and you were snoring on the couch, per usual."

She clutched imaginary pearls. "I do not snore."

"Bitch, the lies you tell."

Emma cackled. "Whatever, continue."

"So we tiptoed past you and when we got upstairs, I think I said something about how I could kiss him all night, and he basically was like, 'Bet.' And then we got naked and he kissed everywhere his mouth could reach."

Her mouth dropped open. "Shut. Up. Z, you are seriously my she-ro." She leaned in, her eyebrows reaching toward her hairline. "How many times he get you right?"

"Chile, more times than I can count. We fell asleep, and then he wanted more."

"Mmm-hmm. And then what did *you* do, you nasty heffa?" Emma twirled a braid around her fingers.

Zora grinned. "I reciprocated, of course."

"You've always been a specialist when it comes to the fellatio." Emma nodded with pride.

"Well, he did such stellar kissing, I couldn't let him think he was more skilled."

"Did you leave the man any of his soul, or is he walking around lobotomized by the master?"

Zora smiled slowly. "A lady never tells."

Emma rubbed her hands together. "So what does this mean? What about Lawrence?"

"He gets back into town this weekend, I think. Reid and I talked about it a bit, but I think that I should just tell Lawrence and see what happens. I still really like him, and I don't want to hide anything. We're not in a relationship. I'm allowed to date who I want."

"So it no longer bothers you that these two are best friends?"

"I don't know. Maybe. Should it?"

"What would you do if one of these guys hit on me, too?"

"I'd talk to you about it, see if you have feelings for anyone in particular. I can always back off."

"Ugh. You're always so fucking pragmatic." Emma rolled her eyes.

"That's a bad thing?"

"I actually think it works here. Besides, I have enough on my plate right now. I'm good with you playing the field with these two fine specimens."

"My priority is this store. And Granny. And you. So I don't

have time to entertain BS. Honestly, I don't really have time to date, but it has been a while, and Reid woke the beast. I don't know which guy I like more, so I think it's reasonable to get to know them better. Reid is quieter and sort of brooding, but Lawrence is so charming and just seems like such a catch. No matter what, I'm going to be honest."

"I'm impressed. You're finally allowing yourself a little time for some romance."

"Well, you weren't exactly going to stop nagging me about having a life outside of the bookstore, were you?"

Emma scrunched up her face. "As your best friend, it's my job to nag you in the right direction. That's what I do." Her eyes bright, she shrugged as if her role was obvious.

"You're impossible."

Emma winked, taking another sip of her coffee. "Thanks, sis. I take great pride in my work."

"Hot date tonight?"

"Two, actually. I'm meeting up with foodie guy first—he wants to go check out some restaurant pop-up by the wharf. Then I'm supposed to go over to Netflix and chill's place."

Zora shook her head. "They don't even get to be referred to by their names?"

Emma side-eyed her friend. "Come on, like you'd remember these dudes."

"What happened to that bartender you liked? She was funny and stupid hot."

"Yeah, I missed my opportunity. She's already booed up." Emma shook her head. "I'm not ready."

"But for some reason, you think I am?" Zora asked bewilderedly.

"You've been ready. You've kept yourself so busy that you don't see it, but you're ready." Emma returned her attention to her work on the computer, while Zora chewed on that last statement.

★ ★ ★

With Emma managing the inventory and Granny attending her monthly poker night, Zora left work while the sun was still out. After picking up groceries and dry-cleaning, she unloaded her bags onto the kitchen counter when her phone buzzed.

Reid: Hey Beautiful. How was your day?

Zora: Hi. ☺ Today flew by. It was busy, but I barely noticed.

Reid: It was like that for me too.

Butterflies swirled in her chest, and Zora wondered if she had that same effect on him. She bit her lip, wishing that they were speaking in person. Everyone seemed to insist she was doing nothing wrong, but she couldn't escape the thought of Lawrence coming home and feeling potentially betrayed—it had gnawed at her all afternoon. She sat down on one of the leather bar stools.

Zora: Are you sure this is a good idea? I don't typically date multiple people, and I'm already seeing your best friend.

Reid: Have you two talked about being exclusive? If so, I'll back off, but I don't want to, TBH.

Zora: We're not exclusive, we've technically only had two dates, but isn't there some sort of bro code about dating the same woman?

Reid: Rules don't apply until feelings get involved. Lawrence and I have been down this road before.

Zora: So...is this turning into some sort of competition?

Reid: I don't know if it'll come to that, but you are definitely a prize, Zora.

She stared at the message for a long moment, evaluating where along the spectrum between swag and running game the line belonged. Deciding that it was swag, her face warmed, the corners of her mouth curving upward. An ellipsis appeared on her screen, and she waited for the next message to appear.

Reid: I want to keep seeing you, Zora. I want you to know my intentions up front.

Zora: You guys are not going to make this easy for me, are you?

She watched her phone as Reid started to type and then stopped, only to restart again.

Reid: If it makes it easier, I can back off until you figure out where you are with Lawrence. Patience is not my strong suit, but I think you're worth the wait.

As generous as the offer was, the pang in Zora's chest let her know that she didn't want him to back off. She just wasn't ready to back away from Lawrence, either. She looked up from her phone to survey the store. Granny sat in her chair reading a children's book to a set of triplets whose mother brought them in once a week for story time. Brian was at the coffee kiosk studying for an upcoming exam. Emma sat cross-legged on the floor—this week she focused on taking inventory of their adult nonfiction section.

She looked back down, trying to think of what to write in response when her phone began to ring. Lawrence's author photo smiled up at her. She froze, her mouth dropping open in surprise. *Pull it together.*

"Hello?" Her voice was an octave above her usual. She cleared her throat. "Lawrence, hi!"

"Zora! How are you?" His smooth voice carried his wide smile.

"I'm good! How are your travels?" Zora could feel her phone buzz—another message from Reid, but he would have to wait for her response. Her heart raced as she willed herself to focus.

"Done for the week—I ended earlier than expected. That's why I'm calling. Are you free tonight?"

"Tonight?" she stuttered. "Um, yeah! I'm free. What did you have in mind?"

"Are you into cigars at all? I know a cigar bar downtown with a great mixologist."

She could hear the hope in his voice. D.C. had a handful of cigar bars, each with a different vibe, and some still fighting to get an evasive liquor license. A couple of locations had prime patio space for outdoor lounging, which was perfect for a September evening. All around D.C., folks with a balcony or front porch would stoop and light up quality sticks from their local tobacconists. Zora wasn't much of a smoker herself, but the scents of tobacco and peaty scotch reminded her of her grandfather. "Sure, that sounds fun. What time and where?"

"How about seven thirty? I could come to your house to pick you up. The parking downtown is awful."

Zora nervously bit her lip. The parking was terrible, but she didn't make it a habit to bring many men around her home. Now that Reid had been there, she felt her guard rising—it

had nothing to do with the fact that it was Lawrence wanting to come by and everything to do with the fact that her
home was her sanctuary—the one place that was off-limits to
people outside her inner circle. Not wanting to give another
person access, she weighed her options. "Why don't you pick
me up from the bookstore? I'll make sure I'm ready on time."

"Okay, sure." His tone muted. "So I'll see you soon."

Zora smiled hard, trying to sound cheerful. "Okay! Can't
wait."

The call ended, and she looked down at her phone to several missed text messages.

Reid: Have I said the wrong thing?

Reid: I'm sorry if I'm coming on too strong. I just like
you, Zora.

Reid: Give me a call later, if you get a chance.

Zora pressed her lips together, fighting the smile playing
at the corners.

Zora: I like you too, Reid. But I also like Lawrence, and I'm
going to tell him tonight about there being something
between me and you. Until I figure things out, I want to
take things slow. Is that okay?

Reid: Of course.

Zora: Want to call me tomorrow?

Reid: I'd like that.

Hours later Zora set her phone on the kitchen counter and made quick work of putting away the groceries and dry-cleaning. Moving upstairs, she stepped into her closet and looked through her clothes, considering what she wouldn't mind smelling like smoke. She pulled on a pair of jeans, a black camisole, and a colorful kimono duster made of thin, flowy fabric that reached her ankles. Her hair was swept into a high bun, and she touched up her natural makeup look with a kiss of highlighter above her cheekbones and an additional coat of mascara. Slipping on a pair of low, block-heeled mules, she posed for herself before the full-length mirror. "Yesss," she whispered.

13

The drive to the bookstore was uneventful. She passed a few joggers enjoying the evening air and a family walking their giant Saint Bernard. She waved to the owner of her favorite Brookland barbecue joint—he always sat on the patio with his boys and a handful of good cigars. She always looked forward to the days they smoked turkey legs and wings for their specials. After parking, Zora headed toward the bookstore entrance but stopped short when she heard her name.

Lawrence pulled up next to her in a black Range Rover, his tinted passenger window sliding down to reveal his smiling face. "Hi! Perfect timing." He pressed a button to unlock the doors.

"Hey!" She pulled open the door and her heart skipped a beat.

His dimples ignited his freshly shaven face. "Wow, you look beautiful." He wore dark jeans and a light sweater that zipped down from the collar. Once she was comfortably in her seat and had closed her door, he leaned over and kissed her cheek. "I'm glad you were free to hang out tonight."

The scent of his cologne lingered as the warmth of his lips left an imprint on her skin, sending tingles down her neck and arms to her fingertips. "Me, too," she replied softly.

He winked at her, intertwining his fingers with hers as he turned to face the road. "I've been waiting all week for this."

Driving down Georgia Avenue, they passed residential neighborhoods, old mom-and-pop storefronts, and office buildings. Families sat out on their front stoops talking and sharing cocktails. As they got closer to downtown, the traffic picked up and the buildings changed to high-rises. Nearing the Capitol building, they lucked out and found parking right in front of the establishment's patio seating. "Let me get your door," Lawrence said, stepping out of the car. He walked around to the passenger side, adjusting his sleeves before he opened her door. He offered his hand as she stepped out, hanging on to it as he locked the car and guided her into the building.

"Welcome back, Lawrence! Great to see you again." The bartender nodded in their direction.

"Hey, man, thanks. It's good to be back." Lawrence waved two fingers back at him.

"Same seats as usual?"

He turned to Zora. "Do you want to sit inside or outside?"

She surveyed the room. Most of the tables were filled, but the room wasn't smoky. "Wow, they must have really good air circulation in here."

"They take good care of us here. I am a member also, so I have a locker here."

"A locker?"

"Yeah, I'm able to keep boxes of cigars in my locker, tools and things like that. Makes things convenient so that I don't have to buy cigars one at a time. I can buy boxes of the things that I like and then store them. The lockers are humidors." He gestured toward the wall.

"Oh, that's cool. What got you into this stuff?"

"My dad." He smiled tightly. "I smoked my first cigar with him."

She squeezed his hand. "Why don't we sit inside? Probably going to get a little chilly out there."

Lawrence nodded, making eye contact with the bartender. "Yeah, can we have my usual table?"

"Sure thing."

Just then, a beautiful hostess walked up to greet them. "Hi, Lawrence!" She threw her arms around him, causing him to release Zora's hand.

"Hey, how are you, Shawna? Good to see you."

The woman tilted her head, pouting her flirty lips. "And who's your lady friend?"

"Isn't she beautiful?" Lawrence asked. "This is Zora."

"She certainly is. It's a pleasure to meet you, Zora. I'm Shawna. Please let me know if there's anything that we can do to make your experience more enjoyable." Shawna smiled widely, showing off perfect white teeth and unexpectedly warm eyes.

Zora smiled. "Thank you, Shawna."

She led the couple to a table in the center of the room. Four leather high-backed chairs framed a coffee table with a large ashtray and a reserved sign. Shawna grabbed the sign, pulling heavy menus from a register counter. "I'll be back with some water for the table and to get your drink order. The menu includes a list of our loose cigars, but you can also walk into the humidor over there." She gestured toward a glass room with shelves brimming with open cigar boxes, their contents wrapped in individual plastic wrappers.

"Thanks, Shawna." Lawrence pulled out a chair for Zora, selecting the chair next to her. "Do you smoke cigars?"

"Rarely, but I can be tempted," she teased. She was a ball

of nerves, trying to figure out how and when to bring up the recent development between her and Reid. She figured playful and light humor was as good a start as any.

"What kind do you like?"

"I like full-bodied, spicy ones. Like me." Zora flipped through the menu, perusing the specialty cocktails and long lists of spirits. When she looked up, she caught Lawrence watching her, his dark eyes drinking in her face and lips.

He tilted his head, his mouth curving into a smile. "Full of surprises. I have something I think you'll like. If Shawna comes back, can you order me an old fashioned?"

"Bourbon or what?"

He laughed. "They'll know." After getting up from the table, he walked to one side of the room, where padded lockers lined the wall. He pulled out his keys and unlocked his unit, exposing several cigar boxes.

"Can I get you anything, Zora? I'm happy to give you some recommendations if you're undecided." Shawna leaned against one of the empty chairs.

"Lawrence asked for an old fashioned."

Shawna nodded. "His usual. And for you?"

"Could I have the Michter's toasted rye with a large ice cube?"

"Of course. I'll get those started, and I'll come check to see if y'all want to order some food."

Zora smiled at her. "Thank you, Shawna."

As Shawna headed toward the bar, Lawrence returned with a few cigars, a torch lighter, and a cigar cutter. He handed a couple of cigars to Zora. "Do you have a preference?"

Looking at the cigar labels, she smiled. "You're testing me."

"I'm just curious." He grinned.

"Mmm-hmm." Zora knew immediately which one she wanted, but she decided to play along. She smelled a petite flavored cigar, which carried sweet scents of vanilla and stone fruit, and handed it back to him. "Fascinating. You keep these in your locker for women who don't like the taste of tobacco?"

He laughed. "You got me. Sometimes people talk a big game, and then they immediately contradict themselves."

Zora eyed the other two cigars in her hand. One was a milder cigar; a brand she sampled when she was first introduced to cigars. The other was her favorite. Its spicy, bold blend of tobacco was earthy and powerful. "I'll take this one. Do you have a V-cutter?"

His eyebrows rose. "I don't, but you might be the sexiest woman alive."

Shawna arrived with their drinks, having overheard the last of their exchange. "I've got you covered." She reached into the pocket of her apron, producing a heavy metal tool. She handed it to Zora, setting bar coasters on the table before putting down their drinks. "Here's your old fashioned, Lawrence. And Zora, your toasted rye with a large cube." She glanced between them. "Can I get you any food?"

"How about an order of smoked wings and the truffle fries?" Lawrence asked Zora. "Did anything else catch your eye?"

Zora scanned the food menu quickly as she cut her cigar, handing the cutter back to Shawna. "Yes, thank you. I haven't eaten dinner yet. Could I have the kale Caesar with the grilled spot prawns?"

Shawna smiled. "My favorite. I'll have that for you shortly. Please enjoy."

Zora turned to Lawrence. "So how was your trip? Where did you go?" She lifted her cigar to her mouth, and he activated his torch lighter, letting the flame kiss the end of her cigar as she drew on it lightly. The tip began to glow a fiery orange.

He swallowed hard, watching her red-stained lips wrap around the cut end of the cigar. "I went from my book events in Atlanta to New York, visiting a couple of indie bookstores up there. I had a couple of book signings and a radio event. I'm sorry that I didn't have much of an opportunity to call you."

She blew out a steady stream of smoke and grabbed her glass. "It's all good. Things have been busy at the store, and then I had the event at Reid's school."

Lawrence lit his own cigar. "Right, the school event. How'd it go?"

"It was fun, and it helped me advertise the *D.C. Speakeasy* contest that we host for young writers in the area."

"Nice."

Shawna delivered their food, and Zora lowered her head to pray. She opened her eyes to Lawrence nibbling on a French fry. The salad greens on her plate were lightly dressed and topped with shaved Parmesan and freshly toasted croutons. The spot prawns had charred grill marks on them, their heads decoratively placed on the tails. She dug into the salad. "Do you have to go out of town often? Mmm, this is good."

"This place has excellent food! And I do have a lot of events coming up this fall. I actually have to leave town again tomorrow."

"Another book event?" Zora cut into one of the prawns, layering it on her fork with kale and shaved Parmesan. She hummed as she took a bite.

"Is it that good?" he asked, grinning at her. She made another perfect bite, extending her fork toward him. Lawrence opened his mouth, meeting Zora's eyes. He kept his eyes on her as he accepted the food, licking a bit of the creamy dressing from his lips. "Okay, wow, that is delicious. And I have an event in Atlanta tomorrow night. I think I have maybe ten more events and then I'll be done with this leg of the tour."

Zora sipped her rye thoughtfully. "That must be really tiring. Is it typical for authors to have so many events?"

He pulled apart a chicken wing. "It can be really exhausting, but it's also energizing to meet so many people who are fans of the series. Some of the events are through my publisher, but I also hired an outside PR person who helps me connect specifically with Black-owned bookstores and speaking engagements for different writing programs at HBCUs and some PWIs."

"How did you come up with your series in the first place?" She rested her chin in her hand, reaching for her cigar, holding it between her middle and forefingers. Puffing lightly, she blew the smoke away from him. "What was the inspiration for Langston Butler?"

"Oh, it's not that interesting." He took a bite, shielding his mouth with his hand. "It was just a random day in college. Reid and I were in the dorms—we were both planning to double major. He focused on English literature and creative writing, while I declared journalism and professional writing."

He set down the drumette and took a sip of water, patting his mouth with a black cloth napkin. "One semester we were both taking a fiction course, and we did some brainstorming together. He ended up writing this mystery with a female lead. I wrote the first draft of what became Book One in the Langston Butler series. It was Reid's idea, actually."

"Langston Butler was Reid's idea?" Zora set down her cigar.

Lawrence nodded. "He thought it was a good idea for us each to write crime fiction mysteries. His was borderline cozy, and mine was closer to a thriller. We wanted to see how the different genres were received by the rest of the class."

"What was the result?"

"A lot of the girls in the class preferred Reid's story—they liked the humor and the main character. There were some romantic elements."

"But there are romantic elements in yours, too."

"Yeah, but they're just trysts. It's nothing that can lead to relationships."

Zora shook her head. "They can't lead to relationships because Langston is stubborn about his bachelor lifestyle. If he'd open himself up to it, I actually think he and Annette could be a really amazing couple."

He scrunched up his nose. "You think so?"

"You wrote the books! You don't recognize the chemistry between them?" Her eyes wide, she lifted her hands incredulously.

He shrugged and sipped his old fashioned. "Almost every female character in my stories is attracted to Langston. It's just who he is."

"Who he is? Oh, my God." Zora rolled her eyes, laughing. "Such a machismo thing to say."

Lawrence's eyes moved across her face. "But it made you smile." He leaned closer, placing a finger under her chin to guide her toward him. He kissed her full on the lips slowly, his breath tickling her skin as his lips parted slightly. Kissing her once more, he ran his thumb over her cheek. "I've been wanting to do that this whole time."

Zora's hand gripped his forearm. "You can do that again."

Lawrence grinned, leaning closer. "I'll admit I'm not a huge fan of PDA, but I'd like that."

She tilted her head slightly but said nothing as he moved to kiss her—a quick peck on the lips. Zora smiled to herself, motioning to Shawna that she wanted a second round of toasted rye.

They finished dinner, chatting about the bookstore and an upcoming event that Zora was hosting. As Lawrence drove them back toward Brookland, he rested a hand on her thigh. *I guess this doesn't count as public.*

He pulled up behind Zora's car and turned off the engine. "I'll be out of town for a couple days, but maybe keep this weekend open? There's somewhere I'd like to take you."

"Oh?" She turned, leaning her temple against the head-rest. "Where?"

"It's a surprise. But I want you to pack an overnight bag."

Overnight? "Really?" she murmured. "Is this somewhere romantic?"

"Maybe." His lips curved slightly.

"Do I need to plan for casual or dressy?"

"No dress code, so just wear what makes you comfortable." He leaned over the center console, pressing his lips against her cheek. "You look good in everything."

"Thank you." She took a deep breath. "Listen, before you make a bunch of plans, I need to tell you that I'm dating some-one else, too."

He shrugged. "That's okay. We're not exclusive. At least, we hadn't talked about that yet."

"True, but there's one more thing."

He nodded, bracing himself. "Okay. Tell me."

"It's Reid."

"Reid?" he asked skeptically. "Cranky high school teacher, Reid?"

"Very funny." She nudged his arm. "But yes, Reid Hughes."

"So I went out of town and he made a move? I had a feel-ing he'd be into you." Lawrence shook his head; a wry smile played on his lips.

Zora was quiet as heat rose in her chest, climbing her throat. "Are you upset? It wasn't something I intended."

Lawrence scoffed. "Not at all. Reid's a good guy and clearly he has good taste. I'm kind of into it."

She scrunched her nose. "Into it?" The astonishment of her tone made him laugh.

"There's nothing wrong with a little friendly competition. Reid and I are different breeds. This happened once before."

"Really? What happened?" Reid hadn't gone into detail, so she hoped Lawrence would.

He nodded. "Back in college, when we were roommates. She chose me."

"And there weren't any sore feelings after that?" Zora bit her lip. "You guys are so…logical."

He bobbed his head from side to side. "We all understood what the possible outcomes were. She refused to date either of us if the dynamic of our friendship started to change. So it didn't."

She watched him. "Just that simple, huh?"

He laughed. "Come on, Zora. We're grown men. We're not going to fight it out in the streets. May the best man win." He turned to watch her with new intensity in his eyes.

"Wow, I thought this conversation would be a lot more difficult." She blew out a breath. "I'm really impressed by the two of you." She pulled the strap of her purse comfortably over her shoulder.

He tipped his head in acknowledgment. "You heading home for the night?"

"Yeah, Emma agreed to close up, and Granny had plans tonight, so I'm headed home. I have some work to prepare for a guest author we're hosting this week." She licked her lips, watching him observe her movements. "Thank you for tonight—I had a good time."

"Text me when you make it, okay?" He gently tapped her hand with his index finger.

Zora nodded, kissing him lightly. The softness of his lips tempted her to linger, but she pulled back, remembering his aversion to public affection. "See you soon." She stepped out of the car, closing the door carefully. Lawrence waited patiently while she started her car and waved as she drove off.

14

The busy bustle of the bookstore kept both Lawrence and Reid from Zora's mind the rest of the week, as she prepared for their featured author on Thursday night. At the checkout counter on the night of the event, Zora and Emma were hit with a line of patrons anxious to purchase books in advance of the event to have them signed; the display of books on Black love, relationships, and life management was depleted so quickly that they carted the last of their stock to the register for people to snatch up when they reached the counter. Granny and Brian were on crowd control, corralling guests toward the seating area, which was packed to standing room only.

Dr. Catherine Clarke stepped into the store right on time; her deep brown skin was probably just as smooth and supple as it had been two decades prior. There was no need for makeup—her cheeks and the bridge of her nose were dotted with tiny moles that looked like freckles. Her long lashes curled naturally to frame brown eyes that crinkled in the corners. She wore a tailored purple dress suit with dark panty-hose and black pumps. Her graying locs were swept into a high bun, and gold rings circled several of her manicured fingers—a large diamond on her left ring finger. "Hi there. Are you Ms. Dizon?"

"Dr. Clarke! It's such a pleasure to meet you—I can't tell you how excited we've been to have the opportunity to host a book event for you. We're huge fans of your work." Zora handed a bag to her customer at the counter and rounded its edge to greet the local celebrity. Dr. Clarke was a marriage and family therapist whose work and research with Black families had been televised and featured on Oprah's OWN network. The line of guests waiting to buy books burst into applause.

Zora extended her hands to Dr. Clarke, who accepted them. "Welcome to Opus Northeast! Your fan base is incredible—half of D.C. is here to see you!"

Dr. Clarke chuckled. "The popularity was something that I hadn't anticipated."

Z gestured toward the throng of people sitting and standing in a half circle toward the back of the store. "Did you always know that you wanted to write books?"

"I did, but I never dreamed of the bestseller list. I always assumed it was rigged." They shared a laugh and she continued. "I just wanted to write something for us, for our community. Something that can help us to love and to grieve and to cope with the struggles that we go through every day. I, for one, got tired of people telling me what my expectations should be when they haven't walked a day in my shoes. They wouldn't dare try my brand let alone my shoes!"

Zora nodded, allowing Dr. Clarke to hold her arm as they walked. The elder woman stepped forward with purpose, her head high and her back straight. She smiled with her mouth closed, accentuating her proud cheekbones, her full lips coated in a matte red lipstick. "I've been watching you on TV and love the contrast that you show between different Black couples and how they navigate obstacles. I like that you bring in everyday people and not just celebrities."

"Well, my dear, underneath it all, celebrities are still everyday people. It's the public who puts them on the pedestal."

Zora's smile brightened. "This is going to be such a good event! Okay, please stand here, and I'll introduce you. I can keep time for you and let you know when we're five minutes away from the scheduled signing, or you're welcome to go over time if you'd like. What's your preference?"

Dr. Clarke leaned close to Zora. "I'm from three blocks over, so let's ride 'til the wheels fall off."

"Yes, ma'am." She turned to the crowd, beaming at the smiling faces clutching books to their chests. "Good afternoon, everyone!"

Zora waited. Several people responded to her in kind, but that was not how she liked to start an event. She stood taller, rolling her shoulders behind her back, and started again.

"Now, y'all know better than that. I said 'Good afternoon!'" This time she projected her voice farther, the sound of it resonating in every corner of the bookstore.

"Good afternoon!" The audience responded in booming unison, several laughing at the increased volume.

"Much better. Today I am honored to introduce our guest to you, Dr. Catherine Clarke, author of *Building Black*, *Worthy to Be Wooed*, and, most recently, *The Roundtable*. Dr. Clarke has committed her career to serving and supporting Black families, Black couples, Black communities looking to build and endeavoring to overcome any obstacle. She has given TED Talks on self-care and cultivating a present mind. She has been featured and interviewed by *the* Oprah Winfrey herself. This winter her Roundtable talks, which include interviews with families from her book's case study, will be featured on the OWN network. Are y'all ready to hear more about *The Roundtable*?"

"Yes!" the onlookers eagerly shouted.

"I give you the incomparable Dr. Catherine Clarke."

The crowd erupted into cheers and applause as the guest of honor stepped forward and squeezed Zora's hand. "Thank you," she whispered. She stepped forward to the podium, folding her hands on the lectern. "Thank you all for this warm welcome. You know, it's good to be home."

Listeners cheered louder, always quick to go hard for the locals. They leaned in, watching Catherine calm those still applauding with a wave of her hands.

"I grew up just a few blocks down Georgia Avenue in what used to be a predominantly Black neighborhood. Times sure have changed, and the community has had some turnover. Gentrification isn't a new phenomenon, young people. It's been happening a long time."

Many people in the crowd nodded.

"After I completed my degrees at Howard—"

"H-U!" a fellow alumnus from the crowd exclaimed, which was met with "You know!" by another.

Dr. Clarke chuckled. "Go Bison! After I completed my studies and was certified as a marriage and family therapist, I sought to pour all of the resources I had into a practice only for Black people. It was my effort to support our community. Do you know what the problem was?"

A woman sitting on the floor whispered, "What?"

Catherine held out her arms, her hands open. "No one came. How many of y'all have elders in your family who don't go to the doctor or don't believe in therapy? They don't trust medical practitioners or believe in the concepts of mental health. Anyone?"

More than half of the people listening raised their hands. Others nodded or whispered their agreement.

"So I had my work cut out for me. Can anyone guess where I started?"

Granny raised her hand. "The church?"

Dr. Clarke smiled. "How'd you know?"

"'Cause that's where I'd start, too." Granny nodded and Catherine reciprocated, indicating their understanding of each other.

"When things went wrong in the household, when someone was ill or had run into some trouble, we went to the church. We'd ask the pastor for counseling. We'd pray. So I went to local pastors who knew me, and I asked them to refer parishioners who needed counseling on a more regular basis or that went into more depth than they were able to provide. That early on, I gave deep discounts to build up a clientele, and the referral system helped me to grow a thriving practice.

"What was most important to me, though, in all of the outreach I was doing, with these books I'd written—I realized that I'd spent a lot of time writing and focusing on the individual and how people come together. *The Roundtable* is where we bring couples who are working hard to *stay* together.

"Many of us are caught in cyclical behavior, and we get lost there until we decide to make changes. Sometimes those changes are painful, and sometimes we avoid them because we assume they'll hurt us irreparably. What we often fail to realize is that we are in a constant state of change. You're changing, I'm changing, and as a unit, we change. But are we consistently willing to put in the work?"

Catherine began to share about a couple from her case study and read passages from her book. "In many ways the couple seemed like they fit well, but neither of them were happy with the other. In surveys they completed, both indicated that they would be happy to be single. Everything about their relationship felt forced, but because they looked good on paper, they stuck it out. It never occurred to either of them to consider what would actually make them happy. They just assumed that their marriage was typical."

She held up a finger. "It wasn't until I asked them what they needed from their partner to be happy—because clearly they thought they'd be happy alone—that we made a breakthrough. We discovered a step that was skipped in their relationship. What was it that was missing? Can anyone guess?"

Spectators looked around the room to see if they could spot who would come up with the right answer, but many of them shook their heads.

"'Like' was missing. They fell in love, everything looked the way it was supposed to look and felt the way it was supposed to feel, so they married, but they grew apart in their marriage very quickly. They didn't take the time to figure out if they really liked each other—they weren't each other's best friend. And you need that kind of like, because there are some days where you won't feel the love, but if you like them—if you value their friendship—you're more likely to try to work it out. If you don't, you'll let things fester. So they didn't work out, and ultimately they split up."

A woman raised her hand nervously, her eyes darting around the room at those turning their attention toward her. "Is that always the result? Can they grow to like each other?"

Catherine clasped her hands together in front of her body. "Anything is possible. It depends on the two people and whether they're really willing to put in the work. A lot of times we get caught up in the rigmarole of life, pulled in so many directions that we lose focus on the people right in front of us. We fall into routines that don't include time with our partners. We're always doing things without prioritizing the time we need to spend together and to really enjoy each other. Often, the little bit of time we have together is an afterthought. We spend it sleeping, or silently decompressing because our days are so filled up with other things." She looked at the woman who asked the question. "Whether it's date nights, or dinner downloads, or the half hour before bed, make time to talk and connect. Put the phones down, turn off the TV, and talk. See what happens."

The talk continued, and other audience members asked questions. As things began to slow, Dr. Clarke turned to Zora and nodded.

Zora stepped forward to stand next to their speaker. "Everyone, thank you so much for joining us for this portion of the event. We're going to start getting people in line for the book signing, but as my helpers set up, I think we have time for one more question."

A young woman stepped forward. "How do you choose?"

"Choose?" Dr. Clarke repeated. "Tell me more."

Likely in her late teens, the girl blushed. "If there is more than one person who likes you, how do you choose? I can't tell which one is right for me."

Catherine considered the issue for a moment and smiled at the girl. "You know, relationships are funny things. In our youth, it's all about excitement, attraction, sex, and emotion. As you get older, you see that some of those things begin to fall away. Looks start to fade. Sex fizzles out. My mother used to say, after all of the sexy stuff falls away, who is the person you want to talk to? Who do you communicate best with? When you're fighting, when you're hurt, when you're grieving, who's going to talk you through it? Who do you want there to hold your hand?" Catherine winked at the girl. "I think you know."

Zora tilted her head at the response as her phone pinged. The crowd erupted into applause, and people stood to begin filing into line.

Lawrence: Hey, Beautiful. I'm back in town. Can't wait to spend time with you this weekend.

Catherine stood beside her. "Your partner?" She gestured to the phone.

Zora shrugged with a half smile. "Maybe." She led the author to a table laden with Sharpie markers and a marquee with her book cover on it. One by one, Zora watched Dr. Clarke as she greeted event participants, took photos with them, and told stories while she signed copies of her books.

Zora wore her event smile, shaking hands with patrons and handing out flyers of upcoming events. In the back of her mind, she chewed on the words the sage therapist shared. *I'll text Lawrence later.*

After cleaning and closing up the store, Zora drove home with PJ Morton's *Piano Album* playing through her stereo speakers. Granny had invited Dr. Clarke to hang out with her and some of her friends to reminisce on what D.C. used to be, and Emma had a date with some guy she met online. Emma had strict instructions to text Zora her location and to use their safe word "froyo" if she needed backup.

At home Z showered to wash the day away, donning a cozy, powder-pink loungewear set of wide-legged pants and a cropped hoodie. In the kitchen she boiled water for pasta as she thinly sliced cloves of garlic and chopped fresh Italian parsley. She melted butter into a pan coated in olive oil and sautéed the garlic with red pepper flakes, salt, and pepper. She spooned in a little of the seasoned pasta water. Once the pasta was cooked

and drained, she tossed it in the sauce, sprinkled the fresh parsley on top, and shaved some fresh Parmesan over her bowl.
After pouring herself a glass of wine, she carried her meal to
the couch, set her wine on the coffee table, and flipped on the
television to a kitchen renovation show. Quiet nights at home
like this were so rare that Zora had to take advantage of them
when she could—the peaceful stillness of the evening coaxed
a reminder that she needed to make decisions about some potential new hires for the store. *These nights don't have to be so rare.*

Zora closed her eyes to pray over her food, and immediately the images of Reid and Lawrence appeared behind her
eyelids. Shaking them from her mind, she spoke over her
meal and the hands that prepared it. Twirling pasta around
her fork, she savored her first bite, making sure she got some
of the crisped garlic, pepper flake, and Parmesan. She moaned
out loud, shaking her head at her bowl. "And no one will ever
experience it," she sighed.

She pulled a notepad and pen from the storage cubby within
her coffee table, sipping her wine as she sat back on the couch.
Still marinating on Dr. Clarke's words, she wondered if she
had enough information to make an educated decision about
who she wanted to date. So much time had passed since her
last relationship, and she longed for the intimacy of having a
partner, but she didn't want to make any rash decisions. She
thought about making a new list of pros and cons for Lawrence and Reid, but then she decided against it. "Better I take
my time getting to know these guys," she surmised.

She took another bite of food, skimming her list once more
as her phone rang. *Lawrence.*

"Hey, how are you?" she asked, muting the television.

"Hello, Zora. I'm well, and you?"

The smile in his deep voice made her face soften. "I'm good.
Are you back already?"

"I am. I just got home and figured I'd call you and see what you're up to."

She pictured him already unpacking his suitcase. He didn't seem like the type to leave tasks for later. "Me? I'm just sitting here with dinner and a glass of wine." She moved the notepad off her lap. "Are you tired from your trip?"

"Eh." He took a deep breath. "It's been a long week, but we're almost to the weekend. I'm ready for our little getaway. Have you packed?"

"Not yet. Do I get to know anything more about this excursion?" Zora pulled her legs onto the couch as she leaned against its arm. She twirled noodles around her fork, waiting for a good moment to take a bite.

"You're not big on surprises, are you?" he asked playfully.

Zora dropped her chin slightly, looking up to the ceiling. "I guess it depends on the surprise."

"You're so alpha, I love it," he chuckled.

"That bad, huh?" She smiled into the phone, taking a bite of food.

"I don't think it's off-putting. I think you're just used to being in control."

"So then surprises are a tool used to get someone to relinquish control?"

"I guess that's true," he laughed. "And yes, I think that this would be my play for a little control over our dynamic here. Maybe you'll be open to surrender just this once?"

"Maybe." She couldn't remember a time that she'd fully let go in the past few years. Everything from the store to her home required her to be on top of things, and though Emma and Granny were fully capable of running things in her absence, she'd always made sure to check in consistently. The store was her baby.

"Are you uncomfortable being away for two days? Or is it the thought of sharing a room with me?"

"*Uncomfortable* isn't the word I'd use, and sharing a room isn't a problem. Why not for a weekend getaway to..." Her voice trailed off hopefully.

He laughed. "Nice try. You'll see when we get there. I'm glad you're giving yourself this time away. You work hard, so you deserve to play hard, too."

"So we're playing this weekend, Mr. Michaels?" She couldn't stop the sultry innuendo.

"There will be some play, but I promise you'll enjoy it." His voice dropped deeper.

The playfulness of his tone made her bite her lip, and she wondered whether Lawrence's bedside manner was anything like his best friend's. "Well, I should warn you that I snore."

Lawrence laughed. "Like a cute little snore, or like an industrial machine?" he teased. "I can bring earplugs if you say the latter."

"I've been told it's cute, but I can't say for sure. I've never heard it." She shrugged. "I just thought I'd give you fair warning in case you're a light sleeper."

"I'm not all that focused on sleep this weekend." The possibilities of what he meant by that statement made Zora shiver.

She blushed. "What will you be focused on?"

His sinister chuckle made her toes curl in anticipation. "I'm going to leave that to your imagination. I'll see you Saturday?"

"Count on it." As they hung up, Zora leaned back to consider the many possibilities of what Lawrence said, but her phone rang again. Grinning, she answered quickly. *Maybe he decided to share after all.* She answered throatily. "Did you change your mind? Want to tell me how we'll occupy our time if we're not sleeping?"

"Uh... Hey, Zora. It's Reid."

Shit. She sat up quickly, her mind racing to find an acceptable explanation. "Reid! Hi. I'm so sorry. I thought you were someone else."

"Yeah, I gathered that." His words were short. "I'm guessing you have plans with Lawrence?"

Zora scrunched up her face, lifting her chin toward the ceiling as she silently cursed herself. "Yeah, Lawrence wanted to surprise me with a getaway this weekend."

"I see. Where are you going?"

"He wouldn't tell me."

"I guess that makes sense. Anyway, I was calling to see if we could plan a date soon, but it sounds like your calendar is kind of full."

"We could do next week!" she blurted out. "What did you have in mind?"

"Something that won't interrupt your sleep hours…"

"Come on, Reid. I'm sorry. You know that I have been worried about this whole situation, with me dating the both of you. I don't want to make things awkward, and I recognize that I just did, but I don't see a scenario where this *isn't* awkward. Do you?"

He exhaled a long breath. "You're right, and I was the one who pushed you to date both of us, so I apologize."

Zora sat quietly for a long moment. "Are you jealous?"

"I don't mean to be, but maybe a little." He laughed lightly. "So next week? I thought maybe we could go to the National Museum of African American History and Culture—they have a new exhibit I've been wanting to see, and I thought you might enjoy it as well."

"I'd love that! I haven't been there in about a year, and I've wanted to spend more time there. Every experience there is edifying."

"I feel the same way. I could spend a week there and still feel like I haven't seen everything."

"I went once and just sat in their video exhibit area listening to Black men describe what it means to be a Black man in America, and I was there for hours. Just being in the building is healing."

"Good for your spirit."

"Yes! And so important in really understanding our history because we sure don't get all of that rich material in school."

"Erasure is real," he agreed. "Cool, so next week."

"Next week! Thank you for thinking of me. I'm really looking forward to it."

"No problem. I hope you enjoy your getaway this weekend." The softness of his gravelly, baritone voice wrapped around her like a fluffy blanket, and Zora thought back to the morning they woke up together and his arms wrapped tightly around her.

"Thank you. I'll see you soon."

15

Zora drove to Lawrence's house on Saturday morning. He still wouldn't tell her where they were going, but he did hint that they had several hours of drive time. The autumn air turned cool overnight, so Zora packed extra layers and some cute boots, just in case Lawrence planned for them to be outside for any extended amount of time.

She sang along with H.E.R. on the radio, bobbing her head to the music. As she passed houses in his neighborhood, she marveled at the fall colors all around. The trees had all turned and were at their most vivid—the maples and oaks sported varieties of red, orange, and yellow leaves, which dotted the lawns of all of his neighbors. She parked on the street in front of his house, but Lawrence was outside when she arrived, and he waved her toward the driveway.

"How are you?" Zora called as she stepped out of her car.

"Hey, beautiful." He closed the gap between them, pulling her into a tight hug—his arms wound around her lower back. "Are you ready for a road trip?" His chin rested against her temple. "You smell nice."

"Thanks!" She smiled up at him as she pulled back. Her black T-shirt was tucked into distressed jeans, which she wore with ankle boots and a faux suede jacket. "I'm ready. Are you all set?"

"We're good to go. I've got some coffees and breakfast burritos in the front seat." Lawrence moved toward the trunk of her car and grabbed her overnight bag. "I'm impressed that you didn't pack more."

She shrugged, laughing. "It's just two days. I tried not to overthink it."

He pretended to shake the oversize tote bag. "You mean to tell me there aren't six pairs of shoes in here?"

Zora giggled. "I hate to disappoint, but there are only three pairs in there. I tried to think about the different types of terrain that were within a two-hour drive of here."

"That's good logic. I promise that I won't have you climbing any trees," he teased.

She snapped her fingers. "Damn, I did pack my shoe spikes just in case."

"Very funny." Lawrence helped her into the passenger seat, and she held her purse in her lap. "Want me to put that in the backseat?"

"Sure, just let me grab my phone."

"Expecting a call?" He raised his brow, his face skeptical.

She shook her head. "Just force of habit for safety and in case you need a copilot to look up directions. Remember, I still don't even know where we're going!"

His shoulders relaxed. "Oh right, we're just headed about two hours out of town to a little bed-and-breakfast I've been to before. The property is beautiful, and there are some fun plans I've arranged for us near there."

Zora regarded him slyly. "You really do like the element of surprise, don't you?"

He shrugged, a smile tugging at the corners of his mouth as he rounded the car to his side and climbed in. "Maybe I like to see the look on people's faces when I surprise them. This might sound selfish, but I feel a sense of satisfaction when I can do things like that."

He started the car and pulled out onto the street, navigating his neighborhood smoothly. Copper leaves swayed in the morning breeze, as finches sang in the sunlight.

"Ah, so your love language is gifts," Zora deduced, smiling at him. "I still don't know what to expect, but thank you in advance for putting so much thought into planning this weekend together. It's been a long time since I've been swept away somewhere."

"How long?"

"My last romantic getaway..." She pulled at her memory. "Maybe six or seven years ago? A long weekend in Jamaica."

Lawrence eyed her quickly before returning his eyes to the road. "Wow, that's a *really* nice trip."

She squinted at him. *Is he comparing his getaway to that trip?* "I'm sure whatever you have planned will be perfect, Lawrence." *Ugh, the male ego.*

He straightened his back, reassured, while Zora pressed her lips together to keep from laughing. "Mind if I put on some music?"

"Please."

They grooved to Jill Scott, SZA, Summer Walker, and Jhené Aiko as Lawrence's SUV glided down the highway away from the nation's capital. They sang along to the music, and Zora giggled as Lawrence attempted to lift his voice into falsetto. He missed the mark, but he kept going as she hummed along. High-rises and monuments gave way to expanses of fields and wooded areas as they continued on.

When Lawrence steered them off the highway, they drove for a long time before turning down a twisting driveway book-ended by large shrubs. Massive oak trees framed a small pond with a spraying fountain; a huge white house lay behind them. They climbed out of the car, stretching their legs and marvel-ing at their surroundings. Zora grabbed her purse from the backseat and slung it over her shoulder as she took in the bay windows and the expansive wraparound porch with rocking chairs and its own porch swing. Blue hydrangeas climbed a trellis on the side of the house. "Gorgeous," she murmured.

A man ambled down the steps to greet them. "Mr. Mi-chaels, it's so good to see you again so soon!"

"Please, call me Lawrence. And this is Zora."

"Ms. Dizon, I'm Terrance. It's a pleasure to meet you, and welcome." He took her hand between both of his and held it. "I understand that you have an excursion planned, so we will take your bags upstairs and see you soon. Your ride is this way." He gestured around the side of the house to a carport, holding Zora's hand on his arm to lead the way. Lawrence followed behind them.

"Wow, is this just for us?" Zora stepped into the cab of the sleek black Sprinter van.

"It is." Lawrence followed her, sitting next to her as Ter-rance closed the door behind them. "I didn't want us to have to worry about driving after our scheduled plans."

"Do I finally get to know what we're doing?" The van made its way back down the driveway to the long expanse of road, retracing some of their steps. Rows of vineyards spanned acres of land before they reached a gate.

"I guess it's okay now." He paused for dramatic effect, a

smile creeping into his cheeks. "We're headed to a wine tasting at a vineyard owned by a good friend of mine."

Zora perked up. "Fun! Black owned?"

"Yes. That's one of the best parts."

"I love that. Wow, this is such a fancy getaway. Thank you." She snuggled against him, and he wrapped his arm around her. "I haven't been treated to anything like this in a really long time."

Lawrence massaged her shoulder, kneading his thumb into the flesh at the base of her neck. "You work hard, Z. Everyone should take time for moments like these. I'm glad I can share it with you." He pulled her close, softly kissing her temple.

"Me, too." Zora turned to him. "How was Atlanta?"

"The turnout was incredible. Way bigger than anything I was expecting, which makes me wonder whether I should do a couple more events there."

"How does it feel to be a celebrity?" She leaned her head on his shoulder.

"Like I have a lot less time to myself these days." The van stopped, and the driver exited to let them out. "That's what makes this getaway that much more special." Lawrence held Zora's hand as she stepped down from the vehicle. "I get to spend some of my time off with you."

They stepped into the main house on the property and were ushered into a private tasting room with a heavy wooden table and twinkling lights. A sommelier walked them through the philosophy of the vineyard and had them sample a flight of their most popular wines to choose their favorite. She then brought them a big cheese and charcuterie board and uncorked the bottle of wine Lawrence and Zora selected.

After the sommelier walked away, Zora took a picture of the board, which was covered with a rose made of thinly sliced Genoa salami, artfully folded prosciutto, and an accordion of spicy soppressata. Dividing the cured meats were triangles of black pepper pecorino, cubes of briny Gorgonzola, a soft pile of Taleggio, and a smoky mozzarella. Dark purple grapes on the vine occupied one corner, and a sweet jelly made with a dessert wine filled a tiny ramekin while another held raw local honey. Thin crackers dotted with black pepper and dried rosemary lined another corner of the board along with green olives marinated with whole cloves of garlic.

Lawrence raised his glass and Zora followed suit. "To our first weekend together."

"Cheers." She blushed. She rolled the wine around her glass before taking in its aroma and sipping it slowly. The juiciness of the cabernet tasted like blackberries and red currants, the wine becoming more dry as it reached the back of her tongue.

"What do you think so far?" Lawrence sipped his wine, rolling it around in his mouth before swallowing it down.

"Is this something you've done with a date before?" Zora asked, nibbling on a cracker covered in Taleggio and raw honey.

Lawrence shrugged. "Once before," he admitted. "This place is just too cool not to share, and I love that we get to support Black businesses in the process."

She agreed. "Thank you for bringing me here. I may just have to subscribe to their monthly wine membership."

He smiled. "I'm a member, so I highly recommend it."

"So is this how you spend your downtime between books? Recharging at a B&B?"

"I wish. I don't really get a lot of downtime lately. I've got a pretty busy promo schedule, and then I've got deadlines for my next two books, so I've always got *something* going on. If I didn't schedule time off, I don't know that I'd actually get any."

"I know for sure I wouldn't have any time off if I didn't schedule it."

"Do you work seven days a week?"

Zora nodded. "I might not work a full shift every day, but

my hands touch something work related every day. Emma and I make a great team, and we're looking to bring on one more person, maybe two."

"Business must be good if you're expanding."

She smiled easily. "We do all right. We have a lot of local support, and when people like you come by, it helps."

He tapped his glass against hers. "Anything that I can do to support Black business, Ms. Dizon."

They relaxed into a comfortable silence, sipping wine and sampling cheeses before returning to the bed-and-breakfast to change before dinner. As they entered their room, Zora took in the clean, contemporary decor. Their bags sat at a storage bench at the foot of a king-size four-poster bed with a fluffy white comforter and oversize pillows. A chaise sat beside a large window with a throw blanket at its foot. On the opposite side of the bed, an oversize couch covered in colorful pillows faced the foot of the bed. A writing desk and a scalloped velvet office chair were against the wall opposite the bed; the television was mounted in the space above the desk. The en-suite bathroom had a claw-foot tub in the center of the room with a rainfall shower behind a glass wall and his-and-hers vanities on either side. A walk-in closet/dressing room entrance was inside the bathroom.

"So cozy," Zora murmured. "That tub looks amazing."

"Perfect for a retreat, right?" Lawrence opened his bag and grabbed a few things. "Do you mind if I take a quick shower first? That way I can be out of your way in the bathroom in case you want some privacy as you get ready."

"Sure, sounds good. Is tonight fancy?"

"I wouldn't say fancy..." He shrugged.

She held up a hand, amused. "Say no more. I think I know what I'm going to wear."

He smiled. "Okay, I'll be out in a few."

Zora grabbed her overnight bag and rifled through it for a flowing maxi dress with an off-the-shoulder ruffle and her travel steamer. The soft, pleated fabric was a deep, shimmering blue, and she loved any dress with pockets. After unzipping the lower compartment of her bag, she pulled out her heeled sandals and a skinny belt to cinch the dress slightly above her natural waist. She grabbed her toiletry organizer and turned just in time for Lawrence to appear wearing nothing but a towel and a smile.

"Um, wow," she breathed.

Water beaded against his smooth brown skin, droplets running down his hairless, muscular torso to gather in the folds of his towel. He ran his hand over his close fade, waiting for her to gather words that she could coherently string together. "You good, Z?" He smiled like a Cheshire cat, ready to get into some mischief.

Zora licked her lips and caught herself, her face flushing as she gathered her things. "Yes! I'm good," she laughed nervously. "I'm just going to..." She gestured toward the bathroom. "I'll be back."

"Take your time, Zora. We don't have to get going for about an hour and a half. If you feel like taking a dip in that tub, I think you'll love the products they have here." He gestured toward the bath caddy tray that extended across the width of the tub, holding bottled soaps and bath salts.

She nodded, grinning. "I just might." Closing the door behind her, she cursed herself under her breath before setting to work steaming her dress, which was only a little wrinkled from its time in her bag. She left the dress hanging and looked briefly at the shower before heading for the tub. Lawrence had said to take her time, and she intended to. She poured a travel-size bottle of botanical bubble bath and some bath salts near the tub's jets and laid her toiletry organizer on the counter of one vanity. Zora wrapped her hair in a silk scarf before easing herself into the steaming bubbles, exhaling deeply before taking in the scents of lavender and eucalyptus. Resting her head on the lip of the tub, she closed her eyes and soaked for a few minutes, trying to remember the last time she'd splurged on a mini-vacation for herself. "This place is worth the drive," she sighed happily.

After taking her time getting ready, Zora opened the door to find Lawrence standing in a deep blue suit at the foot of the bed. The open collar of his starched white dress shirt showed the tiniest sliver of his brown skin. His hands in his pockets, he looked like he was stepping off the cover of *GQ*, and his musky cologne pulled at her nostrils.

"You look stunning, Zora." His eyes were trained on her, so she twirled under his gaze, the skirt of her dress swishing as the pleats fanned out. Her gold jewelry and shimmering eye makeup accentuated her plum-stained lips, and her natural curls were side parted and teased for beautiful volume that kissed her shoulders.

"Thank you, handsome. I like your suit. It's like you knew I'd be wearing blue," she laughed.

He shrugged, grinning. "I just figured it went with everything."

"So where are we going for dinner?"

Lawrence took her by the hand, holding it tightly. "Luckily, we don't have to go very far." They walked toward the main dining area but then pivoted toward a nearly hidden private dining room. Inside, a single table was set with glowing candles and white chrysanthemums. A Black woman with deep brown skin and her microlocs pulled into a high bun stood in a crisp white chef coat. She greeted Lawrence with a handshake.

"Zora, I'd like for you to meet Andrea West, a local celebrity chef from D.C. She's cooked for everyone from the president, to ambassadors, to the Real Housewives. She is cooking something special for us tonight."

Zora shook her hand and pulled her in for a hug. "Wow, it's such a pleasure to meet you!"

"And you as well! Please, have a seat and get comfortable. This is Adel Williams. She will be assisting me tonight and will grab your drink orders. We've put together a tasting menu for you this evening, and under each course there's a wine pairing. There is also a full bar should you prefer a cocktail." She gestured toward a young server with a bright smile.

"Thank you." Zora smiled wide as Lawrence pulled out a chair for her. She ran her fingers over the printed menu and squeezed his hand as he sat down. "I'm blown away! This is too much. You really planned all of this for me?"

He shrugged, his megawatt smile matching hers. "It seemed right to make a grand gesture. I am still vying for your affection, you know."

"Well, you are definitely bringing your A-game, sir."

"Ms. Dizon, Mr. Michaels, welcome. Can I get you something to drink?" Adel smiled broadly at the couple.

"I'll stick to the wine pairings, Adel. Thank you." Zora smiled.

Lawrence nodded. "Me, too, thanks."

Adel nodded and moved toward the bar, while Chef Andrea placed a pristine white plate in front of them. "Tonight we will begin with an amuse-bouche to prestart your courses. Here we have a fresh fig and walnut bite. There's a sheep's milk Roquefort cheese spread on the fig itself, which is wrapped in prosciutto crudo and topped with a toasted walnut half. And, yes, this is something you can pick up with your fingers."

Lawrence looked at Zora and laughed.

"What?" she asked.

"You look like a kid on Christmas."

"I mean, this is my kind of Christmas!" She accepted a glass of wine from Adel and gingerly placed the amuse-bouche onto her tongue. She closed her eyes as her lips wrapped around the morsel, the four ingredients melting together. "Oh, my God."

Lawrence ate his bite, slowly nodding in agreement. "Mmm-hmm."

Round after round, Chef Andrea walked them through the courses, each one even more of a delight to their taste buds. Seared scallops with sea beans and fresh corn. A velvety-sweet potato soup garnished with crème fraiche and watercress. Deconstructed rabbit and dumplings. A bourbon and peach bread pudding with cream cheese ice cream.

"I couldn't possibly eat another bite. Chef Andrea, you've really outdone yourself. This meal was everything."

"I am so glad you enjoyed it! I took the liberty of wrapping up one last bite for you—these are my hazelnut truffles. They do have some hazelnut liqueur in them, so be sure to take your time and enjoy."

Zora stood and hugged the chef. "Thank you again. Do you have a card? I have an event coming up soon and would love to check your availability."

"I certainly do!" She presented one to Zora with both hands.

"Thank you, Andrea." Lawrence shook her hand. "Your food is phenomenal."

"I appreciate you for saying so." She handed each of them a small box tied closed with a ribbon. "Have a great night!"

Zora grinned and waved. "You as well!"

Lawrence offered her his arm, and they made their way back to the room. Inside, Zora kicked off her shoes and moved toward the couch, pulling her legs under her.

"That was the best meal I've had in a long time. Thank you. This has been so much more than just a quick weekend getaway to a B&B, Lawrence."

He released another button of his shirt, curling his finger inside the collar to pull it away from his neck. "You deserve these kinds of getaways, Zora."

Shit. The store. "You know what? I should check in with Emma…"

He shook his head. "No, no, no, none of that."

"No?"

He sat next to her on the couch, pulling her against him. "I don't want you to think about work tonight." He wrapped his arm around her waist, his hand flush against her back, as he kissed her. Angling his face, he ran his fingertips up her back to her exposed shoulder, making her shiver as he kissed her more deeply. His tongue traced her upper lip before gliding against hers, and she moaned softly as his full lips pressed against hers more urgently.

She pulled back slowly, but he leaned forward, chasing her. "I'm going to take a quick shower to rinse off and change into something more comfortable, okay?" She kissed him again, nipping at his bottom lip, before she stood and headed to the bathroom.

"Want some company?" he whispered.

She kissed him once more. "Maybe I have a little surprise for you, too."

"Oh really?"

Zora nodded slowly, her lips curving as she nuzzled his neck. "Be back in a minute." A glance over her shoulder confirmed that he was watching as she walked away, and she smiled coyly at him as he shook his head.

Zora ran the shower, then wrapped her hair, removed her jewelry, and stripped down. The hot water helped soothe her nervous excitement as she wondered whether Lawrence's bedroom skills exceeded Reid's. The lather of the artisanal soap filled the room with the scents of oats and honey. Zora rinsed the soap off, careful to avoid water touching her wrapped hair. She patted herself dry, slathered her skin in cocoa butter, and donned a silky camisole and shorts set that accentuated the fullness of her breasts and made her ass look perfectly round. She pressed her favorite fragrance from a perfume roller against her pressure points and throat with the tips of her fingers and slicked a layer of gloss against her lips.

Zora stared at herself in the mirror, admiring how the casual lingerie hugged her curves, its scalloped lace detail crowning her figure. Lawrence had spared no expense on this getaway, and while Zora didn't need to be lavished with gifts, she was blown away by the thought and care that he had put into their dates. Pressing her lips together, she thought about Reid, and flashes of him kissing every part of her brought a flush to her cheeks. She shook her head, chiding herself in the mirror. "Not now."

Returning to the bedroom, she saw that Lawrence remained on the couch as Zora had left him, though he'd removed his blazer; his eyes lighting up as she returned to her seat next to him. "Damn, you smell good." He pulled her onto his lap, straddling him, as he buried his face in her neck, nibbling at the spot where her neck met her shoulders. "Mmm...do I smell cocoa butter?"

"You like that?" she breathed as his hands squeezed her ass. She wrapped her arms around his neck, pressing her body against his as they kissed softly at first. The kiss intensified as their tongues met, Zora tilting her face in want of more.

Lawrence moaned against her lips, pulling her hips closer to his—his arousal apparent beneath her. She ground her body against it, eliciting another throaty sound from him as his mouth moved toward her ear. Zora's body ached to be touched, and she continued to wind her hips over Lawrence's—the wetness between her thighs beginning to build.

"I love cocoa butter." His deep voice reverberated against her temple. "I even like how it tastes." He gently dragged a strap of her camisole down from her shoulder, exposing one of her breasts. The full width of his tongue licked her bare nipple, making her whimper slightly. He did it twice more, relishing the sound of her. His lips moist, he kissed and sucked at her soft skin. "I need more space to enjoy this."

Taking her hand, he led Zora to the bed. She turned, her ass on the edge of the mattress as she unbuttoned his dress shirt, putting her hands against the expanse of his muscular chest as he kissed her. She pulled the shirt around his shoulders and down his arms, releasing it to the floor as she focused on his pants. He grunted as she unbuckled his belt, the palm of her hand feeling the length of his erection through the fabric of his pants. "My, my," she whispered.

"Yours," he whispered back, pulling Zora's camisole up over her head as she raised her arms. He cupped her breasts, running his tongue over them lazily, rolling the buds of her nipples gently between his teeth. He fished in his pocket and placed a couple of condoms on the bedside table before untying the drawstring to Zora's shorts. He eased them down past her hips, letting them fall to the floor as he admired the curves of her body.

She pulled herself onto the bed, lying back against a pillow while Lawrence took off his pants and pulled down his boxers. His hand on the thick shaft of his penis, he rubbed himself gently, climbing onto the bed. He lifted one of Zora's thighs so that he could kneel between them, leaning forward to suckle her breasts and run his tongue down her navel to the softness of her inner thigh. He rubbed his thumb against her opening before placing his tongue there; the slickness of his mouth and the pressure of his thumb at her entrance made her swear.

He ran his tongue slowly over her clit, sucking on the

smooth flesh as he guided his fingers inside her, making her shudder and buck against him. Feeling the heat and wetness at the seam of her legs, he abruptly removed his fingers and slid on a condom, rubbing his tip against her. "Yes?" he whispered.

"Yeah," Zora breathed, still thinking about his tongue as she touched herself.

"I've got you, Z," he teased, returning his thumb to her clit as he eased himself inside her.

She sucked in a breath, savoring the slow entrance of his full length. She admired his control as he guided himself in and out with a delicious slowness that made her whisper his name, as he continued to graze the pad of his thumb over her sensitive nub. "Fuck."

"Damn, girl." Lawrence's eyes squeezed shut as he began to speed up, and he quickly moved his hands away to steady himself on either side of her.

Zora wrapped her legs around his waist, lifting her hips to meet him as he pushed deeply into her. She wondered what he would feel like from behind as the bed began to creak, the sound of their bodies meeting clapping rhythmically with each thrust.

Lawrence took a couple of deep breaths before dropping to his forearms. He kissed Zora softly as the space between his brows pinched tightly. He grunted, giving two final pumps and growling lightly before he kissed her again. He pressed his lips against her cheek, her throat, her chest, before pulling out of her. "You are amazing," he breathed, climbing up to rest on the pillow next to hers.

Surprised, Zora turned toward Lawrence, reaching for him as he turned away from her and promptly fell asleep. She looked up at the ceiling and sucked her teeth before trailing her fingers down to finish what he'd started.

16

On Sundays the bookstore hours started in the early afternoon, theoretically to allow Zora and Emma the opportunity to sleep in. However, on most Sundays they opted to take Granny out for brunch instead.

Zora and Lawrence had gotten up early to get back on the road—he'd forgotten that he committed to attend an event in Baltimore that one of his sisters planned and had to get back to D.C. to get ready. Zora didn't mind, though she wondered if he was always double committing—if this was something she'd have to get used to if she and Lawrence got more serious. She'd called Emma and Granny on her drive home from Lawrence's house and picked them up for their Sunday ritual.

At a popular restaurant along the Georgetown waterfront, the ladies sat under the awning of an outdoor patio, sipping on mimosas with a smorgasbord of food piled on their plates. "Oh, my God, this stuffed French toast is to die for," Zora exclaimed, covering her mouth as she chewed.

"Dip that fried chicken in the honey sriracha sauce, baby. It'll curl your toes," Granny encouraged. Ms. Marion wore her Sunday best, having attended the early church service. Her floral dress was framed by a colorful cardigan, but her favorite accessories on Sundays were her hats. Granny could give the royal family a run for their money—her relationship with her hatmaker spanned decades. Today she wore a fascinator the color of cranberries tipped gracefully to one side. Its crown was adorned in feathers and a mesh that could be worn down over the face for pure drama. Her hair was pulled tight into her signature chignon.

"Speaking of toe curling," Emma started, taking a sip of her mimosa. "Can we have the details from your trip? Why are you back so early?"

Zora shrugged slowly. "Lawrence forgot about an event he was supposed to go to today, so we came back early. We had a good time, though. It was…nice."

"The sex or the trip, baby? Be specific," Granny chided.

"Yes, ma'am," she responded, shaking her head slowly. "The trip was nice. He really went out of his way to wine and dine me—literally! We drove down to this beautiful bed-and-breakfast, and we were immediately taken to a Black-owned vineyard for a wine tasting. We went back to the B&B to get ready for dinner, and he looked so good in his suit!

"Dinner was phenomenal, and I got the chef's card. She does some catering, and I could totally see using her for an event—" She stopped short when Emma and Granny exchanged a glance. "What? What does that look mean?"

"Sis, even on a romantic getaway, you were thinking about work? That fine man is in a suit dropping all kinds of money to impress you, and the highlight was a chef who can cater an event?" Emma squinted at her friend. "Is his penis small? What is the issue?"

Zora burst out laughing as other women turned at the question. "Please excuse my friend," she cooed, then lowered her voice. "Heffa, will you shut up? And no, his penis isn't small."

"So how was the sex?" Emma stabbed at a slice of strawberry and a piece of French toast. "Somethin' ain't right, Z. I can tell. You didn't come back looking like he broke your back, so what went wrong?"

"He..."

"He what, girl? Spit it out!"

"He was a good size, but he didn't last long enough for me to enjoy it." She exhaled deeply. "There."

"Did he make up for it in other ways? All those words he writes, surely he can make good use of his other attributes," Granny offered.

Emma leaned forward. "Did your granny just ask 'what that mouth do'? Ma'am. Just carry me on to the funeral, because I am deceased."

"Well, what did it do?" Granny's girlish laugh tittered almost shyly, but she raised her eyebrows suggestively. Emma and Zora burst into fits of laughter, high-fiving each other and Granny.

"I can't believe we're having this conversation right now." Zora dabbed at the corners of her eyes with her napkin. "This is too much."

"The sooner you spill, the sooner we can move on," Emma chided.

"Fine," she sighed. "He had some skills, but he stopped too soon, so I didn't finish. He got me close, so I know he's capable, but he jumped the gun in that department, too."

"Did he show any concern about your pleasure after he rushed the sex?" Emma raised a defiant brow. "Because, flag on the play—this sounds damn selfish to me."

"Well, I don't think there was time for him to show concern."

"What do you mean? He finished fast. Y'all had nothing but time after that."

"He went to sleep."

"*Ma'am*. Shut. Up." Emma raised her glass to request a refill from a server walking past with a fresh bottle of champagne. She took a long sip of the effervescent liquid and squeezed her eyes shut. "Zora. He did not go to sleep. Are you serious?"

"Turned on his side and knocked the fuck out. Excuse my language please, Granny."

"Baby, I spoke those words before you were alive. Ain't no need to apologize."

Emma was still stuck. "He went to sleep. Did he try to cuddle?"

Zora pursed her lips, twisting them to one side. "He literally pulled out, turned away from me, and went to sleep. I woke up before him, but he didn't move all night."

"So he didn't even wake up in the morning and try for a second round?"

"He seemed pretty spent after the first one. Besides, he didn't wake up until his sister called him wondering what time he planned to pick her up for whatever this event is today."

"He's got the stamina of an eighty-five-year-old." Emma threw up her hands.

Granny patted her shoulder. "Eighty-five-year-olds are more generous, dear." She winked suggestively as she sipped her mimosa.

Zora raised her eyebrows in surprise. "Well, damn, Granny!"

"So was this a deal breaker for you, Z?" Emma bit into a piece of chicken.

"I don't know. Maybe he hadn't gotten any in a while and just got too excited. Or maybe I'm still building this dude up in my head too much, but honestly, I'd expect more from literally anyone. I think I should give him another shot just to see if that was a fluke." *I sincerely hope it was…*

"Does Reid live up to the hype?"

"Well, Reid is definitely generous, and he really focused on making sure that I got off, but we haven't actually done the deed."

"What are you waiting for?"

"Nothing in particular. We have a date coming up next weekend. He wants to take me to an exhibit at the African American Museum. I didn't want to go during the week—we have too much to get done with these events getting closer." Their community engagement event ahead of the *D.C. Speak-easy* contest was looming, and they still had to secure more donations for the food bank.

"Will you fill the store clerk positions already?" Emma snapped. "You are not beholden to the bookstore the way that you think you are. I'm your assistant manager for a reason, and once we have more help, you'll be able to take the time that you need to have a life, Z. You deserve that."

Ms. Marion nodded in agreement. "Do you think that you're getting closer to narrowing things down between these two gentlemen? Because you know I ain't getting any younger."

"Here we go," Zora sighed.

"Now, I know I'm after you for my great-grandbabies, but I want you to be happy. That's priority number one, Zora." Granny's tone gently chided her granddaughter.

"I do want to narrow things down to one person, but I'm not sure yet. I still really like Lawrence—he's a good guy, he's very generous and intelligent, he was super thoughtful in trying to make me feel special, and he's so ambitious. And maybe it'll take time for us to match each other's stride phys-ically, but that's okay, right? With Reid, a lot of things seem easy—he's clearly intelligent, he's easy to talk to, I think that we have a lot in common, he gives to the community, and he's motivated—but when I think about being with him for the long-term, I remember what a dick he was the night I met him. Who's to say that his behavior doesn't dip to that on a regular basis?"

"True." Emma nodded.

"I just don't know either of these guys very well yet. And I feel like my Spidey senses are firing sometimes."

"Your inner detective is sensing something is amiss? With which one?" Em's eyebrow rose.

"Both, to be honest. I don't know what that's about."

"Well, if anyone can figure out if these guys are hiding something, it's you, Zor-lock."

Z rolled her eyes. "Anyway, I've been planning to read through more of Dr. Clarke's books for advice and have those thoughts I collected on paper."

"A list of pros and cons won't tell you what you feel, baby." Granny tapped her index finger against Zora's hand gently. "That will only get you so far. You need introspection."

Zora shrugged. "But I am attracted to both of them. I don't understand what I'm supposed to feel."

Granny sipped her mimosa. "Sounds like another round of dates is in order."

Emma nodded. "Yep. She isn't there yet."

"Excuse me, I'm right here. What am I missing?" Zora frowned.

Emma turned to her, lips pursed. "You'll know when you feel it. You need more time with them and then you'll know."

"But what if I develop the same feelings for both?"

"You might develop feelings for both of them, but they won't be the same." Emma wagged her finger matter-of-factly. "These guys are so different. Figure out which one you're gravitating toward more. They both seem like good catches."

"And if either of these men turn out to be bad apples, that's what your cousins are for—they're the muscle and will teach someone a lesson if need be," Granny added with a giggle. Zora's aunt—Granny's eldest daughter—had two sons who lived in Baltimore. She didn't see them much outside of the holidays, but they would roll through in a heartbeat if she or Granny needed them. "You know how much they love you, and they been waitin' for a tussle."

Emma's eyes lit up as she mouthed "tussle" to Zora, who hid her smile behind her napkin.

"Hopefully, it doesn't have to come to that, Granny."

"It's always an option, baby."

The blue lights emanating from the computer screen made Zora squeeze her eyes shut. She'd spent the past three hours placing book orders to beef up the store's inventory and to prepare for upcoming book signings. She rubbed her temples, arching her back to stretch and roll her shoulders down from their perch beside her ears.

Next to her keyboard sat a pile of colorful Post-it Notes she'd left for herself as reminders of her constantly growing to-do list. Plucking up the next one—a blue note dated several days earlier—she read the notation: *Call to thank Dr. Clarke.*

Zora smiled to herself, thinking about the talk Dr. Clarke gave at the bookstore—how natural the advice sounded as Catherine described relationship dynamics and setting boundaries to frame reasonable expectations. Glancing at her notepad, she thumbed through to her lists of pros and cons for dating Lawrence and Reid, still unsatisfied because she didn't have the answers she needed. Carefully, she picked up the receiver to her office phone and dialed Dr. Clarke's number.

"This is Catherine," she answered.

"Dr. Clarke! I'm so glad to catch you. This is Zora from Opus Northeast."

"Zora, how lovely to hear from you! How are you, dear?" The warmth in her tone made Zora smile.

"I'm well, thank you. How are you? I hope this is a good time?"

"Of course, and I am hanging in there. Now, tell me, how can I help you today?"

"Well, first, I just wanted to thank you again for such a lively discussion at your book event—I think that the audience would have been happy to stay a couple more hours if you'd allowed for it."

Catherine chuckled. "That's the secret, dear. *Always* leave them wanting more!"

Zora laughed. "I see. Well, you definitely achieved that. I have customers already asking when your next book comes out, because they're hoping you'll join us again."

"I would love to, though my next book isn't scheduled to come out for another year."

"Well, we'll have to have you back before then. Maybe we can celebrate the anniversary of one of your earlier books."

"I love that idea! Thank you." Dr. Clarke's cheerful tone changed to a more pensive one. "But I think that's not the only reason you called…"

Zora bit her lip nervously. "You see right through me."

"It's okay. Tell me what's on your mind."

She blew out a breath. "At the end of your talk, before you sat down for the signing, do you remember the young woman who asked how she should choose between two potential partners?"

"Why, yes! I do."

"Well, I find myself in a similar predicament."

"You need to choose," she guessed.

"No one is pressuring me to choose, but I feel like it would be best for me not to drag it out. They're two good men, but they're best friends, and I am worried that if this goes on for too long, it could create tension."

"Yes, I would assume that it will, too, eventually."

Zora felt like she could hear the gears in Catherine's mind turning over the information that she had shared.

"Do you remember what I told the young woman, Zora?"

"You said that she would know based on who it was she wanted to communicate with, even in hard times."

"Mmm-hmm. Do you know the answer to that question for yourself? When it comes to these two gentlemen, I mean."

"It might be too soon to tell," she admitted. "I'm still getting to know them both."

"Hmm," Dr. Clarke replied. "How do you expect to make a decision if you don't have all of the information?"

Zora laughed. "Honestly, I just keep thinking that it could be easy to develop feelings, and I don't want anyone to get too attached if they're not the one. I don't save a lot of time for dating—work keeps me pretty busy, and I love it. It's impractical for me to spend a lot of time with both of these guys."

"But if you choose too quickly, you might not select the right one."

"But it's also possible that neither of these guys is the right one."

"That's true, but if you thought you were wasting your time, you wouldn't be dating either of these guys," she countered patiently.

"Fair. I just get the sense that I don't know everything I need to know."

"Then you get to be selfish and take the time that you need to feel comfortable and confident. They're not both dating you in an effort to spare *your* feelings," she said matter-of-factly.

"Here's an exercise that I'd like you to try out. I want for you to think about your priorities when it comes to relationships, your career, and what you want for your future. I also want you to consider whether either of these men is someone that you could picture helping you build toward your goals. If the man that can help you build is also the man that you could talk to about anything, then I think that you've found someone worthy of your time. Until then, allow yourself the indulgence of being wined and dined by two eligible suitors in D.C. You know that's a rarity, Zora."

She nodded. "You're right, it is. And it's not like either of them are rushing me into making a decision—it's me."

"Do you think there might be another reason why you're trying to rush the process?"

Zora chewed her lip. "I guess I never really thought about it. Waiting to see how I feel about these guys...honestly? It makes me feel like I'm not in control."

"Is that a requirement for you?"

"I don't think it's a requirement per se, but it's what I'm used to. I run my store. I own my home. Most of my days are spent in environments that I built."

"Uh-huh." Dr. Clarke's tone lifted into a smile. "But love isn't something that you buy or manufacture. It's something that you cultivate over time. Tell me something, Zora. Do you like checklists?"

"I live by them. I even made lists to compare these guys," she laughed, suddenly aware that her list was probably some sort of red flag.

"What did your lists tell you?"

"I can hear the amusement in your voice, you know." Zora smiled.

"I love it when people find their aha moments, and you're very close to one now."

Zora pored over her lists, looking for clues that might tell her what she'd missed. "Well, everything on the list is true. They're observations about each guy. Pros and cons. Likes and dislikes."

"Uh-huh, and what is missing from these lists, dear?"

"What's missing? The answer?"

"No, not the answer. Something you need before you get to the answer."

The silence on the other end of the receiver made Zora's heart pound. "You're not going to tell me, are you?"

"Oh, dear. Trust me. You already know the answer. It will come to you. Anyway, I have to get going. I'm meeting your lovely grandmother and her friends for dinner and a card game."

Zora's face fell. *She's really not going to tell me.* "Thank you so much for your time, Catherine. I appreciate your insights."

"It's my pleasure, dear. Call me if you need to talk again, but I'm confident you've got this."

As the phone call disconnected, Zora brought her lists in front of her, wondering what she'd missed. After staring at it for a long moment, she turned the page, deciding to jot down her must haves and deal breakers, drawing lines from applicable points to each man. Her upcoming date with Reid the following weekend would be a good opportunity to get some questions answered, and Lawrence was going to head back out of town after his event in Baltimore, but he promised to be in touch.

17

Monday and Tuesday went by like a blur—Zora and Emma rushed to put the finishing touches on their coordination efforts with the D.C. Harvest Food Bank—the benefactor of Zora's community engagement event to help promote the *D.C. Speakeasy* contest. Students and teachers from all schools participating in the contest collected food and pantry goods and signed up for shifts to help pack food boxes for local families in need. Wednesday was already upon them—the final day to receive donations—and the bookstore was packed with boxes of goods from local sponsors who donated in support. On Thursday volunteers would help transport all of the goods at the bookstore to the food bank, and Friday was the big day.

"Hey, Zora, we have more boxes to unload. Where should we put them?" Tanesha, Zora's new bookstore clerk, asked, brushing dust from her chambray jumpsuit. She'd walked into the store on Monday looking for employment to supplement the hours that she worked at the Kerri's Coffee storefront.

She'd been to Opus Northeast before to fill in for Brian when he needed time off. A college sophomore, Tanesha was focusing her studies on creative writing.

Zora peered around the store to look for space that wasn't already saturated with pantry goods. "Hmm... I think we have just enough space for those over in that back corner, behind the coffee kiosk. We'd been saving that space for a delivery from Langston Hughes, but I think that when they arrive, we should just transfer their stuff straight to my car. And if anyone calls saying they have more to drop off, please just direct them to take it straight to the food bank."

"You got it!" She smiled brightly. She turned to direct a few high school kids hoisting boxes to follow her.

"Hey, baby. How's she doing so far?" Granny sidled up to Zora with a clipboard in her hand. Though soft-spoken and petite, Granny had a way of getting people to move at her direction.

"Tanesha's amazing! Super organized. I think that she's going to be a huge help—plus, she can also back up Brian when he needs that." Zora had busied herself with drafting some opening remarks for the start of the event on Friday, and she hadn't gotten further than opening a blank page. One distraction after another had kept her moving, but she hadn't gotten to anything on her checklist for the day.

The bell chimed and Zora and Granny turned toward the door. Lawrence strode toward them in a deep red sweater and dark jeans; his hands were laden with bulging grocery bags. "Good afternoon, ladies. How are we doing today?"

Granny stood back from the counter to greet him as he set down his bags. "Just fine, Lawrence, and you?" She let him take her hand in both of his.

"I'm well, Ms. Marion. You sure are looking beautiful

today." He grinned mischievously at her until she popped his hands with her free one.

"Mmm-hmm. I'll leave you two to talk." Marion turned toward the kiosk. "Brian, baby, come collect these bags for me."

Zora peeked over the counter at the bags brimming with canned and dry goods. It looked like Lawrence brought all of it straight from the grocery store. Brian and Tanesha swept up the bags to add to the pile behind the kiosk. "Thank you so much for dropping off a donation! I didn't think you'd have time to come by."

He leaned forward on the counter. "Well, I wanted to surprise you."

She beamed at him. "You sure love surprises!"

He let his fingers graze hers on the table's surface. "I just like making you smile. I'm sorry that I won't be here for the event on Friday—that's a big deal."

She nodded. "Yeah, we've already surpassed our goals. I'm beyond thrilled at this point."

He ran the pads of his fingers over her knuckles while maintaining eye contact with her—it was the tiniest contact that no one else could see, but it was enough to make Zora lick her lips. She was primed to ask for more when a rumbling voice spoke up behind Lawrence.

"Uh, Zora, where should we put these boxes? I think that we have more than can fit in your car." Reid had arrived with two of his students, just as he'd promised. They carried moving boxes full of food.

Zora's attention snapped from Lawrence to Reid and her cheeks grew hot. She pulled her hand away from the counter. "Hey! Actually, Tanesha's got keys to Emma's car, too, and any remaining boxes can be set over by Granny in the seating area."

Granny waved from her chair, and Emma leaned over the

armrest as they watched Zora speak with both men. Z glanced in their direction and widened her eyes for a quick moment before turning and plastering an awkward smile on her face.

Lawrence pushed himself away from the counter, straightening his back before turning round. "What's up, Reid?" Lawrence smiled at his boy, stepping in his direction.

"Whoa, hey, man." They clapped their hands together and pulled each other in for a hug. "I thought you were on your way to the airport."

The tension was so thick that it felt like the two men were talking in slow motion. Zora couldn't hear any of what was being said; Reid seemed a little stiff and made several glances in her direction. She felt frozen in place, like she was ten years old and Granny just caught her with her hand in the cookie jar. They both turned back toward Zora, and she smoothed the front of her jeans. With all the work they'd been doing for the community event at the food bank, she'd relaxed her typical attire for jeans and a knotted T-shirt that read "Got Books?" across the front.

Lawrence stepped back toward the counter. "Listen, I have to get going, but I'll call you to see how the event goes."

She nodded, walking around to the front of the counter. "I'd like that. And safe travels—I hope your events go well." She moved to hug him, but she remembered his feelings on PDA. She gave a little finger wave instead and he winked and turned to go.

"All right, man. I'll send you some content to review for next week's posts," Reid said, his low voice almost inaudible. "Be safe."

"Bet." They clapped each other on the back and the door chimed as it closed behind Lawrence.

Reid stepped forward with his hands in his pockets. His students were chatting with Tanesha and organizing some of the items that they brought. "So…that could have been awkward." His mouth stretched into a slow smile as he ran his hand over his curls.

Z burst into laughter, leaning her hip against the front of the counter. "Could have been?"

He shrugged slightly. "It's fine. We're fine." He stepped closer, resting one hand on the counter near her hip. "I'm really looking forward to this weekend—the event, too. I'm just excited that I get to see you two days in a row." He ran his tongue over the fullness of his bottom lip, and Zora's eyes zeroed in on his mouth.

A small sound escaped her throat, like she was savoring the taste of something and wanted more. She shook her head free of the thoughts running through her mind—of kisses that traveled her entire body—and pressed her palms to her flushed cheeks. "It's like you do that to me on purpose," she whispered.

Amused, he leaned forward to whisper in her ear. "Maybe I do." He planted a quick kiss on her cheek and turned to his students. "Y'all ready?"

His students turned and nodded, though they looked like they wanted to stay.

"All right, we'll see you on Friday," he said to Zora. He raised a hand to wave at Emma and Granny. "Bye, ladies!"

"Bye-bye." Marion's voice carried like a Southern belle on a wraparound porch. "See you soon." Emma waved.

"See you," Zora whispered.

Reid ushered his students out first and turned to wink at Zora before closing the door behind him.

Z took a moment and then turned, clapping her hands. "Okay, now that that's finished, can we sit down to go over final logistics for Friday?"

Marion was already in her usual chair in the seating area,

so Zora waved Emma and Tanesha to follow her. They'd just picked up fresh coffees from Brian.

"Can I ask a question?" Tanesha's hand shot up quickly before Zora could speak. "This might not be appropriate, but who were those two hot guys you were speaking with? Do either of them have a younger brother or a nephew?"

Emma laughed so hard that she snorted. "They're fine, aren't they?"

"So fine." Tanesha fanned herself with Zora's checklist.

Granny's eyebrows bounced behind a closed-lip smile, the apples of her cheeks on full display.

Zora groaned. "If there are more of them, God help us all."

"Good morning, everyone!"

"Good morning!" Coffee-infused voices boomed back in Zora's direction.

"I want to thank you all for being here today both in support of D.C. Harvest Food Bank and our annual *D.C. Speakeasy* writing contest! A few years ago I suggested to Ms. Betty that we add on this service component as a milestone leading up to the contest. I absolutely love that this writing contest allows local students to showcase their skills with the prospect of publication, but when we give back to the community, I want for us to always be thinking more broadly.

"This year I am pleased to share that we have fifty-two schools with students participating in the contest, and every single one of those schools has volunteers who have either been helping behind the scenes to transport donations here or have signed up to work a shift today. We have well over three hundred volunteers total, which is almost double what we had last year!"

The crowd clapped and cheered, nodding along with the good news. Over one hundred people stood in the huge warehouse in comfortable work clothes—many with faces familiar to Zora. Bookstore patrons, local students, and family friends were among the crowd. Reid was present with some of his students—he volunteered to help coordinate all of the drivers' deliveries. Granny was overseeing the pickup tables. Zora, Emma, and Tanesha were coordinating box stuffing assembly lines. Brian was present to manage refreshments.

Zora beamed at the crowd. "Most importantly, the level of sponsorship hit a significant new high. Thanks to our local businesses who came together and raised a total of forty *thousand* dollars, which was five thousand dollars over our goal this year, *D.C. Speakeasy* has agreed to donate an additional ten thousand dollars for a total of fifty—*fifty thousand dollars!*"

The crowd erupted, food bank staff included, some people with tears in their eyes.

Zora's heart threatened to burst. She held out one arm wide as she gripped the microphone in the other. "But how many people does that reach? Well, each dollar provides two meals, so that's one hundred thousand meals. The boxes that we are packing today will feed a family of four for a full week. These financial donations will touch over thirty-five hundred families. And that doesn't even include the hundreds upon hundreds of pounds of food donations that we've received. I—" Zora's voice broke as her eyes filled with tears, but she willed them not to fall. "I want to thank each and every one of you from the bottom of my heart. Our community is strongest when we come together, and I can't think of a better reason than to make sure that our neighbors are fed and cared for. Today we'll be packing and delivering over five thousand boxes of food—that's five *thousand* families being fed for a week. Now who's ready to get to work?"

Hands throughout the warehouse shot up along with a chorus of whoops and hollers. A few people wiped tears from their eyes. Granny fanned herself with her clipboard.

"If you need to find your workstation, please consult one of the ladies with a clipboard." Emma, Granny, Tanesha, and Zora each raised their lists into the air. "All of our drivers, please line up your cars outside of the loading dock. Kerri's Coffee was kind enough to bring out a kiosk for us today to keep everyone fed and hydrated, so please make sure to get some treats for yourself. And DCMV Live Radio is getting set up to go live—they'll be providing us with some music to keep everyone moving. Thanks again, everybody. Let's get it!"

The DJ booth began playing go-go music and everyone in the warehouse cheered and swayed to the beat. Zora began to direct people on her list to load boxes with jarred and canned goods and pass them to Emma's section. Her group added dried pasta and cereal boxes. Tanesha's section added fresh produce—heads of lettuce, broccoli, and cabbage, along with bags of apples and bananas, onions, and potatoes. Finished boxes went to Granny's section for pickup or Reid's section for delivery.

Volunteers arrived for two-to-three-hour shifts, breaking when they needed refreshments or felt like dancing to the music. When the last shift was checked in and the final boxes were stuffed, Zora had Emma take Granny home to relax, and she moved over to the check-in tables to help direct people and hand out boxes. The last of the delivery drivers returned and helped carry boxes to cars of people arriving to pick up food. Reid winked at Zora as he hoisted two boxes into his muscular arms. She smiled, biting her lip as she watched his arms flex from the weight.

When the last box had been placed in a car, Zora walked the warehouse, thanking all of the remaining volunteers for their time. She hugged the students and patrons that she recognized, taking extra time to thank all of the food bank staff who stayed late to see the project through. Reid gave her a big high five, interlacing his fingers with hers before turning to take some of his students back to the campus to retrieve their cars. "See you tomorrow," she said, waving.

"Tomorrow," he replied, his students grinning wide and jostling him as they waved goodbye.

18

Zora flew down the stairs in a rush to turn on the kettle and check the state of her living room before Reid arrived for their date—a Saturday at the museum. Fluffing pillows on the couch, she plucked a piece of lint from the velvet upholstery. "Girl, why are you nervous?" she asked herself in an exasperated tone.

The kettle whistled; a straight line of steam billowed toward the ceiling. She turned off the eye of the stove and poured the boiling hot water into a French press with finely ground coffee from a customer's recent trip to Ethiopia. As the grounds steeped, she stepped into the powder room to fluff her curls and touch up her lipstick.

Emma had worked her magic and did some shopping to add some new pieces to Zora's wardrobe, and just in time—she had cardigans and jackets for days, but she was in dire need for something other than jeans. For the date, Emma selected high-waisted, white linen slacks with billowing wide legs and buttons on the pockets. Zora tucked a sexy, low-cut camisole into her pants, her red lip making her all-white outfit pop even more. She never bought into the faux pas that white was only for summer months—that kind of thinking was exclusionary. Her chambray duster could keep her warm if she needed, but Zora liked the prospect of drawing attention. She looked damn good.

She checked her teeth once more to make sure she didn't have lipstick on them as the doorbell rang. "Right on time."

Reid's eyes widened as she opened the door. "Wow, you look…" He blew out a breath as he searched for the words.

Zora blinked, her mouth falling open. "What? Is it too much? I can change."

He shook his head. "Please don't. You look beautiful, Zora. Stunning, really."

Her mouth opened slightly and then closed as color rushed up her throat to her cheeks. She averted her gaze to his chest. "Thank you. Please come in."

He stepped inside and immediately removed his shoes. "Your place looks different in the daylight. Bigger than I remember."

"You only saw select parts of it last time," Zora chuckled, leading the way to the kitchen. "Coffee?" Though Zora was private about her home, since Reid had already been there once before, she didn't feel that his returning was any violation of her space. Besides, Emma and Granny practically begged to have a few minutes with him.

"Yes, thank you." He sat on a bar stool at the island counter, taking in the aroma. "That smells amazing."

"A gift from one of my customers! She brings me coffee from wherever she travels." Zora put the lid on the pot, plunging the press downward to filter out the grounds. "Cream? Sugar? Oat milk?"

"A splash of oat milk would be great. Thanks. It's cool that your regulars bring you back something from their travels." He leaned forward on his elbows.

She nodded, pouring the dark liquid into two ceramic mugs. She dropped a cube of raw sugar into one and marked both mugs with oat milk. "Here you go."

Their hands touched briefly as Reid accepted the mug. The milliseconds of contact sent a current of heat throughout Zora's body. She squeezed her hand into a fist and then released as her arm dropped to her side, willing herself not to think about how much his touch made her tingle—how their night of kisses lived rent free at the forefront of her mind. How she'd take him upstairs this instant if footsteps on the stairs hadn't pulled her from her reverie. In silence, they both sampled the coffee.

"Seriously, you two, we could cut the sexual tension in here with a knife." Emma padded into the room in a fluffy robe and worn house slippers, her eye mask propped up over her headscarf. Granny shuffled down the stairs behind her; her hair was pinned neatly under her bonnet.

"Granny! What were you doing up there?"

Marion wrapped her arms around Zora, a cheerful expression on her face. "Girl talk, baby. We were up late, so Emma let me crash." She turned her attention to Reid, setting the palms of her hands on the counter. "Good morning, young man. My, you look handsome."

Reid's eyes crinkled at the corners as he greeted them. "Ladies, good morning." His deep, rumbling voice reverberated low in Zora's belly—the sensation traveling lower as she crossed her legs.

"Coffee?" Zora offered, already pouring the last bit into a mug for Emma. She refilled the kettle to make her grandmother a cup of her favorite tea.

"Ugh, you're an angel." Emma grabbed flavored creamer from the refrigerator and poured until her coffee was the palest brown. She held her mug protectively when her eyes met Reid's.

Reid grinned. "You like a little coffee with your cream, huh?"

She shrugged sleepily. "It's the first cup of the day. I need the sugar boost. Then I switch to cappuccinos once we get to the store."

"You sure you'll be okay at the store with Tanesha?" Zora asked cautiously. Their new clerk was beyond capable, but that didn't stop Zora from worrying anyway.

"Seriously, Z, I've got this. I'll have her stocking shelves and putting stickers on signed copies. We'll go over our inventory schedule and some of our vendor systems. She's a smart girl. She'll pick it up quickly. I might have her do some staff recommendation cards, too." Emma waved away the concerns.

Zora nodded, though the pinch she pressed above her nose gave her away.

"Don't worry, baby. Everybody's got to start somewhere, and you don't need to take it all on yourself." Granny patted her arm.

Zora wrapped her arms around Ms. Marion as the kettle began to sing. She moved to pour hot water over loose tea leaves, then set the steeping mug in front of her grandmother.

"So," the elder began, turning to Reid, "I understand you're taking my granddaughter to the African American Museum today?"

Reid's shoulders straightened. "Yes, ma'am. They just opened a new exhibit that I thought Zora might enjoy—it's on Black literary societies of the 1800s."

"That sounds lovely, dear." Granny nodded slowly. "I needn't worry about her while she's in your care, right?"

Her tone was almost always a soothing balm that reached Zora's shoulders and melted the tension down her back. Her question, however, held a firm warning tone that made Zora shudder with memories of childhood shenanigans that resulted in her having to pick a switch from the backyard. Marion's bark was a lot worse than her bite—she rarely followed through once Zora returned with her switch. More often than not, they would talk things out, and Zora never made the same mistake twice. She bit her lip, volleying her gaze toward Reid, who cleared his throat.

"Yes, ma'am. She's safe with me."

Granny removed the metal tea filter from her mug and sipped carefully, holding eye contact with him. "Good."

He looked to Zora, who hid her smile behind her mug. She winked at him, and Emma exhaled loudly. "Maternal wrath is like no other, man." She shook her head and gulped down her coffee. Standing, she gave Reid a few hard claps on the back. "That's my best friend, there, buddy. Don't make me have to get out my Vaseline."

"Understood." Reid's mouth twitched, though he maintained a solemn expression. Turning to Zora, he pressed his hands together. "Ready? Our tickets give us entrance right at ten."

"Let's get going!" she replied brightly, pressing a kiss against her grandmother's cheek. "Love you."

"Love you, baby. We won't wait up."

Emma sucked in a breath, her lips pressed together to stifle a laugh. "Have fun, you two!"

Entering the National Museum of African American History and Culture often felt to Zora like returning home—it was the same feeling she experienced the first time she stepped foot onto African soil in Namibia. There was something about returning to this building that reminded her of all of the history she learned that was never taught to her in schools—the stories of great innovators given lackluster recognition, the truth about medical "innovation" discovered only through torturous experimentation on slaves, the accounts of the Black elite of the nineteenth century. Seeing and hearing accounts of Black Wall Street, Black cowboys, and Black inventors made Zora's chest swell with pride.

They walked the museum for hours, marveling at the updated exhibits, crying and lamenting over parts of their history. Zora did most of the crying, but the Emmett Till memorial exhibition was where Reid broke down. They stood together, taking in the videos playing on the other side of Till's casket, grieving the life of a young man robbed of adulthood. Zora pressed her hand against Reid's back as his tears fell in silence. After several deep breaths, he captured her hand and they continued on through the museum.

As they exited, they stopped to grab food from some local food trucks that gathered near the museum, and sat on the grass on the National Mall. Reid tugged a blanket from the backpack he'd carried with him. "You know, I've lived here on and off for at least half of my life, and I've never done this before." Zora smiled up into the sunshine. "Thanks for bringing the blanket—I could have really had an issue in these pants." She set her chambray duster down as added protection from any moisture in the grass before she sat.

Reid grinned. "I saw the forecast this morning and thought we might want to take advantage of this weather."

She nodded. "It's perfect out today." Zora said a quick prayer as she laid out lobster rolls, Korean barbecue fusion tacos, and pork belly lettuce wraps. Reid set down a mint lemonade for her and a hibiscus lemonade for himself, sitting cross-legged next to Zora. "This is quite the feast."

"I hope you don't mind a girl who can eat." She winked slyly at him.

"I always picture those who go for the tiny salad after having an entire meal at home ahead of time." He tilted his head, jutting his chin toward another couple sitting in the grass about twenty feet away. The woman pushed a fork through a salad that she clearly wasn't excited about while her partner dug into a fat cheeseburger.

Zora grinned. "I know some folks who do exactly that. I've never understood it—if things ever got serious, how would they explain their 'newfound appetite'?" From her purse, she grabbed a small bottle of hand sanitizer and squeezed some into her palm. She offered some to Reid, and he opened his hands to receive it.

"Thank you."

"I'm not a germaphobe, but you never know."

"It's honestly not unreasonable to be a germaphobe these days."

"Facts. So you mentioned that you're from D.C. and your parents were locals, right? What kind of work did they do?" Zora tried to take a dainty bite of the pork belly, but she ended up stuffing the entire bite into her mouth, laughing as she covered her lips with a napkin.

Reid smiled wide. "That was good, wasn't it?"

She nodded, still chewing, but her eyes smiled. The tender pork and sweet glaze mingled with the crisped fat in an unctuous mouthful. "Oh, my God, so good!" she replied as she shielded her mouth with her hand.

"My mom was an English teacher for thirty-five years. She just retired a few months ago. My dad was a jazz musician and a poet." He took a big bite of a lettuce wrap. "Wow, that's amazing!"

She grinned. "Were they ever married?"

Reid shook his head. "I think my pops wanted to, but my mom was stubborn. He toured a lot, and had a lot of local distractions..."

"You mean other women," she corrected.

"Right." Reid blew out a breath. "He had a wandering eye. He loved my mom—he used to ask about her all the time—he just wasn't really the monogamous type." They both picked up half of a lobster roll and tapped them together. "Cheers."

"That feels like a common theme in D.C. The last few guys I dated really seemed to prefer the nonmonogamous lifestyle." She bit into the lobster roll and her eyes immediately closed to savor the sweetness of the claw meat. She licked a drop of butter from her lips as she opened her eyes, which widened as she saw Reid staring at her.

"They said that up front?" Reid's eyebrows shot up.

"One did. He let me know how many people were in his little rotation and everything—all for the whole 'ethical non-monogamy' thing. I'm just not built for sharing long-term."

Reid tilted his head slightly, his expression darkening. "I know the feeling."

Warmth spilled over her cheeks. "You know that it was your idea for me to date both of you, right?"

"I know it, but it still doesn't mean I have to like it." His tone lowered to a rumble.

"I'm not ready to make a choice. I don't know either of you well enough, and I honestly wasn't looking when I met the two of you, so I don't really know what I want."

He leaned closer to her, the sunlight leaving a golden cast across his deep brown skin. "I don't mean to pressure you. It's just… I *know* what I want."

She chewed her lip, knowing the answer, but wanting to hear it anyway. "What do you want?" Her voice hushed with anticipation.

"You." His husky, rumbling voice delivered the word just above a whisper. "The more I talk to you, the more I want to know about you. But honestly, Zora, you don't have to say a word about that right now. I just want to enjoy your presence."

Her lips parted as she looked into his brown eyes glowing in the sunlight like liquid pools of amber framed by thick black lashes. "How can you be so certain?"

He shrugged, and an easy smile crawled across his lips. "When you know, you know. Don't force it. Just let yourself vibe."

"You sound like Dr. Clarke." She eyed him, sipping her drink.

"Catherine Clarke? She's a very smart woman, so I'll take that as a compliment," he laughed.

She chewed on her compostable straw, careful to leave an air hole for sipping, her eyes playful. "You should."

Reid watched her for a moment, his eyes on her mouth. "Come here." He set his hand close to hers on the blanket and leaned over.

Zora lifted her chin to meet his lips, which pressed firmly against hers twice before grazing her temple softly. She nuzzled his neck, taking in the scent of his cologne. "Why do you always smell so good?" she whispered, her lips barely touching his skin.

He shivered at the contact. "Remember, I'm trying to impress you. I can't be out here just rank and expecting positive results."

She burst out laughing. "I suppose that's true." She cupped his face in her hands. "Thank you for not being rank out in these streets."

They shared another kiss, this time a lazy, languid one without a care given to those around them who might see. The hibiscus from his lemonade awakened her senses—the combination of the tart floral spiced with cinnamon and his citrusy cologne made her hungry for another taste.

"Are you ready to get out of here, Z?" Reid's mouth hovered over hers and she snuck a quick peck.

"I am." She stretched as he stood. He grabbed her hands and helped her up from the blanket.

"Good. I have one last surprise."

19

Reid drove them to his condo—a two-bedroom in Petworth, which was maybe a twelve-minute drive from the bookstore. "I have to warn you. My apartment is on the top floor and there's no elevator."

Zora's eyes widened. "A walk-up? How many floors?"

He winced. "Four. Is that okay?"

"Whew, I'm sure glad I wore flats today," she laughed. "It's fine. Don't worry! I might be a little out of breath when we get up there, but I'll survive. These thighs are strong." She patted her leg and grinned, watching his eyes travel downward.

He squeezed her hand tightly, pulling into a parking space behind the brick building. "It's a small place—eight units total. One big studio is on the basement level. Mine is the entire top floor, and I also have half of the rooftop."

"Your own outdoor space? Nice! That's one thing I was missing when I had a condo in Brookland. I still miss living in that area, though."

"I know what you mean. It's so lively right there, and I heard they just opened a comedy theater near your bookstore." He stepped out of the car and walked around to let Zora out. "You ready for this hike?"

"If we didn't get our steps in at the museum, I guess we're about to get them in now!" She grinned brightly at him, throwing her duster jacket over her arm, but he pulled it from her before she began to climb. "Such a gentleman," she teased.

Inside, the walls were painted brightly in primary colors with one brick accent wall. A floating staircase wrapped its way around a central wall; the stair treads were thick slabs of smooth, dark wood. Reid retrieved his mail from a row of metal mailboxes near the lobby entrance, leading the way to the foot of the stairs. He stood, waiting for her to step in front of him.

"Back there to enjoy the view?" She walked past him and began to climb.

"Maybe."

She turned to look back at him as she continued up the steps, her hand on the railing against the wall. The stairs were more gradual than steep, and they made it up the stairs to Reid's door quickly. His eyes never left her backside. "Not bad, just a little hot," Zora breathed.

He laughed easily. "To be fair, you were hot before we climbed the stairs." His smile widened as color crept into Zora's already flushed cheeks. "Let's get some fresh air on the rooftop."

As they stepped into the apartment, Reid gestured toward a narrow staircase just inside his front door. He grabbed a bottle of wine and two stemless glasses, nodding at her to lead the way. A glass door at the top opened to a well-kept garden, patio furniture, and a fire pit. "We can do a tour of the apartment later, but we should enjoy the view before the sun drops too low."

"Wow, this is beautiful," Zora whispered, admiring the signs marking various herbs. She strolled around the space, taking in the view of the surrounding buildings—slabs of concrete and brick towering over single-family homes, row houses, and duplexes. As the sun began its descent, she shivered, pulling on her jacket.

"Here, this should help warm you up a little." Reid poured wine and handed her a glass before pouring another for himself. "Would you like to cozy up with a fire?"

"That sounds perfect." She sipped on her drink as he turned on the fire pit and gestured toward the patio couch, with its plush blue cushions and a throw blanket over the arm. The gas-fueled fire burned blue and then orange, its warmth tickling her skin. "Do you spend a lot of time up here?"

"I do. The weather's been so nice that I'll come up here and read or write. It's also a nice spot to enjoy a cigar." He sat on the couch and immediately stood to remove a notebook from the cushion beneath him. "See? I'm always thinking about something."

"Can I read something you've written?" Zora sat next to him and playfully reached across him to get to the spiral-bound book. She batted her lashes at him. "Pretty please?"

Reid laughed, setting the notebook on the other side of him, his body acting as a barrier.

"Oh, it's like that?" Before she could reach for it, he turned toward her, blocking it from view.

"Yeah, I could probably let you read something. Come here first." He wrapped his arms around her and pulled her against him, pressing his lips against her temple. "It's hard being so close to you all day and not being allowed to touch you the way I want, you know that?"

"Mr. Hughes! I had no idea." She lifted her chin to kiss his lips. "Tell me what you've been tempted to do all day."

His mouth trailed lower; his tongue teased the sensitive skin just below her ear. "Or... I could provide a live demonstration."

The warmth of his breath on her ear made her shudder; she squeezed her eyes shut tightly. "That's also an option," she concurred throatily, turning her face toward his.

Reid's hooded eyes focused on Zora's lips, though he took his time making his way to them, planting soft, sweet kisses against the apples of her cheeks, the tip of her nose, the center of her forehead. As his mouth met hers, his gravelly voice caught in his throat somewhere between a moan and a grunt, his eyes closing to savor the taste of wine still on her tongue. Cupping her face, he tilted her head for greater access, and her hands rose to cling to his forearms.

Gasping for breath, he trailed his lips to her throat, pressing them against the space where her neck met her shoulders. He breathed in the subtle notes of her perfume, pressing his face against her hair, kissing her curls. "I love that scent you wear."

Zora opened her eyes as Reid leaned back; her head rested against his chest. "Thank you," she whispered.

"The sun is starting to set, Z. That's why I wanted to bring you up here in the first place."

"Wow," she breathed, unsure whether her response was to the kiss or the sight. The sky above formed an ombre of color—shades of indigo and blue melted into purple and orange. Feathery clouds the color of pink taffy stretched slowly across the sky as if they were yawning before bed, and streetlights glittered up and down the neighborhood still bustling with evening activity.

As Zora wrapped her arms around Reid's waist, her hand touched something hard—his notebook! She curled her fingers around it slowly, sneaking a peek at him as he marveled at the sunset. "Aha!"

Startled, he laughed. "It's really that serious, huh?"

"Don't you want to share what you're eventually going to publish?"

"I don't know that I'll get to publish it, honestly." He shrugged. "It's still rough anyway. That's been in this couch for months and has not been edited or anything yet." He gestured toward the book.

"I'm not going to judge you, Reid." She willed him to look her in the eye. "I promise."

He nodded. "Go ahead."

"Do you want to tell me about it first?"

"It's a mystery series that I'm working on. I haven't plotted this out as thoroughly as I probably should have, so I've been fumbling my way through it, but it has a Black female main character. She gets discharged from the military due to a medical injury, and she struggles with some trauma, but she uses her MP training to investigate a series of murders in her neighborhood."

"Oh, that sounds interesting. Is her trauma from her military service or something from before?"

"A little bit of both."

"Hmm." Zora nodded. "This sounds like something I'd read. I love strong female characters."

"You mentioned that before."

"Are you sure you're okay with me reading it? I really don't have to if you're not comfortable."

He waved his hand. "It's cool. Go ahead."

She thumbed through the pages, waiting to see if something would jump out at her.

"Hmm… Ooo, okay." She cleared her throat playfully, winking up at Reid. "'Serena quickened her pace, sensing that someone was in the shadows that crept behind her. Reaching into the pocket of her coat, she wrapped her fingers around the kubotan attached to her key ring. Her grasp tightened around the thick aluminum rod, and as the sound of measured breaths inched closer, she pulled it out of her pocket, careful to keep it concealed. Clutching it tightly in her fist, she held the weapon close to her chest, remembering her self-defense training.

"'As a hand clamped onto her shoulder and spun her around, Serena thrust her arm in the direction of the assailant's face, connecting the blunt tip of the kubotan that extended from her fist with his front teeth. With a deafening crunch and a yelp of pain, the man disappeared back into the shadows, leaving behind broken incisors and two droplets of blood.'"

As Zora finished the passage, a twinge of familiarity prickled at the back of her neck, awakening her Spidey senses. If Emma were there, she would have welcomed Zor-lock to the party.

"Well, what did you think?" Reid nudged her gently, watching her face. "And my grammar can be off sometimes, so please don't judge this early draft too harshly."

"No, no, I love how strong and bold she is." Zora's smile didn't reach her eyes. "The grammar was fine! It reads like a page turner so far." *But have I turned that page before?* The story felt so familiar.

With Zora still leaning back against Reid on the patio sofa, she was grateful that her bluff wouldn't be questioned. Granny reminded her on a very regular basis that she was never to join Granny's friends for a round of poker.

The setting sun dipped farther below the horizon, intensifying the colors in the sky. Reid flipped on strings of Edison lights, which hung from the wooden pergola. Holding hands, they sipped their wine, the alcohol and the smell of Reid's cologne lulling her into a calm sense of familiarity. He nuzzled her neck, and Zora forgot all about her sleuthing intuition.

As the sun faded out of sight, she shivered, and Reid led her back downstairs into the apartment.

Reid gave Zora the quickest of tours once they were inside. The apartment had an open floor plan with a kitchen and breakfast nook, a dining table laden with papers and books, and a wide sofa. The second bedroom doubled as office space and a fitness room, with a Peloton Tread against one wall and a yoga mat spread out on the floor. Zora followed Reid into his bedroom and took in the massive king-size bed and matching dresser. The windows were shaded with velvety-blue blackout curtains, and a barn-style sliding door led to a walk-in closet and an en-suite bathroom.

The tour clearly finished, Reid turned to wrap his arms around Zora's waist, then trailed his lips lightly from her throat, across her collarbone and pressed gently against her shoulder. "I've been wanting to kiss you all day. When you opened the door and I saw you looking like this..." He held her hands away from his body so that he could get another look. "I have never seen anyone or anything more beautiful."

A flurry of butterflies tickled her stomach and sent shock waves farther south. "Thank you. I feel beautiful," she whispered. Remembering how he'd looked at her the last time they were alone in her bedroom, she shivered with anticipation.

"Well, let me see some more, then." His lips curved as he leaned forward, wrapping his arms around her, pulling her close. He kissed her parted lips, teasing them open with his own, gliding his tongue against hers. Nipping at her mouth, his hands roamed her backside, cupping her ass. "Let me see," he whispered.

Slowly, he helped her out of her duster, and he watched as she unbuttoned her linen pants, tugging her camisole over her head. Emma once told Zora that there was power in eye contact, so she kept her eyes trained on Reid as she disrobed, standing proudly in her nakedness. His eyes traveled excruciatingly slowly over the terrain of her body, appreciating every curve. He licked his lips like he had been starving for a meal and she was the feast set before him. She hoped that his hunger would translate into action, because she was ravenous at the thought of her disappointing encounter with Lawrence.

She lifted her head higher, feeling just as hungry as he looked. "Your turn." Her voice was hoarse, her throat dry as he lifted his sweater over his head, followed by a white undershirt. She admired his physique; his washboard stomach peeked through the thin material.

He unbuckled his pants at a glacier's pace, and Zora broke eye contact just quickly enough to see a bulge emerging beneath heavy denim. "We finally get to finish what we started last time." His pants slid down his legs, and his boxers immediately followed, and Zora bit her lip to keep her jaw from dropping along with them.

Reid's deep chocolate skin glowed in the warm light of his bedside lamp, each muscle looking like it could have been etched from stone but for the occasional twitch or contraction. Thick shoulders led to a broad chest and rigid abs, and Zora's knees weakened as her eyes traced the muscular lines leading down in a V from his abs to his stiff erection. His muscular thighs twitched, and she licked her lips.

"I like the way you look at me, too." Reid's hand instinctively wrapped around the thick shaft of his dick.

"It's hard not to look at you right now," she admitted, her eyes trained on him. Stepping closer, he slid his hands along her hips and grabbed her ass as she wrapped her arms around his neck. She let him guide her toward the foot of the bed and gently seat her on its edge.

He leaned over her, kissing her earlobes, biting her bottom

lip, running his tongue lazily over her collarbone and breasts before kneeling on the floor in front of her. "I'm still not over the first time I tasted you, Z."

Her eyes darkened at the thought. "Then maybe it's time for you to have seconds."

A glint in his eye flickered like a flame. "I think you're right." He pressed his hand against her sternum until she lay back on the bed, skimming his fingertips down her body. He dipped low to bring his shoulders under her thighs, their flesh resting on the breadth of his muscular frame. The heat of his mouth pressed against the flesh near the inside of her knee; his tongue painted an excruciatingly slow trail toward the heat building at her core.

Zora squeezed her eyes shut, savoring each sensation shooting through her body. She clutched the comforter tightly and gasped as his soft lips closed around her clit. He licked and lapped her sensitive bud hungrily until she cried out, grasping at the back of his head to keep going because she couldn't find the words. She bucked against him, encouraging him to double down on his efforts. His hand rested on her stomach; the other pulled at her thigh to make room for him to continue as her body shook and tensed. Climaxes came to her wave after wave until she convulsed, digging her nails into Reid's shoulders.

He followed the same path up her body that his hand had trailed, placing butterfly kisses along her torso, sucking at her breasts, and tenderly licking her collarbone. He pulled a condom from the pocket of his jeans on the floor and put it on before leaning his weight on his hands placed on either side of Zora's body. He ground his thick shaft against her sensitive nub, and she bit her lip as he leaned forward to kiss her. The muscles in his chest and shoulders contracted, and she scraped the tips of her nails against his deep brown skin.

As he rubbed against her, his soft lips locked tenderly with hers. They angled their faces to take more of each other in, and he moaned against her mouth as she lightly slid the tip of her tongue across the length of his. "Zora, can I—"

"Yes." Impatient, she throbbed with anticipation. "Please."

Reid ran his fingers down the length of Zora's torso, tormenting her for a little longer. He squeezed her breast, running his thumb over her nipple as she squirmed. As his hand moved lower, she sucked in a breath as the same digit grazed her clit and moved lower to her damp center. "Damn, Z," his low voice growled like thunder. "So wet."

Tugging at the length of his dick, he rubbed the cloaked tip against her opening and upward, driving Zora crazy. With each movement, she lifted her hips, ready to meet him, but he relished in teasing her. "Give me what I want, babe," she whispered, her voice thick with wantonness.

"And what's that?" He watched her, devouring her with his eyes as his movements turned into slow circles.

Their eyes met, and Reid sucked in a surprised breath as Zora moved to her knees and pushed him onto his back next to her on the edge of the bed, his feet resting on the floor. Climbing onto his lap, Zora took control, pleased at Reid's wide-eyed expression. "You know what I want," she breathed, wrapping her fingers around his length. She guided him to her entrance, inhaling through gritted teeth as she took in all of him.

"Shit," he whispered, gripping her hips as she rode him slowly, her hands on his chest. Staring up at her, her curls fanned into a mane framing her face, he cupped her chin, wanting to taste her lips. Instead, she turned her face toward his hand, taking his thumb into her mouth.

As she sucked on his finger, she wound her pelvis in a slow circle until Reid moaned. Zora reached for him, pulling him into a sitting position, resting her arms on his shoulders as she picked up the pace. Rocking back and forth in his lap, he grasped her ass, pulling her onto him to go deeper. She wrapped her arms around his neck as he buried his face in her breasts.

"Come here." He hoisted her up, before turning and laying her on her back while he stood. Pressing her knees toward her chest, he drove into her, bringing her to the brink of climax again before slowing, teasing his heavy dick in and out slowly. He moved his thumb back to her clit, massaging it gently as he moved inside her.

"I'm close," she whimpered, wrapping one of her legs around Reid's back as the other hung over his shoulder.

"Me, too, baby." His fingers continued to massage her as he pushed inside her wet mound. "Now come for me." He leaned over her, grinding deeper into her, his thumb slick and gentle against her pulsating core.

Zora squeezed her eyes shut, her senses overwhelmed as her thighs began to shake. She bit back a scream as she arrived at the brink of orgasm.

"That's it, Z." He licked at her nipples, gently rolling one between his teeth. "Come for me."

The words were barely out of his mouth when her back arched, heat exploding behind her closed eyelids, the muscles between her thighs contracting and throbbing as Reid pumped in his last deep thrusts. She lifted her hips, inviting him in, fully meeting each burst forward as their bodies clapped together. He tensed and fell against her, gasping for breath as she opened her eyes. He lifted his head to look at her, still trying to catch his breath, and she smiled up at him, trying to read his expression. "What?"

"Nothing. You're. Wow. That was..." he huffed.

"It was," she agreed, wrapping her arms around him. She

planted a kiss against his forehead, giggling as his beard tickled her skin.

He lifted himself up, slowly pulling out of her and disposing of the condom. "Water?"

"Sure." She crawled toward the head of the bed, pulling back the comforter and leaning against the pillows, dazed and thoroughly satisfied—her appetite quenched.

He returned with two glasses, one half full as he guzzled the cool liquid. Handing her a glass, he pulled back the covers and climbed into bed next to her.

Zora took a big gulp of water and set the glass down on the nightstand. She dropped her head onto his shoulder, and Reid wrapped his arms around her.

He kissed the top of her head. "Please tell me we're going to get to do that again."

She grinned. "Do you really think I'd deprive myself of all of this?" She gestured toward his body. "I'm both exhausted and wide-awake."

He laughed. "Me, too. Come here. You're so warm." He pulled her soft body down by her middle to be his little spoon, burying his face against the back of her neck. She wiggled against him to get comfortable, her ass brushing against his semiengorged flesh. "Keep doing that and you're going to make me hard again, Z," he groaned.

She craned her neck to look back at him. "And what's wrong with that?"

20

The sounds of the bell chime on the front door of Opus Northeast were dulled by the coffeehouse music playing through Zora's noise-canceling headphones. Deep in thought, she attempted to concentrate on the invoices in front of her—one of many tasks on her checklist. Too bad she couldn't focus.

"Make it make sense," Zora muttered to herself. All morning she had replayed the section of Reid's book that she read in her head. *Why did that passage feel so familiar? Where did I—what the...* A hand waving in her periphery made her jump. "Jesus, Emma! How many times do I have to tell you that these are noise *canceling* and not *soundproof*? Knock or announce yourself, or I swear you'll be wearing that doorbell."

Emma ignored her dramatics. "You talkin' to yourself again, Z? You really ought to talk to someone about that, you know."

Zora frowned. "I just can't stop thinking about the other night."

Emma's eyes widened. "Your date with Reid? I didn't get

to ask you about that yesterday, but don't think I didn't hear you sneaking in the house yesterday morning, you little minx." She winked.

Zora rolled her eyes. "Oh please. I knew you heard me come in. You're so obvious."

Emma pretended to take offense, clutching fake pearls. "Me? How?"

"Because normally your snoring is much louder."

Emma clicked her tongue, chucking a paper clip at Zora's deadpan expression. "So you obviously spent the night. How did it go? Did you actually get yours this time?" Emma's approval of Lawrence had declined sharply after the bed-and-breakfast. She didn't believe in giving second chances for bad sex. Zora tried to correct her that the sex wasn't bad, just incomplete, but that argument didn't have the strength behind it that she'd hoped. *Neither did Lawrence's lasting power, but a girl could dream.*

Zora looked around to see if anyone was in earshot before returning her attention to Emma. "I did," she whispered, and she and her friend immediately burst into a simultaneous fit of cackling. Brian craned his neck from the coffee kiosk, where he was helping Granny with a crossword puzzle.

Emma twiddled her fingers together, leaning forward. "Ooo, you betta spill, ho."

"Shut up!" Zora chided in a hushed tone.

Emma's eyes widened and she spat her words through gritted teeth in a sharp staccato. "Start. Talking."

"The museum was amazing, as expected. And then we stopped by the food trucks and sat on the National Mall for some sunshine."

Emma feigned a snore, emitting the same nasally snort she did the morning before as Zora snuck upstairs. "Okay, Vitamin D, but I want to hear about that *D*!"

"Shut. Up."

Emma rolled her eyes and they both burst into mischievous laughter conspiratorially.

"So we went back to his place and watched the sunset on his rooftop patio. We had some wine, and he let me read some of his writing." She raised her eyebrows but continued. "Then we went back downstairs and had a whole lot of sex."

She and Em slapped five, interlacing their hands in a victory shake. "Ooo, did you get enough for me, too?"

"More importantly, do you think you could be pregnant?" another voice interjected—the hopeful tone unmistakable.

The girls both whipped their heads around toward the office door to see Granny Marion standing in the doorway with her hands clasped with hope and stars in her eyes. Zora groaned. "Come on, Granny. That is absolutely not possible."

"Are you sure?" she asked sweetly. "Condoms aren't 100 percent effective."

"Ms. Marion!" Emma scolded. "You are the only person in the world who is hoping the condom broke!"

"Seriously!" Zora exclaimed.

"All right, well, I'm sorry. It's just that I'm not going to be here forever, you know?"

"Granny! You can't play the whole 'sunset years' card again for the rest of this month."

Marion sat gingerly in the chair beside Emma's. "Well, fine. Let's hear it, then." She gestured for Zora to continue.

Emma's eyes bulged.

Zora blinked. "Are you sure you want to hear this, Granny?"

The matriarch batted her lashes, speaking in a calm, matter-of-fact tone. "Sweet child, I get more play than you and Emma put together. Out with it."

Trying to shake that particular revelation from her memory, along with Emma's reactions of shock and approval, Zora exhaled deeply. "The sex was mind-blowing. We did it twice last night and twice this morning."

"Damn, are you raw?" Emma shrieked.

"Emma!" Zora clenched, aware of customers likely in earshot. "No!"

"Ah, so then he knows the importance of lubrication." Granny nodded, her gentle statement of fact again catching the two younger women off guard. "Continue."

Zora's mouth dropped open as Emma pressed her lips together tightly, literally buzzing with energy. Z squeezed her eyes shut. "So to continue, the sex is great, he's very attentive, the date was thoughtful, but… I think we might have a problem."

"Bad hygiene? Weird fetish?" Emma guessed. "What could be the problem? He seemed like the perfect gentleman when he came to the house, and the date went well, so…"

"I think he's a plagiarist."

Emma's brows sank as she squinted at Zora, poking out her lips. "Of all the things we're concerned about, how did plagiarism make it to the top of the list?"

"While I was there, he let me read some of his writing. Remember? He said he was really into writing and hoped to eventually be published like Lawrence. And he's such a great teacher, so I've been excited to read his work."

"Who did he plagiarize? I need more information." Emma sank back in her chair.

"I'm not sure yet, but I know I've read something similar before." Zora raised both hands and shrugged. "I don't want it to be true, but I had that twinge of suspicion kick in the moment I read the passage—I got that feeling at the pit of my stomach. Something about the attacker, no, a man who 'disappeared into the shadows, leaving behind broken incisors and two drops of blood.' It felt familiar to me."

Emma looked meaningfully at Granny and then turned to Zora. "Z, listen. I know I love to tap into your Zor-lock skills from time to time, but are you sure you're about to uncover some big mystery here? Is this just you not wanting to make a decision about these guys?"

"Or," Granny added, "is this you knowing your decision but pushing them away so that you can focus on the bookstore?"

"Oop!" Emma raised an index finger toward Granny, who tapped it with her own.

Zora prickled. "Listen, I haven't made any decisions about these two guys, but I'm telling you, I've read this before." A stack of books on the corner of her desk caught her eye, and she grabbed the one on the top of the pile. "Could it be that obvious?" she muttered to herself.

"What?" Emma leaned forward.

The book in Zora's hands was Lawrence's most recent thriller—the one he discussed at his signing. "Annette, the character who helps solve all of the main character's investigations gets attacked in one of the chapters. She uses a different weapon to defend herself, though." Her fingers flew through the pages, stopping three quarters of the way through the story. She planted her index finger against the passage. "Here."

"What does it say, baby?" Granny asked, pulling her glasses from the designer chain around her neck and placing them on the bridge of her nose.

"It says 'As a hand latched onto her shoulder and spun her in the other direction, Annette jabbed her arm in the direction of the attacker's face, connecting the blunt tip of the baton that extended from her fist with his front teeth. With an ear-splitting crunch and a yelp of pain, the man disappeared back into the shadows, leaving behind broken teeth and two droplets of blood.' See? That last line is almost verbatim."

"Why are you so good at this?" Emma exclaimed. "And what does this mean for you and Reid?"

"Well, obviously, I'm going to have to talk to him about it. Maybe he just read Lawrence's book and doesn't realize he pulled that language, or maybe he's using that as a place-holder, or—"

"Or maybe he stole the line intentionally," Granny concluded. "I don't know, baby. Something ain't right. My intuition tells me there's more to this story. Just talk to him."

"Wait, so one is a liar and bad in bed, and one plagiarizes. Does that mean they're both out?" Emma looked back and forth between the other two.

"What lie?" Granny put her hands on her hips.

"It's nothing, Granny, seriously." Zora waved away the thought.

Emma gestured to Zora. "Z, you said he was making you a home-cooked meal, but you suspected that he ordered that from your favorite restaurant."

Zora nodded slowly. "But trying to impress a woman with cooking versus selling stolen words? I think one is a lot worse here. And Lawrence isn't bad in bed. We just haven't found our rhythm yet."

Emma's eyes rolled back hard. "Name a woman that hasn't made that excuse about a man and I'll buy your lattes for the rest of the month."

"I told you, our coffee is already expensed through the store." Z pinched the skin at the bridge of her nose.

"Then two months." Emma put her hands on her hips.

"Ugh. You're insufferable." Zora sighed, shaking her head at her friend, though the corners of her mouth pulled upward.

"Love you, too." Emma winked and walked out.

Lawrence: Hey beautiful, how is your week going?

Zora: Hey, handsome! So far, so good! Where are you now?

She surveyed the pile of completed invoices on her desk and the number of check marks on her task list. There was still more to be done, but she was satisfied with the progress. Emma was out on the floor with Tanesha, teaching her how to log inventory. Granny had gone for a walk in the sunshine with one of the regulars, while Zora took advantage of the quiet to complete new book orders and pay the bills.

"Hey, Z." Brian stood at the threshold of her office with a fresh latte. "You looked like you were on a roll, so I brought you another."

"You're a real one, B." She waved him in and he set the drink on her desk with a lemon madeleine. "Everything going smoothly out there?"

"Yeah, it's been quiet, but the afternoon rush should be coming soon."

"How'd your test go?"

Brian shrugged. "She hasn't given back our exams yet, but I think it went well."

"Good."

She nibbled on the madeleine as she stared at her phone. Ellipses crawled at the bottom of her screen, indicating that Lawrence was typing a response.

Lawrence: Back in Atlanta, but I'll be in town by the weekend. Think you might have a free night to be wined and dined? We had to end our getaway so abruptly, and I've been wanting to make it up to you. Can you take a night off?

Zora: I think that I can make that happen. ☺ Saturday?

Lawrence: Perfect. Dinner by the waterfront?

A shiver of anticipation whispered up her spine. Complain as Emma might, Lawrence was a good guy who put a lot of thought and effort into his pursuit of Zora—his favorite restaurant and cigar bars, weekend getaways, and private dinners with local chefs. She thought back over past relationships, none of them recent, and tried to remember a time that someone had even thought to make plans in advance. Her last serious relationship ended with her twenties, and Zora's ex had been in the process of establishing himself professionally, working long hours, so if she received any pampering, it was by her own initiation. She wondered how much of this generosity was incorporated into Lawrence's love languages and how much of this was just to compete with Reid, a teacher, who was probably underpaid.

Zora: You really are trying to spoil me, aren't you?

Lawrence: Someone should. ☺

She couldn't help but smile. She could hear Emma's voice shouting, "Treat yo'self, sis!"

Zora: Thank you, that sounds amazing. So did you decide to double your efforts with the book crowd in Atlanta?

Lawrence: Great! And yes, had to hit a few more locations. Sales had a nice boost from my last trip, and there were some indie bookstores that I didn't get to visit last time, so my PR team thought a return trip would be a good idea.

Zora: You've got them waiting at the door, huh? ☺

Lawrence: LOL no one is searching for me with a flashlight yet.

Zora: But maybe they should.

Lawrence: Would you?

Zora: Guess we'll find out when you come back to town.

Lawrence: Such a tease.

Zora threw back her head and laughed, forgetting for a moment where she was. Outside the windows of her office, she caught glimpses of Emma and Granny craning to see what was so funny and composed herself.

Zora: You think so?

Lawrence: You don't think you teased me on the trip? All of that beautiful, soft skin on display. And that dress? I couldn't wait to touch you that night. I want to touch you again.

Zora: What would you touch if you were here right now?

She bit her lip, resting her elbows on her desk as she cradled her phone in both of her hands. *Are we really about to start sexting right now?* Her eyes fluttered closed as she pictured Lawrence in her office with all of the blinds drawn and lifted her chin to stretch her neck. Her breath became shallow as she anticipated what he might say next.

"Heffa, are you in here sending freaky texts?" Emma whispered incredulously. "Why are your eyes closed?"

Startled, Zora almost fell out of her chair as she snapped her eyes open. "Jesus!"

"Nope, just Emma." She grinned, pointing at herself.

"Ugh, sometimes I hate you."

"Girl, shut up. You know you love me." She advanced into the room, shutting the office door behind her. "Now, spill, because I know that face. Who are we texting, and are there pictures?"

Zora's face flushed hot. "No, there aren't any pictures. Lawrence is texting me from Atlanta."

"Wasn't he just there?"

"He said the market is good there, so they went back to boost sales." Her cell phone pinged, and Emma snatched it before Zora could block her.

As Zora's best friend, Emma knew Zora's passcode to unlock her phone. As she stared at the phone, her mouth dropped open.

"Well, what did he say?" Zora hissed.

"He said he wants to touch whatever will handle this." Emma turned the phone slowly, revealing the head and shaft of a deep brown erection.

Zora's eyes bulged. "No, he didn't!"

"Um, yes he did! Damn, girl, you didn't tell me that's what he was workin' with!"

"Well, my time with it was limited. Give me that!" She snatched the phone out of her friend's hand.

Emma cocked her head to the side. "I prefer ones that have a little curve to them. That sucka is dead straight." She held up her hand and pumped her fist.

Zora grinned. "I can't believe he sent this."

Emma nodded to her. "Well, what are you going to say back to him?"

"I don't know! No one's sent me a dick pic in years, and I haven't dated this much in a decade. What would you say?"

Emma dated someone new almost every week. She liked to keep her options open, and she said the novelty of a new guy kept her on her toes. Ever the social butterfly, she maintained a rotation that made Zora dizzy to the point that she stopped trying to remember names and instead remembered the function or purpose that Emma assigned each of them—her Netflix and chill guy was for sex, then there was the shopping fanatic, the one who always had tickets to great shows, the foodie, the one who could fix her car, the one who was into yoga and spa dates. She joked that a blend of all of these guys could make the perfect man, but he'd still never stack up to the perfect woman. Though bi, she never added women to her roster—she said that the men were for play and she'd let go of the entire squad for the right woman, but only when she was ready to fall in love. Emma's eyes hooded slightly as her lips curved mischievously. "Tell him that he should use it to hit the spot he missed last time."

"Girl, I'm not saying that to that man!" Aghast, Zora looked down at her phone like he could hear them conspiring, pretending to clutch her pearls.

"Why not?" Emma's pointed expression implied that this was the most obvious response.

"Won't that crush his ego?"

"Hell no, it gives him a goal. I'm tired of women who won't tell men the truth. If it's small, they don't need chicks out here telling them that they're about to put someone's eye out when it barely does more than rest on his balls. You can have a whole relationship where you don't get off if you want to, but trust and believe that won't be me!"

"Ugh, well, how do I say that without being an asshole?"

"Did you just call me an asshole? You know what, never

mind, I'll take that. Give me your phone." She held her hand out expectantly.

Conflicted, Zora pursed her lips, mulling over the possible outcomes of relinquishing her phone to her silly best friend.

"You know we both have work to get to, right? Time is money, my friend." She gestured again for the device like a parent or teacher ready to confiscate some contraband.

"Shut up. You're already at work." Blowing out a breath, she gave the phone to Emma and immediately regretted it when her bestie cackled with glee.

"This is about to be good," she crooned, typing feverishly into the phone.

Zora craned her neck to see what Emma wrote, but she couldn't read the message upside down and Emma turned the phone facedown in her lap when she finished.

"So what happened with Reid? Are we focusing on Lawrence now?"

"How am I supposed to focus on anything when you just sent something freaky in response to a dick pic?" Zora rolled her eyes when Emma's only response was a pointed stare. "Okay, okay. I haven't talked to Reid yet, but I think I'm leaning toward Lawrence. Fundamentally, I just don't see how Reid and I could work if he's really willing to steal from his own best friend."

"Are you going to see him again?"

Zora nodded. "We have a dinner already planned this week. I think I might try to bring it up. See what he says."

"Ballsy to go the confrontation route. I still think there's some logical explanation for that. When are you supposed to see Lawrence again?"

"This weekend."

Her phone pinged again, and Emma turned it over, her face lighting up like a display window. "Well, you should anticipate that he's gonna try to blow your back out this time. You're welcome, by the way." She dropped the phone into Zora's hands and sashayed out.

Zora hurriedly unlocked her phone to see what damage had been done.

Lawrence: I want to touch whatever will handle this. [photo attachment]

Zora: I have a spot you can aim for this time that needs some attention. I promise the more you hit it, the sweeter the sounds I'll make for you. Think you're up for the challenge, big boy? 😏 ♥

Lawrence: Damn, Zora, like that? I won't stop until I do. 😈

"Hmm. I guess we'll see," Zora said wistfully. Looking out the window, she caught Emma's eye and winked at her.

"So I'm not fired?" she called from the checkout counter.

"There's always tomorrow!"

21

"You should consider yourself blessed, sir, because this doesn't happen very often." Zora tied on an apron and pulled a block of Parmigiano Reggiano out of the refrigerator. The scents of garlic and tomatoes and basil wafted through the air.

"You don't like to cook in this big ol' kitchen?" Reid smiled at Zora from his seat at the kitchen island.

"I just don't have a lot of time. I'll throw together a salad or something, but Granny loves to cook and often leaves me little care packages in my fridge. Her smothered pork chops are to die for." Her eyes rolled back just thinking about them.

"Oh, wow, does she do those over rice or with potatoes?" He leaned forward, resting his chin in his hands.

"Both. She'll smother some potatoes in the gravy, too, and then put everything over rice with some greens or string beans. Her Sunday dinners when I was a kid were epic." She chef kissed the tips of her fingers.

"Sounds amazing. So what is it that you're blessing us with this evening?" He peered across the island at the feast she'd prepared.

"We have some spinach and prosciutto ravioli with grilled shrimp in my walnut pesto sauce, some fresh bruschetta using tomatoes from my Granny's garden out back, and some creamy burrata cheese with an olive tapenade. I'll tell you about dessert later."

"This is so fancy. I've never had a tapenade. I don't even really know what that is."

"It's a spreadable paste made of diced olives, capers, and anchovies. It's a bit salty, but it balances really nicely with the cheese." She spread a small amount on a slice of baguette and cut into the burrata, exposing its creamy center. "Here, try this."

He wrinkled his nose, accepting the bread gingerly. "Well, here goes!" He bit into the baguette, immediately closing his eyes as he chewed quickly at first, his mouth slowing as the flavors melded together on his tongue. His eyes brightened. "I've never tasted anything like that!"

"You like it?"

He nodded. "May I?" He pointed to the bruschetta.

"Of course!"

"What's in this?" He sniffed the toast point, making her laugh.

"Fresh tomatoes, olive oil, garlic, basil, parsley, a little salt."

"That's it?"

"Yep!"

The toasted bread was small, so he shoved the entire piece into his mouth, chewing slowly. His eyes closed. "Mmm. The food is so simple, but it's got so much flavor. This is delicious, Z!"

"Thank you! There's something about Italian food that I find so comforting." She dropped store-bought raviolis into boiling water and wiped her hands on her apron. "Six minutes, and we're ready to eat! Would you like a glass of wine?"

"Sure, that sounds great."

"Emma picked up a really nice vermentino for us." She pulled the bottle from a wine fridge near her pantry. She handed Reid the bottle and a corkscrew. "Would you mind uncorking this for me while I get our ravioli plated?"

"I think I can handle that for you." Their fingertips brushed, and Zora drew her hand away quickly, as if she'd been burned.

"You okay?" Reid raised his eyebrow.

"Yeah, I'm fine!" she replied brightly, her voice a little too high to be believable. Knowing she didn't have a poker face, she turned and busied herself with the ravioli, lifting them from the rolling boil with a slotted spoon. She bounced the spoon to relieve any water droplets before distributing the ravioli between two shallow bowls. Carefully, she ladled a bit of pesto sauce onto the steaming pasta, topped them with grilled shrimp, and shaved fresh Parmigiano Reggiano to crown the dish.

"We should take a picture." Reid's eyebrows lifted in awe as his eyes widened. "No one has ever cooked something like this for me before."

Zora carried the dishes over to his side of the island, placing one in front of him and placing one in front of the seat next to his. He hovered his camera above his dish, trying to capture the food at the right angle and then showed off his photo with pride.

He grabbed her hand and pulled her to him, kissing her softly on the lips. "Thank you, Z. This is really special."

"You're welcome," she replied shyly.

He pulled out her stool so she could sit and waited. "Should we say a prayer?"

"Would you like to do the honors?" She watched him.

"Of course." He clutched her hand again. "Heavenly Father, we thank You for this day and the opportunity to be together. We thank You for the food that we are about to receive, and we ask that You bless it, let it be nourishment for our bodies and souls. Please bless the hands that prepared this meal. Bless her business. Allow Your Son and Your truth to be at the center of our lives. In His name we pray. Amen."

"Amen." She watched him, thinking of the word that stood out to her most during the prayer. *Truth*. She rinsed and wiped down two white wine glasses and placed them on the counter.

Reid poured the wine and pushed the cork back into the bottle. Lifting his glass, he turned to Zora, his eyes crinkling at the corners. "To you, for making this beautiful meal."

"Aw, thank you." She tapped her glass lightly against his and took a small sip. "Please, dig in!"

Reid cut a ravioli in half with his fork, taking one half with a grilled shrimp as his perfect bite. The look of contentment on his face made her smile. "This is some of the best food I've had this year, Z. Wow."

"Thank you." They quieted as they ate except to murmur observations about the food, the silence between them comfortable, though Zora couldn't push the nagging thought from her mind. "Can I ask you a question?"

"Of course." He directed his gaze toward her between bites.

"How long have you been writing that book that you shared with me?" She started slowly, still trying to figure out how to broach the subject delicately.

"Oh, I started that one like a year or two ago. There are others I've started and shelved, but I'm most excited about this one. My main character is so cool, and I love thrillers. I've just been so busy, I haven't devoted a lot of time to finishing the draft, but the story is fully plotted." He smiled easily, unsuspecting.

Zora nodded. "What are your thoughts on a writer borrowing pieces from another author's work?"

His chewing slowed as the skin between his brows pinched together. "Something happen at work today? Some publishing scandal that I didn't hear about?"

She laughed awkwardly. "No, no big scandal. It just came up in conversation, so I thought I'd ask you for your take." She looked at him intently, waiting for a tell that would give him away. *Please tell me you wouldn't do what I think you did.*

He remained quiet for a long moment, still chewing his food. "I mean, do I think it's right to intentionally plagiarize? No, of course not. But do I think that there are distinctly new concepts out there that no one has ever written? My answer would also be no."

"Tell me what you mean." She waited patiently as turmoil built beneath her skin. She wanted him to say something that would quench the fire of accusation that swirled in her chest.

"Everyone borrows from somewhere. Whether it's tropes, or a retelling, or a concept—it's all been done before. Writing these days is really trying to find a new angle to tell the story from—not a new story altogether."

"So you think that sometimes people might unintentionally pull from others?"

"I think that's inevitable. How many versions of *Cinderella* are out in the world? Or *Pride and Prejudice*? How many enemies to lovers stories can there be? The possibilities are infinite!" He gestured broadly, extending his open hands out to his sides.

"But actual word choice, the description of a scene. Is that fair game?"

"Of course not!" he laughed. "That's plagiarism. Concepts, structure, sure. Exposition or dialogue, absolutely not." He turned to face her, searching her eyes for some sort of explanation behind the topic of conversation. "Tell me, what's this really about?"

She poked at her food until she couldn't take it anymore. "Truth?"

"Please." He set his fork down on the plate. "I wouldn't lie to you, Z." His reassuring tone was accompanied by a squeeze of her shoulder.

She nodded, but still, his words didn't comfort her the way that she had hoped. *He says he wouldn't plagiarize, so maybe he didn't. But how does that explain these identical scenes?* "I recognized a passage from your notebook in Lawrence's most recent novel. It sounded really familiar to me, and I just wonder how it could be that your story includes almost identical words for one of the attack scenes."

He stilled, but he never broke eye contact with her. He nodded slightly. "That part is from the beginning of the notebook. Lawrence has been over a million times, and he liked that phrasing, so he asked if he could pull it for his story. I just haven't gone through and edited to update. I do that later on when I type everything out."

He shrugged like it was nothing, but the feeling in the pit of Zora's stomach didn't go away. "So he took *your writing*, not the other way around?"

"I'm confident in my writing, Z. I have no need to pull from Lawrence. I promise."

Nodding, Zora decided to shake it off and accept his explanation, though something told her there was something more he wasn't telling her. "Thank you for telling me that. I'm sorry if I made things a little awkward."

"I'm glad you asked. I wouldn't want you to worry that I'd do something like that. And to Lawrence, of all people." He reached over and squeezed her hand as it rested on the table.

"I just get these gut feelings sometimes. Anyway, please eat.

I have so much food here," she laughed. She took a long sip of her wine and they proceeded to finish their meal. After, she directed him toward the couch, refilled their wineglasses, and carried them over along with her box of hazelnut truffles from Chef Andrea. "Are you a chocolate fan?"

"I love it."

"I met this amazing chef and I'm thinking about hiring her to cater our short-story contest event. She made these." Zora unwrapped the box carefully, lifting the lid to show four identical truffles studded with crushed hazelnuts.

"Wow, these look delicious. Thank you for sharing them with me." He scooted closer to her, nudging her with his shoulder.

The sensation sent a warmth toward her belly, different from the twisty angst she still felt in her chest. The closer he got, the lower it traveled, sending jolts of electricity firing through every synapse. They each picked one up and grinned as they tapped them together. "Cheers."

Reid took a bite, careful not to drop any pieces of hazelnut on the floor or couch. "Oh, my God."

Zora peeked at him through the corner of her eye as her teeth sank into the truffle. "Mmm." The creamy, rich dark chocolate was softened with a punch of hazelnut liqueur in the center; a whole roasted hazelnut sat at its liquidy pool. "I wonder if she freezes the liqueur to get it into the center."

"If you were at all unsure whether you should hire that chef, I'm going to vote in favor of doing so. This is beyond!" He popped the other half of his truffle into his mouth and closed his eyes, humming as he chewed. "They're so rich, you really only need one, but they're so good that you want to eat all of them."

She nodded in agreement, eyeing the last two. "Truly."

He fell over, laughing. "I see you, Z. Don't worry, those two are all you."

She blushed, but the chocolates were too good to share. "I want to feel bad for wanting the last two to myself, but I don't. I'm going to run a hot bath and let these truffles melt away my stress."

Reid tilted his head to admire her form. "Want some company?"

Yes. "No, I shouldn't tonight. And it's been such a long week, and I'm sort of tired," she lied.

"Oh, of course." He stood, sensing that she was ending their evening, but the somber expression on his face said it all. He nodded and made his way toward the door to put on his shoes.

Zora followed quietly, not wanting to put her foot in her mouth, but wanting to reflect on their conversation and her suspicions. She offered an apologetic smile when his shoes were on and he stepped in her direction.

"Are you sure you don't want me to stay? I could help you relieve some of that stress, you know." He wrapped his arms around her, pulling her close.

So tempting. Zora squeezed her eyes shut, taking in the scent of his cologne as she willed herself to stay strong. "Sorry, love. I have an early morning tomorrow. If you stay, there's no chance of me getting a full night's sleep."

He pulled away from her, chuckling, his arms still locked around her waist as he gazed down at her. "I do have some self-control, Z."

"Yeah, but right now I don't." She batted her lashes at him and they both laughed.

"All right, if you're sure." When she nodded, he brushed his lips against hers, planting another kiss against her temple. "In that case, thank you again for dinner."

She rested her chin on his shoulder. "You're very welcome. Let me know when you make it home, please?"

"You got it." She opened the door for him and watched him walk down the front steps toward his car. A drafty breeze made her shiver as she leaned against the front door. She waved to him as he started his car and drove away.

Shutting the front door, she shook her head as she plopped back down on the couch, having no intention of taking a bath. She flipped on the television and put her feet on the coffee table. Dipping her fingers back into the truffle box, she muttered to herself, "Who needs men when truffles exist?"

Reid: Hey, it's me again. I know I left you a message earlier, but I've been a little worried about how we left things last night. Did I do something wrong? Can we talk?

Two days after their date, Zora had yet to respond to several missed calls and texts from Reid. She'd have to respond at some point, but not when she was getting ready for her date with Lawrence. Fresh from the shower, she moisturized with shea butter and coconut oil, massaging it into her limbs and torso.

Then she turned her attention to her hair, which she wrapped in a worn T-shirt to catch excess water or moisture from the hair serum and curl cream. She'd been paying more attention to skincare lately, and it had paid off, resulting in supple, glowing skin. With a foundation brush, she swirled on some light coverage before adding definition to her brows and running a spoolie through her lash extensions. Emma finally dragged her out to Vienna for an appointment, and she was right—her lash stylist was everything. Zora loved how the added volume framed her eyes and eliminated the need for eye makeup. She brushed on a peachy blush above her natural contour line and fanned on a bit of highlighter for a touch of shimmer.

As she worked, her mind wandered back to Reid. On one hand, she believed he was telling her the truth when he said he wouldn't plagiarize, but on the other, why would he just agree to let Lawrence, an established writer, use lines from the novel he'd been working on for himself? Something still didn't add up.

Maybe I'm thinking about this the wrong way. Her Zor-lock senses tingled and she felt like she was right on the edge of piecing everything together. *But how?*

She removed the T-shirt from her hair, blotting out some of the remaining moisture. The more her curls air-dried, the tighter they would become. She would fluff them with a hair pick to add some body once she'd gotten dressed. She sat on the edge of her bed in a satin robe, the plum-colored fabric cool and whisper-light against her skin. Lawrence's book sat on her bedside table.

Zora reached for it, skimming the pages until she found the passage again. Reading it through, she felt like she was looking right at the smoking gun, but couldn't put her finger on what it was. Thumbing through the pages, she read a different scene with the main character, Private Investigator Langston Butler and his assistant, Annette. Something about Annette pulled at her—the essence of her character felt bigger than the side character she was relegated to play, but Zora couldn't shake loose what was familiar about her. The mystery would have to be solved another day.

She dropped the book back on the night table. "I don't have time for this," she muttered.

"Z?" Emma knocked at her door.

"Hey, come in." Zora felt through her hair for dampness. *Almost dry.*

Emma bounced in with a matching crop top and sweat-pants on. Her braids were twisted up into a bun on the top of her head, like a beautiful crown. She had a bag of trail mix in her hand, half of which would be wasted—she only ate the almonds and dried cranberries.

Zora frowned. "I thought you had a date?"

Emma plopped down on the bench at the foot of the bed. "I do."

"But you're in pajamas…"

"Oh! Tonight is Netflix and chill guy. We ain't goin' no-where. I'll just be at his place, so it's not like I need to dress up. I'll get mine, though. Can't let you have all the fun." She winked, popping an almond into her mouth. Surveying the scene, she eyed Z's hair. "I like the side part. Your curls look juicy."

Zora touched her hair. "Thank you! I should have washed it a little earlier, but it's fine. By the time dinner ends, it'll probably be fully dry."

"Are y'all going to his place after or coming here?"

"I hadn't really thought about it. We'll probably come here. It's easier for him to get away if he doesn't want to stay the night." She pursed her lips. *That's what I would do if I wanted the ability to make a quick exit.* "Even better that you'll be over at dude's tonight—we won't be trippin' over each other."

"Why wouldn't he want to stay the night?"

"I don't know. He might. I just have a weird feeling."

"Please tell me you're not still Zor-locking these two." Emma rolled her eyes. "What is it that you think you're going to uncover here, girl?"

"I'm not quite sure, but I feel like it's all about to come into focus. Are you sure about this dress?" She held up the thin, burnt-orange fabric with its barely there straps. "This isn't overkill?"

"Girl, I'm always sure when it comes to clothes. That color will pop against your skin, and it will hug every single curve in a way that primes Lawrence for a nightcap."

Zora waggled her eyebrows. "Let's hope."

"And why would you be worried about overkill? Sometimes you gotta flex on 'em, Z. Remind them who you are. Apply that pressure, sis. Bet the bedroom is a whole new experience this time."

Zora smiled mischievously. "I guess it is the right time to flex a little more."

"Let 'em know."

22

"Wow, you look gorgeous, Zora," Lawrence breathed. Zora had decided to let down her walls and invite Lawrence to pick her up at home. Yes, he probably lied about cooking her dinner, but in the grand scheme of things, he made a lot of effort trying to impress her. If that was the worst that he did, she'd allow him to front for a little while and pretend he could cook. She stepped out of her front door in the flirty, burnt-orange sundress and heels, a wrap tied to the strap of her purse in case the evening cooled down. The thin straps of her dress plunged to a generous neckline that displayed her curving décolletage. The warm air enveloped her as Lawrence embraced her shoulders lightly, dropping a quick kiss on her cheek. *Right. No PDA.*

"You look damn good yourself," she said, gesturing toward him.

"Thank you." He smiled. Lawrence's dark gray dress shirt and black slacks were complimentary to her dress, making her stand out even more. His lips curved as he pulled a bouquet of long-stemmed red roses from behind his back. "These are for you."

Zora's eyes lit up. *Full of surprises.* "Lawrence, these are gorgeous! Thank you. I'll just put these in some water really quickly." She rushed back into the house, but Emma met her near the door, obviously having heard the exchange.

Emma stuck her arm out to take the flowers. "I'll take care of these for you. Hey, Lawrence!"

He waved quickly as Zora shoved the roses into Emma's hands. "Nosy heffa," she whispered. Turning back toward the door, she called out, "Enjoy your date tonight!"

"I will. Luv youuu." Emma smiled and waved, burying her nose into the bouquet.

After slamming the door, Zora turned her attention back to Lawrence. "Ready?"

"Emma's got a hot date?" He turned, and she followed him toward the sidewalk. She wondered if he felt naked without a blazer or tie. His musky cologne lingered in Zora's nostrils as he led her toward his car, which shone as if it had just received a fresh coat of wax.

She shrugged. "Yeah, she won't be back until tomorrow. How was your flight? You got in this morning?"

He ran a hand over his chest as if to smooth his shirt. "I did. We had a slight delay, but everything after takeoff went smoothly. It's good to be home."

"Did you accomplish what you'd hoped in Atlanta?"

He helped her into the car and closed the door behind her as the cicadas began their song. He hopped into the driver's seat. "Atlanta is starting to feel like my second home. We've scheduled another set of events there in a couple of weeks."

"Wow. I didn't realize there were so many independent bookstores in Atlanta! Would you mind grabbing business cards for me? I love to connect and coordinate with fellow indies." Often, if one indie was supporting an author's book tour, Zora would try to do the same. It helped the author coordinate their travel, and it also gave the stores the opportunity to cross-promote. The number of Black independent bookstores wasn't nearly high enough, so every chance she got, she tried to highlight the work of her peers, and with D.C. and Atlanta being such big hubs for the Black community, it made sense to have a strong network in both major cities.

Lawrence cleared his throat and looked into his rearview mirror. "Sure, I'll be sure to do that this next trip."

Zora glanced at him, her brow furrowing slightly, but she turned her head and looked out the window. The drive to the Georgetown waterfront was uneventful. Lawrence played one of Zora's favorite Miles Davis albums on the ride, so she zoned out to the music while staring at the changing colors. They valeted the car and walked toward the waterfront, the sky beginning to shift to a dusky blue and burnt-orange ombre. Ducks swam lazily on the Potomac as thin clouds turned cotton-candy pink.

The restaurant's impeccable service was clear from the entry—they were greeted by a team of hostesses clad in black. Zora and Lawrence took in the starched white tablecloths and watched as a barrage of waitstaff descended on a table simultaneously to present the main course to a party seated nearby. To avoid the mosquitoes hovering at dusk, they opted to sit inside at a table against the window so that they could watch the sunset as they talked.

They sipped on Aperol Spritzes, marveling at how much the leaves had changed now that they were in October. Over orange and fennel salads, and Chilean sea bass with blistered tomatoes, olives, and caper berries, they grew quiet, savoring the flavors that played on their tongues, hitting sweet, savory, salty, and bitter notes across their taste buds. Anytime Zora did her happy wiggle, Lawrence laughed and squeezed her thigh under the table—she would have welcomed more contact, but Zora respected that Lawrence still found a way to touch her in public.

Zora's eyes crinkled at the corners. "Have you ever read Reid's writing?"

A forkful of orange supreme paused in front of Lawrence's lips, and he shrugged. "Sure. Been a while, though." He slid the fork between his lips, rolling the sweet fruit with his tongue.

"He's very talented."

He laughed, close to spitting out his food. "He's all right. He was better when we were in college."

Ouch. "He shared with me that he's writing a book."

Lawrence threw back his head in raucous laughter. His eyes squeezed shut as he held a hand to his chest, trying to calm himself. "Reid? Write a book? That was a long-deferred dream. He thinks about it from time to time, but he'll never follow through on it."

"You don't think so?" Zora tilted her head, remembering Reid's excitement at the prospect of having his story out in the world. "When he talked to me about it, he seemed really motivated."

Lawrence grew quiet, the last shakes of laughter fading. His eyes unreadable. "Nah, I swear—he goes through these phases. Besides, with his teaching and the work that he does for me, he doesn't have time to write a book. Plus, he'd still have to find representation and someone who'd want to buy it if he intended to go the traditional route."

Zora squinted her eyes at him. "You sound like you don't want him to try."

Lawrence held up his hands. "It's not that I don't want him

to," he protested. "Trust me. He's my best friend. He doesn't have time."

She bit her tongue. Lawrence may have been his best friend, and while she'd only known Reid a little while, she knew he would make time for his dream.

"Wouldn't it make more sense to hire an assistant for all the social media stuff he does for you? Some college student that needs some spending money?"

"Teachers don't make a lot of money, and it lets me help out my friend in a way that he'll accept. He doesn't want money from me as a friend, but he'll accept pay if he's working for it."

Zora's Spidey senses pulsated in her chest, and she wanted to cry bullshit, but she didn't know why. "Well, maybe I'll ask him for some advice. I'm always trying to increase our following, and he might have some pointers."

"Yeah, maybe." Lawrence had a faraway look in his eyes, and she suspected he was tired of speaking about Reid. *This is supposed to be a date.*

She reached over and touched his knee under the table. "Hey. Want to get out of here?" She winked.

He looked at her, eyes brightening. "You have no idea." He gestured for the check and had paid and requested the car in mere moments.

On the drive back to Zora's, in the privacy of Lawrence's tinted windows, he kissed her fingertips one by one and traced his thumb along the flesh just inside her knee. Keeping his eyes on the road, he let his hand travel higher, squeezing her thigh, the heat building inside her to the point that it took her entire being not to spread her legs and let his fingers explore the slick folds between them. His thumb stroked back and forth against her skin, and she squeezed her eyes shut in anticipation.

They barely made it inside the front door before they began

to remove each other's clothes. Lawrence turned Zora around to hug the wall as he pulled the zipper of her dress down at a deliciously slow pace. As he let the straps fall away from her shoulders, he trailed his lips up her spine to the base of her neck. The warmth of his breath against her skin made her shiver, and her mouth dropped open as he ran his tongue just behind her ear. "I don't think we're going to make it upstairs," he whispered, his fingers hooking under the sides of her thong as he pulled it down from her hips. She stepped out of it, kicking off her shoes in the process.

As she turned to face him, Lawrence pinned her against the wall, her hands above her head. He held her hands there with one hand, reaching behind her back with the other to unfasten her strapless bra.

"So fucking sexy." Her bra fell away from her breasts, and he squeezed one, lifting it to his mouth. He dragged his tongue across her nipple, the peak of it stiffening, and she moved at the sensation. "Already squirming." He smiled against her lips, kissing her with an urgency he didn't have the last time. Releasing her breast, his fingers slid down her body and between her thighs, grazing her most sensitive spot.

Zora moaned against his lips, tilting her head to let more of him in as their tongues collided. His musky cologne melded with the scent of her perfume into a woodsy fragrance that intoxicated her as his deft fingers moved into and out of her slowly, slicking her wetness across her clit. He pressed inside her again, and Zora rode his hand, whimpering as she neared orgasm, the pressure inside her building until he removed his hand without warning.

"I want to be inside you," he whispered.

You just were. Slightly disoriented, she led him to the couch, pulling his hand back to where it had been. "I was so close," she whispered encouragingly, her eyes snapping shut as he moved his thumb against her sensitive skin, moisture accumulating between her thighs. Her eyes fell open as the stimulation stopped—Lawrence removed his clothes quickly, his erection thick and ready. Tearing a condom from its package, he slid it down the length of his dick, holding it in place as he guided the tip toward Zora, rubbing it against her.

Her back arched at the contact until she lifted her hips to accept him; she ached to return to the brink of that orgasm. "That's right. I know you want this." He pushed inside with a slowness that made her want to beg.

Eager to avoid a repeat of their last encounter, she tried to channel the sultry demand of Emma's text message. "I do. Now hit that spot for me." She wrapped her legs around him, lifting her hips to meet every thrust as he accepted her challenge. His slow teasing turned to deep pounding; his steely arousal pummeled into her, searching for the sweet sounds she'd promised. She moaned, gasping as he got closer to her spot, the pressure again building low in her abdomen. Before she could warn him or cry out, he slowed.

Lawrence gave one final thrust with a growl before rolling off her and onto the sofa on his back. "Did you come this time?" He gasped for breath, turning his head on an accent pillow.

Staring at the ceiling, she screwed her mouth to the side, before telling the truth. "No, but I was close for a minute." *That minute is all you gave me.*

"Have you considered the possibility that maybe you're too in your own head? Maybe you're not letting go enough for it to happen." He propped his head up in his hand.

"Excuse me?" *This is my fault?*

"Come on, I'm not trying to offend you. I'm just saying, there are so many women out there who say they have a hard time with orgasms. They overthink it and basically get in their own way. It's nothing to be embarrassed about." He held his hands down as a sign of peace, but his words struck a nerve.

"I'm not embarrassed! Are you really mansplaining the female orgasm to me?"

"Well, we keep trying, and you can't seem to get off."

"And so the obvious answer to you is that *I'm* the issue?"

"You have to let yourself relax more."

"If you want me to relax into it, you have to give me more time!" Zora's eyes widened and she bit her lip. "You know what? I shouldn't have said that."

Lawrence sat up on the couch, looking down at Zora, with her curls in a halo around her face on the pillow. "Oh, so you're saying it's my fault? Well, tell me, Zora, how much time do you need to get off? And since when is your orgasm my responsibility?"

The fuck? Her eyes narrowed. "Clearly, I need more time than you do. But what am I supposed to do when you don't give more than two licks of head, and our two sexual experiences add up to a grand total of almost satisfying six minutes?" Zora was fuming. She should have listened to Emma—no second chances when it comes to bad sex. "Why don't you go ahead and see yourself out, because obviously I'll *again* have to take care of what you started but clearly couldn't finish."

"Oh, I could finish it. You just aren't comfortable enough with your body to let yourself release."

"Excuse you? There is nothing wrong with an inch of these curves, and I dare you to say otherwise. My orgasm isn't your responsibility…the fuck? Was I laying there having sex with myself?" She stood proudly in her nakedness, hands on her hips. Her eyebrows turned upward in a scowl as she stared him down.

"You misunderstand me. I don't have an issue with your curves, but I think you do. Maybe you don't realize that you're insecure."

"Sir, if you don't get the fuck out of my house!" Zora grabbed a throw blanket slung over the arm of the sofa and wrapped it around her body. "Take all your li'l clothes and get out!" She enunciated the last two words for effect, throwing his shoes out the front door. "Insecure? If you don't take that minuteman bullshit somewhere!"

Shocked by her sudden anger, he relented. "Look, maybe I didn't say that right. Maybe we can resolve this." He pulled on his pants, his dress shirt slung over his shoulder and his socks in his hand. He held them up as his flag of surrender.

"Tuh! Not tonight we can't." She shook her head emphatically, gesturing out the door. "In the meantime..."

"Fine, I'll go. Take a few days and then maybe we can get to the root of this." He walked through the door, picking up his shoes, which had landed on the porch. Before he could turn to elicit a response, she closed the door behind him, locking the dead bolt. "That's really mature," he called through the front door.

Inside, Zora picked up her shoes and scattered clothes and carried them upstairs. "That man knows *nothing* about women." And then it hit her—the entire puzzle fit together. "Well, I'll be damned," she muttered.

23

"Zora." Reid looked at her with wary, unsmiling eyes. They weren't cold or unkind, but she longed for his laugh and the crinkles at the corners of his eyes. He stood in Lawrence's driveway as she walked up from the street. She had just kicked Lawrence out of her home the night before, and she hadn't been in contact with Reid for several days. Thankfully, when she'd messaged him and asked that he meet her at Lawrence's house, he'd responded right away.

A weight formed in the pit of her stomach. *Just talk to him.* "Hi, Reid."

He didn't respond; he just watched her.

She stepped closer to him, facing him finally. "Listen, I'm sorry that I didn't get back to you. I've just had a lot on my mind." She touched his arm and he bristled at the contact. She lifted her hand away, holding it up in apology. "You know what, I deserved that."

"Did I do something?" he asked. He searched her face for

an answer, his arms hanging lifelessly at his sides. "I really thought we had something happening between us, and then all of a sudden you ghosted."

Zora blinked. "I—I think you should come inside with me. I want to talk to the both of you." She reached for his arm and thought better of it.

"You made your decision. Is that it?" Reid blew out a breath. He shook his head and looked at the ground. "If you're choosing him, I don't need to be there for that."

"That's not what this is about, Reid. I swear, I was confused about a couple of things, but I'm pretty sure I figured it out. I promise, I'm not choosing Lawrence, okay? Please?" She beckoned him toward the door, not bothering with the formality of the doorbell. "Lawrence?" she called.

By the time he'd returned home from their date, Lawrence was already texting and leaving messages to apologize. Zora decided to sleep on it, finally responding to his text the next morning, agreeing to meet with him and talk. She definitely didn't want to talk about their last tryst in front of Reid, but they had bigger fish to fry. A reluctant Reid trailed behind her.

"I'm in the kitchen," Lawrence called. As she turned into the room with Reid in tow, Lawrence's eyes darted between the two of them and his forehead wrinkled. "What's going on?"

"Lawrence, I know we said we would talk about some other things, but first there's something I want to address with the two of you." Zora put her purse down on the edge of the dining table before standing in the center of the room. Reid stood off to the side, his arms closed tightly across his chest. "I've had something that's been on my mind, and I think it's important to just get it out there so that we can all be on the same page."

Lawrence stood on the other side of the kitchen island, facing the two of them. He looked from Reid to Zora to Reid again, searching for a hint on one of their faces. Finding none, he squinted at her. "You know, I'm not really down for a throuple, if that's what you're here to propose."

"No, but thank you for clarifying." She glared at him; the sternness in her voice reminded her of her mother's anytime Zora dared to say something slick. He raised his hands in apology, and Reid cracked a smile that fell away when she turned to face him. "Now remember, you said you'd never lie to me."

"And I never have." His response was immediate.

"You sure?"

He nodded slowly, but his face wasn't convincing.

"So then tell me. Everything in that notebook, you wrote all of that?"

"Of course I did. Every word." His arms dropped to his sides, letting his guard down, but he'd underestimated her.

"Then do you want to tell me what else you wrote?" She pulled Lawrence's signed book from her purse, tapping her index finger against the spine.

"I—" Reid blinked, stammering to find the words, but it didn't matter.

Zora turned to Lawrence. "You didn't write those books, did you? Reid wrote them." The answer was so obvious to her after Lawrence left her house. He never seemed to understand the references that she made to Annette's character strengths—he honestly didn't seem to understand women at all—and she suspected that if he had written the books, Annette would be mansplained to death by the all-knowing male main character. "Even the family memoir—all of this is Reid's writing. Isn't it?"

Reid continued to blunder. He held up a hand for her to stop and wait for him to explain, but she couldn't. She needed to know the truth, but she was pretty sure she'd already figured it all out.

"Annette is Serena, right? I just don't understand. You allowed him to take your strong, complex lead character and make her a sidekick. Why did you go along with this?" she asked Reid, planting her hands on her hips. "And how could you take credit for his work?" She turned to Lawrence with disapproval all over her face. "How did y'all even dream up this arrangement?"

Lawrence's face contorted with anger as his eyes bored holes into Reid. "You told her? You know I'm going to sue you, right? I'm going to fucking bleed you dry," he spat through gritted teeth.

Reid's face went slack. "I didn't tell her. Never. She figured it out. I did *not* breach the contract."

"You expect me to believe that? You wanted to win her, so you told her. Made me look like the bad guy." Lawrence rested his hands on the stone counter, leaning forward on them as he hurled accusations.

"If I told her, why would I leave out the part about signing an NDA?" Reid shouted. "I didn't tell her."

Stunned at the exchange, Zora could only watch it unfold as if she wasn't even there, realizing that she hadn't anticipated the nondisclosure agreement or the threat of litigation. She never predicted that her discovery would turn into a yelling match between the two of them.

"Let's see if a judge believes you," Lawrence sneered. "Get the fuck out."

Reid stared at Zora before stalking off toward the front door, his expression unreadable.

Her heart dropped. *What did I just do?*

"How could you speak to your best friend that way?" she asked, bewildered by the exchange.

Lawrence turned to face her. "You know, you don't need to lie to me, Zora. I know that he told you." He smiled, but it didn't reach his eyes, which were narrowed and trained hard on her.

"But he didn't! He was telling you the truth." She gestured toward the front door, which Reid left standing open.

"I don't believe that for a second. We had our little issue last night, and you two decided to conspire against me. He wants out of his contract, like you said, and he wants you, so it makes sense for him to use you to get his way."

"That doesn't even make sense! He's your best friend! He wouldn't do that to you, Lawrence." Zora's heart was pounding out of her chest. She tried to think of something that could convince Lawrence that there was no conspiracy.

"You don't know him like I do. He's always been jealous. Since the last time we were both interested in the same girl—in college."

"You can't believe that," she whispered. "Don't just let him leave. That's your best friend since college."

"Not anymore."

"Reid, wait! Please." Zora rushed down the front steps and grabbed hold of his arm as he walked away. "Please!"

The afternoon air turned brisk and Lawrence's neighbors had begun to decorate their homes with Halloween decorations. Red and yellow leaves swirled on the sidewalk in the breeze, and Zora pulled her cardigan tighter around her shoulders with one hand as she held on to Reid with the other.

He tugged his arm from her grasp, retreating from her. "What am I waiting for, Zora?" His voice was strained and his hands clenched into fists. "For you to actually believe me when I told you I would never steal Lawrence's writing? Is this why you started acting funny? Why you basically *ghosted* me?"

Shit. She took a deep breath. "Well, at first I thought that you had plagiarized Lawrence's book. But then when I asked you about it and you said he took your lines, something just didn't feel right. It felt like you were hiding something. I just had to figure it out to be sure. I needed some space until I did, and now here we are." She lifted her palms and then dropped them to her sides.

"Okay, Nancy Drew, well, thank you for solving a mystery that didn't need to be solved and potentially bankrupting me in the process." His sarcasm sliced through her like a blade.

"I'm sorry! I didn't know about your arrangement. I just felt like something was off, and I wanted to address it with the two of you. How was I supposed to know—" She gestured wildly, a knot growing in the pit of her stomach. It took everything in her not to throw herself at him; she ached, wanting to wrap her arms around him and assure him that she would never intentionally do anything to hurt him.

"Me telling you that our working relationship is complicated wasn't code to start snooping around, Zora. Why couldn't you just leave it alone?" He motioned with open hands toward her, his eyes wide with frustration.

Zora stood firmly. "Why did you have to lie? You've been feeding me bullshit about *social media* all this time, and I knew you were hiding something. Was I supposed to just ignore that?"

Reid stared at Zora for a long moment. "You literally can't help yourself, can you? You're still poking around, trying to get to the bottom of some great mystery." He stepped closer to her. "This isn't a game, Zora, or one of Lawrence's books. This is real life. I should never have let you in, or let you read that stupid notebook, but I promise, there's no romanticized reasoning behind this agreement—Lawrence didn't want people to know he needed a ghostwriter. It's that simple."

"Is his writing that bad?" She scrunched up her face, picking a poor moment to be funny.

His eyes bored into hers, and she fought the urge to lean forward. He remained silent, his stillness almost unnatural as the leaves of the cedar trees around them rustled in the breeze.

"Okay, so humor wasn't the way to go." She shrugged. "Please talk to me." *Please let me fix this.*

"What is there to say, Z? You don't trust me, but you're willing to put my whole situation on blast, which not only ends the money that I was receiving for the work but also puts me at risk of a lawsuit."

Her eyes watered. "I thought that I was helping. If Lawrence could see that he was taking advantage of your talents, I thought that he would encourage you to go after your dreams and could get you closer to publishing your own work. In your name." She longed to reach out to him, for him to hold her. The looks of anger and disgust on his face twisted her heart, threatening to tear it to pieces.

"And how spineless do you have to think that I am to just blindly go along with Lawrence taking credit for my work?"

"Clearly, I didn't think this all the way through. I'm so sorry, Reid. I should have trusted you, but I was trying to defend you. Can't you see that?" *Please.*

"What made you think that I wanted or *needed* your defense?" The darkness in his voice made her step backward.

There it was, the tone she hadn't heard since their very first meeting at the bookstore all those weeks before. He was completely closed off—the wall that he'd barricaded around himself at Lawrence's signing erected before her eyes. Reid's tough exterior was impenetrable to her pleading eyes. He glared at her, through her, his gaze piercing her like the freshly sharpened daggers used by the villains he'd written about in Lawrence's books, though no one would ever know.

Zora held back tears, trying to think of a way that she could right things between the two of them but also between Reid and Lawrence. Reid took a step back, apparently satisfied that there was no good answer to his question. She looked up into his face, willing away the pinch between his brows. "Come back inside," she begged. "We can get to the bottom of this. He's not going to sue you, Reid. You're his best friend. This is my fault."

"You're damn right it is," he retorted. "And why would I go back in there? He told me to leave. I'm no longer welcome." He ran his hand over his mouth and beard, shaking his head.

"He didn't mean it." She tried to wave it away, but Reid stepped closer, lowering his face to eye level. She looked into his eyes; not an ounce of care was found in those dark pools. "Please, please stay with me," she whispered. *I love you.*

His voice was barely above a whisper. "Don't you think you've done enough?" Reid turned toward the street without another word or glance in her direction. Each step away from her was another twist at Zora's heart.

24

"Lawrence." Zora took careful steps back into the kitchen, unsure what she'd find inside.

He sat at the dining table, drinking a glass of wine. He wasn't looking at her, but he was aware of her presence. "What now?"

"I just want to talk to you. Would you rather I leave?" She sat at the opposite end of the table carefully.

He shrugged, taking another sip of wine. "What more could you possibly have to say? You've just ruined a business arrangement that had been working for both of us for a decade. I mean, I appreciate that you've brought Reid's breach to my attention, because I will definitely make a nice chunk of change for that, but what else is there, Zora?"

"Come on, Lawrence. Are you really going to sue your best friend?"

"He's not my best friend. Not anymore."

"You're willing to lose him because I figured out that he wrote your books? He has to mean more to you than that."

"I mean, what do you know, Zora? I still don't believe you figured this out on your own. I know he told you, and I'm going to prove it."

"What could he have gained by telling me?" She threw up her hands. "That doesn't even make sense. You think he masterminded what just happened—just to win my affection?"

"That's the only explanation. Reid was never cut out for the limelight. That's why he sold me his stories in the first place—he wanted his small little existence with his students and his classes. He wanted his characters to be out in the world, but didn't want to have to do the promo. I bet he figured that if you knew that I didn't write those stories, all that interest that you had in me would go to him instead."

Taken aback, Zora stared at him for a long moment. "Lawrence, yes, I'm a big fan of the series, but once I met you, the books weren't the reason that I liked you. I'm not a clout chaser—I genuinely liked getting to know you as a person."

He scoffed, but she continued.

"I'm serious! You're charming and charismatic, you're well traveled, you have excellent taste in food and wine, you're funny and intelligent and handsome. But you know all of that. I would have liked you without the books—that was just a bonus."

"But you don't like me now that you know the truth."

"I don't like your behavior—how quickly you've turned on your friend—y'all have known each other for almost twenty years! How can you cut that off so quickly without even having a real conversation? He didn't tell me anything. I swear!"

"You really expect me to believe that you read a couple of passages and magically it all came to you. Deduction would have to be your superpower for that to be true."

"But you see, that type of thinking is how I figured it all out—you are *clueless* when it comes to women. You literally tried to mansplain a female orgasm to me. You had no pride in the female character in your own book being such an integral part of your main character's success. You had no idea that Reid made her to have that kind of lead potential because she was based off of a lead herself, or that she was made that way *because* Reid sees that Black women are the backbone of the community. And you don't even bother to ask him for that background, which honestly would do a lot to enrich your talks at book events.

"You took the creativity of your friend as your own because your ego is so big that you think you deserve the accolades while Reid, that humble teacher, sits back and lets you take it. How can you call yourself his friend? Maybe he chose not to be in the limelight because you so clearly wanted it for yourself."

"You don't know the whole story, Zora. You may think you're some modern-day Sherlock, but I assure you, sweetie, you're not." He sneered at her, looking her up and down as if his assessment held some value.

"Sweetie?" Her eyebrow arched. "Now, look here. I don't know who you *think* you are, Lawrence Michaels, but I assure you that you're not God's gift to anyone. Maybe someday, you will be, but you need some work. You have money, and you flaunt it generously, but that's because you're deficient in other ways. For instance, yes, you're good-looking and charming, but you have the stamina of a string of hiccups and your generosity clearly does not extend to your sex game. How about you invest in some lessons on the female orgasm before mansplaining it to a lady? Or get yourself some of those little blue pills and practice getting past the first song on the playlist before nutting, playboy? In any event, you're no longer my concern."

He shook his head bitterly. "All you bitches are the same."

Zora stood slowly, resting her fingertips on the table as she looked him dead in his eyes, unblinking, her head high. "I will be that bitch for *you*, Lawrence. Don't try me."

He opened his mouth to say something but shut it again. *Good boy.*

She slung her purse over her shoulder and turned toward the door. "That's what I thought."

"What am I going to do?" Zora's eyes were swollen from crying as she lay on the sofa between Granny and Emma. Her head rested in Marion's lap, and her legs were draped over Emma's. Granny ran her hand over her granddaughter's hair to soothe her in the same way she'd done when Zora was little.

Zora arrived home from Lawrence's house and immediately sent up the bat signal. Emma and Granny rushed home from the bookstore, leaving Tanesha to handle business for a couple of hours only after she promised to call if she needed any help.

"Can I ask a question without you thinking I'm not on your side?" Emma tilted her head.

Zora sniffled. "What?"

"Why didn't you take this information to Reid first? You'd been icing him. Once you figured out the whole truth, you had no reason to stay quiet."

Zora's chest heaved. "Well, in retrospect, that was clearly the better option," she sobbed. "Everything happened so fast, and I—" Her words became an unintelligible mumble.

Marion eyed Emma, shaking her head, so Emma zipped her lips. "It's okay, baby."

Z wiped her eyes with the cuff of her sleeve. "I was just thinking on a macro level. I thought that if I pointed out that I knew, and that they didn't have to hide their arrangement, then we could move forward honestly."

"Did you still want to try with Lawrence?"

"Well, no, but see this is how hindsight is 20/20. I should have contacted Reid first, but Lawrence had been blowing up my phone to apologize for the night before."

Emma tapped Zora on the thigh. "What happened on the date this time that he was trying you on speed dial anyway?"

"Ugh…remember the goal we gave him?"

"Tell me he achieved the goal this time at least."

Zora raised her head from Marion's lap to look Emma in the eye. "Not only did he not achieve the goal, but he told me that I was insecure in my body and that's why I was having trouble orgasming."

Emma pushed her braids away from her face, cupping her hand to her ear. "Excuse me, say what now?"

"Seriously. I thought I was hallucinating when he said that shit."

Granny tapped an index finger against her cheek. "And what did you say in response, baby?"

Zora laid her head back down. "I told him that I need more time than he does to get off and that our combined sexual experiences add up to a total of six minutes."

Emma's mouth dropped open, and her chest heaved with laughter, but no sound came out. When she finally took in a breath, she shrieked and cackled until Zora and Granny fell into fits of giggles, too. Emma laughed so hard that tears fell from her eyes. "And then what happened?"

"I threw his shoes out on the porch and told him to get out of my house."

"Did he have clothes on?"

Zora shrugged. "Pants. That was enough."

Granny chuckled. "Well, that explains why the neighbors were worried this morning. They stopped by as we were leaving to ask if everything was okay. They overheard y'all arguing."

Zora rubbed her temples. "Yeah, he yelled that I was being

immature when I slammed the door in his face. I'll bake them some cookies or something, and they'll forget all about it."

"Maybe. It's not easy to forget a half naked man being locked out of the house across the street, baby. Lawrence is a lot of things, but he's still quite a looker."

Zora groaned, covering her face with her hands.

Emma was still piecing together the story. "But how did you get from that to figuring out that Reid was Lawrence's ghostwriter?"

"It just became so clear to me that he knows nothing about women. He couldn't have possibly written Annette with that kind of intentionality, because he doesn't even believe women to be that capable. That's how I knew it wasn't just a few lines Lawrence stole. It was the whole book. The whole series of books."

"Your Zor-lock skills are next level, girl." Emma shook her head.

"Well, they didn't help me see that I was addressing this in the wrong way." Zora sat up, putting her feet on the floor. Granny leaned her head on her granddaughter's shoulder. "He's going to understand, right? That I didn't mean for it to happen like this?"

"I'm sure he already knows that, my sweetie," Marion murmured. "Just give him time."

She sniffled reluctant acquiescence. "You're right."

Granny patted her leg. "You need to eat something, baby." She pushed herself up from the sofa and headed toward the kitchen.

Zora snuggled against Emma. "What are you gonna cook?"

"I thought I might make your favorite. Want some smothered pork chops?"

Emma's stomach gurgled and growled before Zora could

answer. Zora frowned up at her friend who covered her stomach with both hands.

"Well, damn, Granny, I think Emma's stomach just asked if it could get in on the action, too." Zora cracked a smile that turned into a giggle.

Emma laughed until her stomach began to growl again. "I think it's yelling at me."

Zora doubled over, laughing so hard that tears fell from her eyes. "When was the last time you ate something, heffa? It sounds angry!"

"I had to abandon my pastry to get back here, weepy!" she retorted, her eyes popping wide as her stomach continued its angry gurgling. She pushed Zora off her. "Back up. It might force me to eat you in a minute."

Zora fell off the couch and lay flat on her back, convulsing with laughter. "If the alien pops out of your chest, I'm running for it."

"Bitch, shut up, it's getting you first for taking its pastry."

Between fits of cackles, Zora sat up, wiping her eyes. "You're right. I'm fucked."

25

Zora: Please talk to me, Reid. I'm so sorry for what happened.

Zora hated the fact that, just days before, she'd given this same silent treatment to Reid. The lack of response physically made her body ache, and if his feelings were anything like hers, she regretted putting him through such unbearable torture. At home she sat on the sofa as dusk claimed the sky, casting shadows through the windows. She watched her phone, hoping to see an ellipsis pop up.

Nothing.

"Z? What are you doing sitting here in the dark?" Emma opened the front door as she and Granny arrived home from the bookstore. "Everything okay?"

"He still won't respond to me."

"Give him time, my baby. He just needs a minute." Granny sat next to her on the sofa and patted her thigh. "Just think of this from his perspective. You tanked his writing career and might have gotten him sued in the process. That's a lot to forgive." Never one to sugarcoat the truth, Marion didn't attempt to now.

"But I didn't *mean* to!"

"Of course you didn't, my sweetness, but it's still a lot."

"You basically got him fired from a job, Z," Emma spoke up. "If you messed with my money, I'd be pretty pissed off, too. Granted, I do work for you, and the only way you'd mess with my money is if you fired me, and of course that will never happen...but this isn't about us. This is about you here. I digress."

"Okay, I know y'all are trying to help me, but I was better off sitting here in the dark. Maybe you should let me wallow." Zora shut her eyes, tired from overthinking what she could do to fix things for Reid.

"Now, that is simply out of the question," Granny said gently. "You are a Dizon, and you will carry yourself accordingly, young lady. Now, pick yourself up and stop feeling sorry for yourself. No, you didn't intend to hurt him, but you have, so keep trying and make it better. Besides, it's not like no one else would ever have figured out their little scheme—it just took someone to pay attention. Someone would have caught on eventually."

"Yes, ma'am," she mumbled, looking at the floor.

"I'm sorry, what?" Granny's eyebrows rose slightly, but it was enough for Zora to get her act together.

"Yes, ma'am." She cleared her throat, sitting up straight. "I just have one question, because I'm all out of ideas."

"Now what's that?"

"How do I make it better? Because I'm sorry, but he won't know, because he won't even read my texts or answer my calls."

"Maybe he just needs a minute, Z. You took a beat when you thought he was stealing Lawrence's work. You just need something to distract you for a little while," Emma suggested, leaning against an armchair.

"Yeah, what am I supposed to do until then?"

"We could do a weekend getaway. Maybe a spa weekend or something?"

"Both of us? And who's going to run the store? No. We can't do that."

"Why not? You own the place, Zora."

She bristled. "That's not the way you run a business."

"Zora. People will survive for two days. Or, you could have Tanesha just open the store for limited hours. That girl could pull a six-hour shift in her sleep."

She pursed her lips, mulling it over. "You really think she'd be okay?"

"Are you kidding? She's a pro! You've barely seen her in action. You've been so busy balancing two men along with the books. She's ready."

Granny clapped her hands together. "Then it's settled. Girls' trip!"

"You'll come with us, Granny?" Zora hugged her close.

"I wouldn't miss it. Besides, this one is my treat. I have a friend who owes me a favor."

"Jesus, this is what people do for you when they owe you a favor? Do I want to know what you did for them?" Zora leaned back in her lounge chair, feeling the sun warming her face.

The Chameleon Resort and Spa was nothing short of spectacular. A five-star resort nestled in the heart of Virginia, the Chameleon was the ultimate spa experience on a massive estate. The resort's acreage included a barn and stable of horses for riding, hiking trails, indoor and outdoor pools, a healing garden, a state-of-the-art spa, four restaurants, three bars, a vineyard, the hotel itself, and a slew of luxury condominiums toward the border of the property.

The ladies were welcomed like VIPs, put up in a massive suite where they shared a common living space but each had their own bedrooms and bathrooms, and were treated to every luxury the spa could offer. On the first day they enjoyed facials, scrubs, seaweed wraps, and massages. The second day they had morning mud masks before enjoying a leisurely afternoon by the pool. Luckily, they'd made it to the resort the week before the outdoor pool closed for the season, and the weather was still unseasonably warm and beautifully sunny.

"Oh, the owner and I go way back. In fact, when we were younger, I taught her daughters their first dance lessons. And when her granddaughters were ready for dance, I gave them private lessons though I'd already retired." Granny leaned back, her wide-brimmed visor protecting her face from the elements. She wore a long-sleeved shirt over her bathing suit, having no intention of actually getting in the water. "We've known each other for over forty years, and she's been asking me to come for a visit since she opened the place. She was delighted when I called her to tell her I was bringing my granddaughter and bonus grandchild."

"You think of me as a bonus, Granny?" Emma sat up, a wide smile spreading across her face.

"How could I not, my darling?" Granny pressed her index finger against Emma's, opening her arms to embrace Zora's best friend, who was visibly moved by the admission. "I've known you since you were six years old and snaggletoothed. You came over to bring Zora candy on her birthday and have been best friends ever since."

Emma's parents still lived in California, and she went home for the holidays to visit, but she'd been warmly welcomed into Zora's family. She had been there with Zora when both of her parents passed, and though Zora had her half sister, she always considered Emma her second sibling.

Zora watched their exchange, amused. She felt good in her high-waisted bikini, which had a colorful ruffle over her bust, flattering her curves. *This was exactly what I needed.* "Stating the obvious, but okay."

"Oh, shut up, Z." Emma stuck her fingers into her glass of cucumber ice water and flicked the cool droplets at her. "You finally look like you're feeling better. Find your Zen, did you?"

"Yes, I found my Zen. Apparently, my Zen is having a scrub and massage by a very strong and sexy woman named Zoe. That woman was so fine she had me questioning my own sexuality."

"Oh, my God, yes," Emma gushed. "Zoe did my seaweed wrap and if I didn't think this was such a classy establishment, or that it could get back to Granny's friend who owns the place, I would have busted it open right on the table for her."

Granny covered her mouth with her hand as she giggled.

Zora snorted. "Shut up. You know, I can't stand you! Do you even know if she's into you like that?"

"Of course I know. It's not my first time!" Emma dug into the pocket of her spa robe, which hung on the back of her lounge chair. Her boy-short bikini showed off her strong, muscular thighs. "She gave me the digits."

"Oh, well, all right! Does this mean that you're officially about to disband your little roster?" Zora sipped on a green smoothie.

Emma sipped her water thoughtfully. "I don't know, maybe."

Zora's mouth dropped open. "You said you wouldn't do that until you were ready to fall in love. You sayin' you're ready?"

She nodded. "I think I might be. I mean, look at you. You didn't think you were ready."

Zora balked. "I'm still not ready."

"Tuh! The lies you tell." Emma walked to the edge of the pool and tested the water with her toes. Satisfied, she sat down on the edge, dunking her legs into the crystal-blue surface. "You love Reid. Why else would you be sulking in the dark when he doesn't respond to you?"

"I just feel guilty. That's all. It's not love."

"I don't buy that for a second, but if that's the story you're going to stick to…" Emma shrugged and then hoisted herself into the water, holding her breath as she plunged toward the bottom. When she came up for air, she flipped her braids up and out of her face, sending sprays of water in Zora's direction.

Zora sat with Emma's words, allowing the cool water to entice her into the pool. She jumped into the water next to Emma, lifting her torso so that she floated on her back. Gliding her arms along the surface, she thought about Reid and the prospect of never hearing from him made her gasp for breath. Still, that was a reality that she might face.

And what if he does call you back? What will you say? She lifted her head and guided herself to the edge of the pool, where she rested her head on her arms. *Can you trust him?* NDA or not, he'd still lied to her face about the work he did for Lawrence. She had more questions than answers, and she hated being unsure of herself.

The one thing she was sure of was that Emma was wrong. What she was feeling was not love. Not possible. She wiped the thought from her mind as she patted her face with a corner of a towel. The writing contest was coming up. Reid's students were participating in the event, but that didn't mean that he'd show up or respond to one of her messages. Maybe it was best that he didn't. The last thing Zora needed was drama as she announced the winners. What mattered most was that the event was going to put a spotlight on young writers in the community and help put her store on the map. She needed to make sure that everything went off without a hitch so that she could prove once and for all that she was the right person to take over the *D.C. Speakeasy* event moving forward.

26

The bookstore was filled to capacity with young writers and their families, buzzing with excitement as they awaited the announcement of the contest winner. Granny navigated the room, greeting the various family groups, and inviting them to partake of refreshments laid out near the coffee kiosk.

Chef Andrea described the various hors d'oeuvres and truffles that she was contributing to the evening. She had been delighted to receive Zora's call, and when Andrea heard about the event, she offered to donate food as a sponsor. Having been born and raised in D.C., Andrea was thrilled to hear that local students would win and be published, giving them more incentive to follow their creative dreams, so she whipped up some of her favorite bites to celebrate the contest winner.

Zora stood waving at guests. Recognizing some of Reid's students, she walked over to greet them and was met with big hugs.

"Hi, Miss Zora! Thank you so much for putting on this

contest!" A girl in pink camouflage pants and a hot pink tank top embraced her.

"Hi, Nicole. I'm so glad y'all made it!" She hugged the girl back, opening her arms to some of Nicole's classmates, too.

"The whole class participated, so everyone is on their way." Nicole's hair was swept back into a hefty ponytail, with all of her baby hair laid in perfect swirls.

Zora nodded. "I'll keep a lookout for others. Help yourself to some food, and see if you can grab a seat." Emma and Brian set out folding chairs in every open spot, attempting to keep a clear walkway for guests.

Granny reached for Zora's hand and leaned close. "I've never seen the store this full, baby. Your parents would be proud to see what you've done here."

Zora squeezed her hand. "You think so?" Her breath caught in her chest as she surveyed the store. People sat with little plates on their laps, marveling at the gourmet bites of food and the rich truffles, while others held stacks of books to purchase after the announcement was made. Emma worked all morning on a display table of anthologies from previous years that included her contest winners, and almost every one of Reid's students had picked up one or more to devour when they got home.

"I know it. And they're not the only ones, sugar." Marion squeezed her hand. "I am so proud of you for following your dream and building something that you love so much. Watching the way that you care about this place is what's always had me convinced that you would be a great mom..."

Zora readied herself for another impassioned plea for great-grandbabies.

"But even if you decided not to have children, this place has been your baby, and watching it grow and your business expand brings so much joy to so many people. You've really found your purpose, baby."

Zora's eyes filled with tears as she hugged her grandmother tight. "Well, it wouldn't be what it is right now without you, and Emma, and Brian, and Tanesha. And Tessa and Safina. And Mama and Daddy. This has been a dream come to fruition, and I'm just grateful." She dabbed at the corners of her eyes with the pad of her finger, one arm still wrapped around Granny.

"Well, I'm gonna take my seat. It looks like everything is about to get started. You ready?" Granny cupped Zora's face, wiping away one final tear. "Your makeup's fine, baby. Go on and get up there."

Her granddaughter smiled, sniffled, and kissed her grandmother on the cheek. "I love you."

"Not nearly as much as I love you, dear heart."

The microphone emitted a high-pitched wail when Emma turned it on. "Hi, everyone. How are y'all doin' tonight?" The crowd erupted in cheers and applause. "Thank you for joining us at Opus Northeast! I am Emma, the assistant manager here. We're going to get started in a few minutes, so if everyone wants to come close to the sitting area, we set out more chairs."

Granny found her seat, which some of the students saved for her. A regular patron seated next to her struggled to eat some food while holding her toddler in her lap; her niece was one of the contestants. Granny scooped up the baby so the woman could eat, and Zora rolled her eyes when Granny pointed in her direction and then hugged the little boy tightly. She nuzzled his neck and he smiled big, as onlookers crooned over his toothsome grin. Then her eyes widened, and Zora turned to see her niece ambling toward the seating area. Zora wrapped her arms around Safina, who looked more grown every time she saw her. "Hey, college girl."

"Hi, Auntie. You know I couldn't miss this. I heard you spoke to Mr. Hughes's class." Safina's petite frame was clad in a GW sweatshirt and some ripped jeans.

"I'm glad you made it, sweetie."

"Mom wanted to make it, too, but she had to stay late at work."

"Oh, that's okay. This is a long hike from Baltimore after a full workday. We're just about to get started, so go say hi to your granny." She watched Granny hold the baby in one arm so that she could hug Safina with the other—Marion practically glowed with love for her great-granddaughter. Zora made her way over to Emma, whose eyes seemed trained on someone near the door. "You good?"

"Mmm-hmm. But really, I should be asking you that question."

"Why?"

Emma signaled by lifting her chin in the direction of the front door. Zora's eyes scanned the crowd until they locked on another pair looking directly at her.

"Reid," she breathed.

"You gonna talk to him?" Emma asked in a hushed tone, wary for once of all of the people.

"Seems inevitable."

"Why don't you sound happy? You wanted to hear from him." Emma rested an elbow on the nearest bookshelf, turning toward Zora.

"How can I trust anything he says?" *What if he's hiding something else?*

"You've been wanting to hear from him, and now he's here."

"And I want him to forgive me, but do you think that he sees that he did wrong, too?" Zora's feelings were all over the place once she saw him. She wanted to hug him and kiss him and shake him.

"You'll kick yourself if you don't hear him out. If you have feelings for him, maybe give him a chance to explain. You don't have to decide anything today, right?"

She nodded. "You're right. Okay, well, let's focus. I've got awards to announce."

Emma grinned. "That's my girl. Okay, here are the envelopes with the winners. Be sure to thank our sponsors and nudge people toward refreshments because Chef Andrea brought a shit-ton of food."

"Got it." She took the envelopes and tried to remember all of the sponsors who contributed. *I should have written out a note card.* "Do I have any lipstick on my teeth?" She bared her pearly whites to make sure her matte lipstick hadn't lifted.

"Nah, you good."

"Thanks, sis."

Zora picked up the microphone and turned it back on, turning toward the crowd. Zora was surprised to see that Reid had taken a seat next to Granny—one of his students vacated the seat to go and stand with her friends toward the back of the room. The anxious, hopeful faces of high schoolers kept her focus off Reid. "Good evening."

Granny, Reid, and several of the adults responded. "Good evening."

Zora put her hands on her hips and side-eyed the crowd, whose laughter boomed in response. "Y'all know better than that! Now, I said good evening!"

"Good evening!" the crowd shouted in response, several of the teens tittering with their friends.

"Thank you all so much for joining us tonight! As you know, this contest is something that's very near and dear to my heart, and we have a lot of people to thank for helping us to put this together now for the fourth year in a row!"

The crowd whooped and applauded, and out of the corner of her eye she saw Reid whisper something to Granny that made her nod in approval. *What did he say?* She caught herself and looked down at the envelopes in her hands. *Sponsors!*

"Before we announce the winners, and I say *winners* because we had so many incredible submissions that *two* writers were selected, we need to recognize our sponsors. Huge thanks to the *D.C. Speakeasy*, DCMV Live Radio, Kerri's Coffee, Corner Bistro, author Dr. Cathy Clarke, and Chef Andrea West for their generous donations and support—we would not be able to offer this contest without you, nor would we be the community that we are without you. To the *D.C. Speakeasy* in particular, thank you for being the impetus for these annual anthology publications that highlight up-and-coming D.C. voices—you are helping to motivate and inspire our young people. To DCMV Live Radio, thank you for helping to publicize our event. To our patrons and proud parents, thank you for your support both of Opus Northeast and of your incredible kids who are the reason for this contest. I hope that this is something that we can offer for many more years to come.

"And with that, I'll stop stalling." She smiled out at the crowd as they chuckled. Emma popped one of Chef Andrea's truffles into her mouth and rolled her eyes so hard that she turned away from the stage. Zora bit her lip to stifle a laugh and slid her finger under the flap of one envelope to reveal the embossed card inside. "This year our winners will have their stories published along with other local contributors in the *D.C. Speakeasy's 'Young Writers Anthology'* and five hundred dollars. They'll also be interviewed on DCMV Live Radio. Our first winner is… Nicole Brown."

One of Reid's writing students, the girl in pink camouflage, covered her mouth in shock, her eyes wide. As her mom shouted her support, Nicole made her way to the stage to accept her envelope. Reid whooped and stood to his feet, applauding the young author.

Nicole shook Zora's hand and then hugged her tightly as her emotions began to take over. Zora squeezed her tight and whispered, "You killed it, great job! Stand up here while I call the other person up, okay?"

Nicole nodded, wiping happy tears from her eyes.

"Huge congratulations to Nicole! Now for our second winner. Drumroll please." People in the audience clapped their hands against their knees to invoke the sound effect. "The second prize goes to… Stephan Miller."

Another of Reid's students stood back toward the coffee kiosk with his mouth hanging open. A tall, lanky kid with his locs tied back from his face and a pair of rainbow-colored frames perched on his nose pointed one finger to the sky and tapped his chest lightly. As he neared the front, he went straight for Reid, slapping him five and then allowing Reid to embrace him tightly, clapping a hand against his back.

Zora sucked in a breath. Stephan made his way to the stage and fist-bumped Nicole before putting his arm around Zora's shoulders. She tugged Nicole to her other side, raising one of each of the winners' arms in victory as the crowd cheered and snapped photos. Looking again toward her grandmother, her eyes stopped when they met the gaze of a pair looking back at her through wire-rimmed glasses.

The crowd erupted in applause and cheers. "Congratulations to our winners and all of our entrants—this year was especially tough because there were so many strong pieces submitted. DCMV Live Radio is going to start playing some music, and as you enjoy refreshments, please walk around to the story displays around the store—we've highlighted the winners as well as some of this year's runners-up. Again, thank you all so much for coming and enjoy!"

"Zora." Reid's eyes searched her face as she stepped toward him. He kept his arms by his sides, his hands shoved into the pockets of his jeans. His V-neck T-shirt pulled tightly across his chest and strained against the muscles in his arms.

"Hi, Reid." Zora's mouth tightened. *Why does he smell so good?* His citrusy scent lingered in her nose, drawing her a step closer.

"Listen, I know that I should have responded to your messages, but I needed to get my head right first." He looked at her hopefully, readjusting his glasses.

She nodded, trying her best to be detached from her feelings, assuming he'd only have the worst to say. "Sure, I understand. I mean, I did the same thing, right?"

"Yeah, but that doesn't make it right. I just wanted to apologize. I should have stayed and talked to you, but I was so focused on Lawrence and his threat to sue me. I didn't react the way that I should have, and I want you to know that I'm not mad at you for bringing everything to light. I'm sorry. Can you forgive me?" He licked his lips, watching her reaction, waiting. His hands were clenched tightly by his sides.

Zora took a deep breath. "Honestly, I've been trying to ask you for forgiveness, too, because I really feel terrible for putting you in a position where you're losing a financial opportunity and possibly being sued because of me. I should have come to you first, and instead I got caught up in thinking that I could fix a part of the dynamic between you and Lawrence, though that really wasn't my business.

"Can I forgive? Sure, but that's because it's a waste of energy to carry a grudge. But I am more worried that I will have a hard time trusting you. I keep picturing you walking away from me, and maybe that's my hang-up, but I've lost too many people I care about to be okay with people who deal in half-truths."

"But Z—"

She held up a hand. "You told me that you knew you wanted to be with me, but you couldn't tell me the truth. Instead, you lied to me, giving me the same story that you gave everyone else. That doesn't exactly sound like the start of a healthy relationship, now, does it? I don't know how we move forward." *Even though I want to.*

He swallowed hard. "Please give me a chance. I don't have any excuse for what I did. Even with the threat of the lawsuit, I should have trusted you with the truth. You deserve that."

"Damn right I do."

"I don't want to lose you, Zora." His dark eyes implored hers to open up to him. The scent of his cologne tugged her toward him, but she wasn't ready to stop resisting.

Nicole and Stephan joined them then. "Mr. Hughes, Zora, can we take a picture with both of you?"

Zora turned her attention to the students, her smile bright. "Of course!" She guided the students to stand between her and Reid, who watched the exchange. She beckoned for a nearby patron to take the photo with Nicole's iPhone.

They all smiled, and after several snaps of the phone's camera, the four turned toward each other. "Zora, thank you so much for this opportunity. I didn't think that I'd ever be published, at least not while in high school. You just helped one of my dreams come true." Nicole teared up, and Zora wrapped her arm around the girl's shoulder.

"It's my pleasure. But really, the level of your writing is the result of your talent and your teacher. I just created an outlet for people to see what Mr. Hughes was already seeing." She gestured toward Reid, who smiled at Nicole and nodded in agreement.

Stephan looked between Zora and Reid, clearly suspecting that they'd intruded on a conversation already in progress. "Come on, Nic, let's go check out those truffles." He turned to Zora, his hands pressed together in front of his chest. "Thank you again."

She smiled at him. "It's my pleasure. Congratulations."

The students walked off toward Chef Andrea, and Zora again felt cloaked in Reid's nearness. She avoided eye contact, instead looking around the room and offering a friendly smile to those who looked her way.

Reid stepped closer, whispering so that only she could hear. "Please, Zora. Give me a chance, even if it's just as friends. Let me make this right."

Zora looked down, trying hard not to emote as she looked up into Reid's eyes. "I swear to you that I'm not trying to be difficult. I just can't stop thinking about everything that's happened and wonder if there's another secret to be revealed later on. I'm not sure that I trust how I feel right now. It's not that I don't want you, because I do. But I'm scared. I need some time," she whispered back. Feeling a wave of sadness threatening to wash over her, she turned and walked toward her office, leaving Reid to watch her retreat.

27

"Remind me why we're doing this again?" Zora muttered through clenched teeth as Emma dragged her by the arm down a bustling K Street.

"Because we're not going to just sit in the house and pout after letting go of a man that you could have had if you'd wanted him."

"I'm not pouting after him," she sulked.

Emma stopped short so quickly that Zora bumped into her. Staring her friend in the eye, Emma moved within inches of Zora's face. "Tell your face that you're not pouting, because it doesn't seem to have gotten the memo. Your lip is poked out so far it's halfway down the block." She pointed at Zora's bottom lip. "Fix your face, dammit! I'm not taking you into this event looking like someone stole your damn dog."

Zora side-eyed her friend but relaxed her face. "Fine. Let's get this over with."

Emma put her hands on her hips. "You know, you used to love open mic nights. What changed?"

"I'm just not in the mood to go out, Em. I don't want to see people."

She rolled her eyes and began to drag Zora by the arm again, her braids swept up into a high bun. "By people, do you mean Lawrence or Reid? Or men in general? It's a ladies' night event, so unless one of them is performing, I think we're in the clear."

"Ugh, fine."

They entered a local bookstore café that often hosted open mic nights and poetry slams, Emma nodding at the security checking IDs. After having their hands stamped, they went straight to the bar for cocktails before finding seats close to the stage.

"We don't have to sit this close."

"Are you going to complain about everything?"

Zora sucked her teeth and sat down, taking a sip of her martini. A live jazz band was playing a set before the event started; signs on the wall indicated that the poetry reading theme for the night was love. Inwardly, she groaned, but the drink was strong and the music loosened the tightness of her shoulders. The thrumming of the double bass and the drum brush against the cymbals caught hold of her, and she relaxed into the rhythmic melody.

A server brought them another round that they hadn't ordered, and the girls surveyed the room to see if they could find who sent them. Shrugging, they toasted each other and leaned back as the first acts began to bare their hearts and souls on stage under a shining spotlight with nothing but a microphone on a stand and their notes for reference.

A teenage girl with a heart-shaped face and a bright pink outfit took the stage then smiled and waved in Zora's direction, and Zora's face lit up. "Oh, it's Nicole!" she whispered excitedly to Emma. "She was one of our contest winners. Her writing is beautiful."

"This should be good," Em whispered back.

On stage Nicole's long ponytail hung over her shoulders, framing her face. She moved the hair behind her back, closing her eyes and taking a deep breath before stepping up to the microphone. "Hey, y'all, I'm Nic. I'm working on a collection of poems right now that's currently titled *Spellbound*. Each poem is a spell that captures a moment in time in the life of a young person coming into their own. The emotions, the growing pains, the comparisons, and the many ways in which we build our identities are what I try to capture in each piece. This particular spell is called 'Lust.'"

She looked out into the crowd as a chorus of fingers snapped in response. "All right now, Nic," one woman called out, encouraging the young lady.

Everyone in the room grew quiet as Nicole lifted her hands, opening them near her eyes as if a vision were coming into view.

"That moment when we make eye contact.
Across the room.
Air crackling.
Senses heightened.
Catch these eyes.
As they sweep in your direction.
And these hips.
As they sway with intention.
And with one glance.
You've already pictured.
In your mind's eye.
A nude prelude.
Lives, lips, tongues, limbs.

Entwined in an erotic embrace.
That touched your soul.
Caught your breath.
And curled your toes.
But it wasn't meant to be.
Because I wasn't alone.
So you nodded hello.
And you watched me walk away.
Still under my spell."

Nicole smiled broadly to the audience, who snapped and cheered as she exited the stage.

Zora slapped her five as she walked by. "So good!" she whispered.

The emcee went up to announce the next performer. "All right, y'all, everyone enjoying themselves?"

Everyone cheered, several people holding up their cocktails to salute. Emma turned toward Zora. "Wow, she was amazing!"

"Right? That was some sexy shit for an eighteen-year-old."

"Listen, these kids are grown, girl. I tell you, some of them are out here living their best lives."

"You ain't neva lied. I need one of them to teach me, okay?"

"Mmm-hmm, girl. I—"

"All right, well, we're going to have our next creative take the stage. He's been here a couple times before, so some of y'all will recognize him. I want everyone to give a warm welcome to Mr. Reid Hughes."

Zora's head snapped forward at the mention of his name. "Shit."

There he was. His charcoal-gray pullover sweater hugged his body over his dark-wash denim jeans. As he stepped onto the stage, he adjusted his glasses on the bridge of his nose. He gripped a piece of paper in his other hand.

"Dammit, he looks like he smells good, too," Zora muttered under her breath. "Ow!"

Emma's elbow had connected sharply with her rib cage. "Just make sure you hear him out, okay?"

"Wait, did you know that he was going to be here? Please tell me that you didn't plan to ambush me with some bullshit." Zora glared at her friend as she rubbed her side.

"Now, it's not bullshit, and you've been in a mood all week. You need to hear him out and have an open mind. You're not doing yourself any favors by putting up this wall. What good is it doing you?"

Zora was tempted to get up, but she didn't want to make a scene in front of a bunch of strangers, and she knew Emma wouldn't let her leave. She looked back up on the stage and her eyes immediately connected with Reid's. He cleared his throat as he stepped closer to the microphone.

"Good evening, everyone." He pushed the cuffs of his sweater up toward his elbows. "Wow, it's hot up here under these lights."

"Good evening!" the crowd responded. A couple of ladies in the front pretended to fan him to cool him down.

He smiled. "Hey, thanks. So tonight, given the theme, I wanted to share something new that I've been working on. I'd like to dedicate this to a potential new love—a love that may have been cut short because recently I made the wrong choice. But that's the thing about love, right? If we don't shoot our shot, we'll never know what could have been. I just know I'd regret not taking the chance, not telling her how I feel. Y'all okay with me getting this off my chest?"

The audience murmured their agreement with him, while others searched the audience to see who Reid might be talking about. One man in the back of the room called out to him. "Speak your truth, brotha!"

Zora sucked in a breath, a million butterflies swirling in her chest.

He brandished his paper. "So this poem is called 'Intertwined.'

"Her heartbeat against mine
Our souls intertwined
The way fingers lace together
The urgency of now or never
There's sweetness in her lips
A poetry to her hips
After all is said and done
That night we became one

Her heartbeat against mine
Our souls intertwined
Our future's at stake
A mistake I did make
But I'll fight for your love
It's worth heaven above
A smile on your face
I still long for the taste"

Someone in the audience cried out at his words, garnering shushing from some in the audience and laughter from others. Zora didn't hear any of it—her eyes remained fixed on the man on stage.

Reid read on, glancing at her from time to time, her gaze seeming to give him courage.

"Her heartbeat against mine
Our souls intertwined

Her heart I'll gently carry
One day I see us married
She's all that I need
To build and succeed
The mentality to grow
Tells me what I need to know

Her heartbeat against mine
Our souls intertwined
What else can I do
To show that I love you
I'd bend on one knee
I'd do anything
My lighthouse in a storm
My heart you've transformed

Her heartbeat against mine
Our souls intertwined
I'll re-earn your trust
Quell my temper—a must
I'll knock down my walls
If it means that you'll fall
I promise my best
From this life to the next

Her heartbeat against mine
Our souls intertwined."

Zora watched his face as he pressed his lips together, the corners of his mouth curving into a tentative smile. He stepped down from the stage to offer his hand to Zora, who stood as he came closer. She placed her hand in his, and he squeezed it tightly as he gazed into her eyes. "I'm sorry, Zora. I won't keep anything from you ever again. You have my word. Just, please, give me another chance. I love you, Z."

"You mean that?" she whispered.

He nodded. "Every word."

Zora looked up into his eyes, the force between them simply too strong to resist. Grabbing the front of his sweater, she pulled him in for a kiss, the audience cheering with approval. "Good." She held him tightly, hoping he'd stay true to his promise and never let her go.

28

"I missed you," he whispered against her lips. Their bodies were inches apart—too far for his liking—so he pressed against her.

"I missed you, too," Zora breathed, leaning back against the passenger door of Reid's car. The warmth of his breath teased open her lips as she curled her fingers around the lapels of his coat. She kissed him slowly, languishing her tongue against his, sucking on the fullness of his lower lip. "We should go to your place."

His lips curved. "Are we going to make it to my place?"

She searched his eyes for a moment, watching the corners crinkle as he smiled. "Probably not, but it's worth a try." Her hands deftly moved inside his coat and under his shirt; her nails gently grazed his back.

His eyes jerked shut as he gasped. "Your hands are freezing! Jesus, if that isn't motivation to get us home…" The October air had transitioned to a brisk chill almost overnight, and Zora had forgotten her gloves.

Zora burst out laughing. "Okay, fine. Turn on the heat so my hands will be nice and toasty when we get there."

"We're closer to your place." Reid turned onto Georgia Avenue and headed toward Z's neighborhood. "We won't have any interruptions, right?"

"Nah, Emma was planning to ditch me after the event anyway so she could go hook up with her Netflix and chill guy. Granny is out with friends for her poker night."

"She really be livin' it up, huh?" He grinned.

"Granny is the life of every party she attends. Just wait 'til you see her dance!" They laughed at the thought and grew quiet. Zora ran her fingertips over the palm of Reid's hand, which sat faceup in hers. The warmth and pressure of it in her lap sent tingles to the juncture of her thighs as she thought about what he could do to her with just one hand. She squeezed her legs together, thankful they were only a few minutes from her house.

He turned into her neighborhood, and as familiar houses came into view, he smiled over at her. "I feel like I've been holding my breath, like anything that I do to disturb the universe might make me wake up from a dream."

She pinched the skin on the back of his arm and his eyes widened in surprise. "Nope! You're awake. Guess you're stuck with me." She gave him her sweetest smile and they both burst out laughing.

He pulled over, parking the car in front of her house. "I'm going to get you back for that, Z."

"No!" she shrieked, running for the front door.

He chased after her, wrapping his arms around her middle as she unlocked the door, planting a kiss on the side of her neck. "But maybe that will have to wait."

She turned to look at him as she pushed open the door, and he followed her inside. Their eyes locked, she closed the door behind him, and they removed their shoes. "That's probably a good idea."

"Yeah? Why is that?"

"Honestly? Because I can't stop thinking about your mouth on me."

Reid stepped closer to her, planting a kiss on her lips so searing hot that she moaned against him. He nudged her backward, lashing his tongue against hers as they made their way up the stairs. Articles of clothing were strewn in every direction as Zora lit a candle on her dresser, the flickering flame casting shadows of their bodies as they grew closer together. Reid nipped at her shoulder, pressing himself against her naked backside as he ran his fingertips over the front of her body.

Zora leaned her head back against his chest as he cupped her breasts in his hands, teasing light circles over her erect nipples.

"Where is it that you want my mouth?" he breathed against her ear, sucking on her earlobe.

She steadied herself against the dresser, pushing herself backward so that she could turn to face him, his hands gliding gently down her back to squeeze her ass. "You know where."

Reid dropped to his knees before her, kissing her stomach, her hips, her thighs. "Tell me what you want." He slid the candle farther down the dresser before pushing Zora back against it. He crawled closer to her and she lifted one thigh over his shoulder as she half stood, half leaned against the dresser.

"Eat my pussy," she whispered, throwing her head back as his roaming fingers made their way to her heated core, its folds slick with desire. Her knees grew weak and she was thankful to have the dresser to hang on to, her fingers gripping its edge as Reid's lips and tongue surrounded her most sensitive spot. She whimpered as he touched and tasted and licked and lapped. She moved against his mouth, riding his face as he suckled her clit, crying out when he pressed two fingers inside her.

As his fingers increased their speed, Zora's hips rocked against him until she tensed and shuddered, white lights firing behind her eyelids like fireworks. "Shit," she breathed as he kissed the flesh on the inside of her thigh. Her body jerked as he slid his fingers out of her, his thumb continuing to massage her clit.

He watched her regain control of her faculties, as she licked her lips, raised her head, and looked down at him. He continued to wind her up, gently moving his thumb in a circular motion, kissing and biting at her warm flesh.

She pushed her hair back from her face, and giggled at the sight of steam evaporating from his glasses. She pulled them from his face, setting them on the dresser as he stood. Zora placed her hands on either side of his face, bringing him close to kiss his lips. "Sorry that I steamed up your glasses." She grinned.

He slapped her ass, kissing her again, letting her taste herself on his tongue. He kissed her until he stole her breath. "You should get used to that, Z."

"I should?" She smiled, her eyes heavy with sedation.

Reid nodded, biting his lip. "You'd be mistaken if you thought I was done. You should get comfortable." He led her to the bed, laying her down on her back and splaying her knees wide. "That was only the first course."

Zora lay in the crook of Reid's arm, their cheeks pressed together, their breath becoming less staggered as their heart rates slowed. Her eyelids hung low with exhausted contentment after Reid made her body a four-course meal. "I can't believe you're here."

"Nowhere else I'd rather be." He kissed her forehead, his breath blowing a curl that tickled her ear.

"I'm glad." She closed her eyes, still processing the love they made. Opening them, she turned onto her side, resting her arm against Reid's chest and her chin on her hand. "I meant what I said in my messages, you know. I really am sorry for what's happened with Lawrence, and I never intended for things to blow up the way they did. The lawsuit—"

"Don't worry. He's not going to sue me." Reid held up two fingers to slow her down before pushing a wayward curl behind her ear.

Zora's eyes widened. "Are you sure?"

He nodded. "We talked. Took a few days for him to hear me out, and we did have to get lawyers involved, but I did the thing you're never supposed to do."

She lifted her head. "What's that?"

Reid smiled slyly. "I called his mother."

"The mama card?" Zora cackled. "No, you did not call his mama!"

"I did what needed to be done. I've known that dude since we were seventeen. I spend every Thanksgiving with his family, and this year will be no different. There's no way she'd let him sue me."

"So how did your talk go?"

"He sulked most of the time because his mom really went in on him."

"Well, good, he deserved that."

"He did. We agreed on some terms. I'd already started the next book, so I've agreed to finish that book and then he will hire someone else to continue ghostwriting for him. I know you never would have told anyone about our arrangement, but you were right. I was holding back. That's why I was so unbearable that night at the reading—it was time for this arrangement to come to an end. I was tired of seeing my work published under someone else's name. Anyway, I should be done with the draft within the next two months, and it will be up to him to see through the edits."

"Can he handle that? You never answered me when I asked about his writing."

"He's a good writer, but he's not confident in his abilities, and he's never had to see it through. He's always had others he could rely on." Reid looked up toward the ceiling, chewing on his bottom lip.

"What about your friendship, babe? Are you good?" Zora's eyebrows furrowed.

Reid rubbed her shoulders and back. "We'll be okay. It's going to take some time, but he'll come around. He did like you, you know."

Zora grimaced. "I was kind of mean to him, but he really deserved it."

"I heard about that," he laughed lightly, nodding against her temple. "Knocked him down a peg."

"A few pegs, maybe, but he provoked me." She smiled.

"He's always had an ego, but I don't think anyone has ever been less concerned with stroking it than you. He liked that—described you as fiery."

"Well, there are plenty of others out there who will be honest if he takes the time to listen, but I'm taken." She nuzzled Reid's neck, taking in the scent of his intoxicating cologne.

Reid grabbed Zora's arms and pulled her on top of him, kissing her lips. "Yes, you are."

29

One month later

The evening air whispered against the back of Zora's neck, making her shiver. November weather had rolled in and all of the beautifully colored leaves had turned brown and fallen from the trees, littering the streets and sidewalks. Zora pulled her coat tighter around her as she waited for Reid to round the car to get to her.

"What are we even doing here, babe? This place doesn't open for weeks!" He'd parked outside a dark restaurant that had a grand opening scheduled for the end of the month. Zora recognized the pitch-black building as Chef Andrea's new brick-and-mortar restaurant, Morsel—her first attempt at running her own shop. They received an invitation to Andrea's grand opening, to which they'd happily RSVP'd.

"I told you. It's a secret. You know that we have to celebrate your big accomplishment." He grasped her hand, leading her toward the entrance.

"But how are we going to celebrate at a closed restaurant?" Nothing about the restaurant gave off the appearance that it was open. The windows were dark, the doors appeared to be locked, and there weren't any cars in the side of the parking lot that was visible from the front of the building. The entire street seemed quiet, which was unusual for a Friday, but the cold autumn air likely changed a lot of plans at the last minute. Zora wouldn't have minded staying home and snuggling under a blanket herself.

Reid had insisted that they go out to celebrate, as just three days earlier Zora learned that she was being included in D.C.'s annual Forty under Forty as a successful local entrepreneur who built a reputation by supporting local youths and the neighborhood community. DCMV Live Radio broadcasted the announcement and invited Zora for an interview, and much to her delight, she was able to plug Opus Northeast and the annual short-story contest to garner more support for the next year.

Supposedly, Reid made a reservation for dinner to take her out and celebrate, which she balked at, because she wanted Emma and Granny to be a part of the festivities. Both of them were busy and assured Zora that she and Reid should go out and celebrate anyway, but clearly, Reid dropped the ball. *I'm so hungry!*

Zora tried not to pout as Reid led her toward the front door. "Seriously, babe? This place is closed."

"Or is it?" Reid pulled open the door with confidence, stunning her.

What is going on?

They stepped into the foyer of the restaurant, Zora more confused than ever. "Are you sure we should be here?" She pictured an alarm going off and flashing red and blue lights illuminating the street. "The last thing we want is for someone to call the cops on two Black people breaking into a closed restaurant."

Reid side-eyed her, unamused. "Will you just trust me?"

She raised her hands in apology, pretending to zip her lips closed.

Squeezing her hand, he led her farther inside, the only light streaming in from the streetlights outside. They passed an empty dining room and headed toward the back of the restaurant, where sliding doors with opaque glass stood before a private dining room.

As he reached for the door, Zora tugged at his arm. "Are you sure this is a good idea? This is creeping me out."

Reid wrapped his arm around her. "I've got you. I promise." He kissed her temple. "Come on." He slid open the door and nudged Zora to walk in front of him.

As she took her first steps into the private dining room, the warm lights of chandeliers flashed on, and a stunned Zora jumped as a crowd shouted, "Surprise!" at the top of their lungs, laughing and taking photos of her dazed expression. When the cameras stopped flashing, Zora squealed as she saw Granny Marion, Emma, Brian, Tanesha, Chef Andrea, Dr. Catherine Clarke, the DCMV Live Radio crew, Nicole, Stephan, and some of Reid's other students, all standing there. She turned, and in walked Tessa and Safina, each grinning from ear to ear.

"Oh, my God!" she exclaimed, laughing as she wrapped her arms around each person present. "What? I mean how?"

As she embraced Chef Andrea, Reid walked closer. "The minute they announced you as an influencer on the list, I reached out to Chef here to get you some truffles. She came up with the idea of doing a soft opening for the restaurant with a small group to try out some new menu items, and Emma and Ms. Marion did the rest. Some of my students asked if we were doing anything to celebrate, because they wanted to be here to thank you, so I brought them along, too."

Zora cooed. "Oh, hi!" She threw her arms around Nicole and Stephan, and a few other students came in for a group hug. "I just can't believe this is for me. I'm so happy that all of you are here."

"You deserve this recognition, Zora." DJ Trev put an arm around her shoulder. "That anthology published by the *D.C. Speakeasy* gained national attention, and what you've done to encourage students to write here in D.C. is a big deal. You had over four hundred kids submit a story."

"That's right," Granny Marion piped up. "The *D.C. Speakeasy* has decided that next year all anthology contributors will be selected through your contest at Opus Northeast."

Zora's mouth fell open. "Are you serious?" Her eyes welled with tears as she pressed her hands together against her mouth. "We get to do the whole thing?"

Reid nodded. "The whole thing."

"The whole thing!" Zora's friend, Sheila, from *D.C. Speakeasy* piped up behind her.

"Oh, my God! I'm so happy to see you!" Zora wrapped her arms around her. Sheila's schedule had been so hectic that she had only been able to keep up with Zora via email or phone calls. "How were you able to talk them into giving me the whole anthology?"

"When you put up numbers like you did this year, Zora, you make my job really easy." Sheila held Zora's hands in her own. "Ms. Betty told me to tell you that she's proud of you."

"She did?" A tear fell down her cheek as she tried to process the magnitude of the recognition she'd received. Overwhelmed, she threw up her hands. "We're gonna have to start earlier!"

"Okay now, hold your horses, Z, because I can already see that you're about to plan the next year of our lives. Tonight just let us celebrate your vision for Opus Northeast," Emma said gently. Chef Andrea handed the adults champagne and the students a bubbly mocktail. "This bookstore started with the thanks of your parents, rest their souls, and you are building a legacy not only for your family but for the D.C. community. I don't know anyone as selfless, driven, or as humble as you are, Zora. You deserve, sis." Emma's face crumpled as she began to cry. Zora wrapped her arm around her friend's shoulders as she tried to regain her composure. Emma lifted her glass tearfully. "To Zora's Forty under Forty!"

"To Zora!" Everyone clinked glasses together and began to take their seats around a long table set for a family-style meal.

A hand landed on Zora's shoulder, and Dr. Clarke greeted her with a kiss on the cheek. "It's so good to see you again, Catherine. Thank you so much for coming!"

"I'm honored to be invited, Zora. Your grandmother has become such a dear friend. You know, she's kept me apprised of your dating these past few weeks."

"Has she?" Zora figured. Granny and Catherine had gotten close and saw each other weekly.

"She has. Did you ever figure out what was missing from those lists you were making?" Catherine leaned forward, an amused curve to her lips.

Zora smiled widely. "Feelings. The things you need to have before you have an answer are feelings."

"Exactly right, dear. I love to see people figure it out." She eyed Reid. "It looks like you came to a decision."

Zora nodded. "I didn't realize that I'd developed feelings until we almost lost each other. And even then, I had to let go and trust myself. Just like you said."

Catherine squeezed her hand. "I'm glad. I'm going to go sit near Marion, but let's grab lunch sometime soon."

"I'd like that." Zora sat between Emma and Reid, across from Tessa and Safina, as Chef Andrea directed a waitstaff that had been hiding in the kitchen until after the grand entrance. As soon as everyone was seated, servers swooped in with heaping plates of roasted wild boar and turnips, with a caramelized peach and stout coulis, over a kabocha squash puree; wild salmon herb-roasted on a cedar plank with a lemon-mustard vinaigrette; a mushroom risotto with shaved white truffle; crispy Brussels sprouts with guanciale lardons; and a fall harvest salad with sliced apples and fresh goat cheese.

The room grew quiet as the feast arrived. Chef Andrea joined the table as Granny blessed the food, and everyone dug in. Each delectable bite was worth savoring, and Zora and Emma gasped, exclaimed, and danced each time they tasted something new. Reid watched with amusement, but Zora caught him.

When he took his first bite of risotto, his eyes closed slowly and his chewing slowed. Opening his eyes, he turned to see Zora grinning at him. "What?" he laughed.

"You're in love with her cooking, too! It's okay to admit it."

"The food is hittin'," he admitted.

She shook her head. "I still can't believe that you did all of this for me. What did I do to deserve such a grand gesture?" She looked into his dark brown eyes, his glasses reflecting light as he leaned closer to her.

"That's easy. Because I love you." He leaned forward and kissed her lips gently.

She pressed her forehead against his, exhaling slowly. "I love you, too, Reid."

His eyes widened at her admission before a huge grin spread across his face. He leaned toward her, his mouth near her ear.

"Took you long enough, Ms. Dizon. Just remember who said it first."

"Yes, Mr. Hughes." She giggled, resting her head on his shoulder. Catching her grandmother's eyes across the table, she winked at her.

Granny Marion nodded in her direction and then cupped her hands close to her mouth. "Great-grandbabies," she whispered, crossing fingers on both hands.

★ ★ ★ ★ ★

Acknowledgments

First, last, and always, Father God, I thank You for another day and another opportunity to connect with and love on others.

To Veronica Park and Jemiscoe Chambers-Black, my incredible agents over the course of this story coming to fruition, I couldn't be more grateful for you both. I appreciate and value your insights, your encouragement, your friendships. V, thank you for seeing the vision and believing. Jem, thank you for your warmth and fierce advocacy. To film agent Debbie Deuble and foreign rights agent Taryn Fagerness, thank you both for your enthusiasm and for believing in my projects. To everyone at Andrea Brown Literary, thank you all so much for the warm welcome, love, and support! I'm so blessed to have a powerhouse team of women supporting me.

To my editor, April Osborn, thank you so much for loving Zora, for helping me to see her more clearly, and for giving me space to tackle this mysterious love triangle. To the incredible team at MIRA: Gigi Lau, Erin Craig, Sean Kapitain, Laura Gianino, Ashley MacDonald, Randy Chan, Lindsey Reeder,

Ana Luxton, Kathleen Mancini, Nicole Brebner, Puja Lad, and others behind the scenes, I am so grateful!

To Cathy Charles-Williams, I am in awe of your talent—thank you for bringing Zora, Lawrence, and Reid to life!

To my family: Mom and Pop, thank you for cheering me on, for reading scenes that I'm sure made you uncomfortable, and for being okay with me not killing off a character on page. To Uncle Stuart, thank you for always being there. To Uncle Kirk, Kira, Jess, Mykel, Grett, Yvette, Ariana, the McCoys, the Welches, the Adamses, the Harts, the Grimeses, the Batistes—I am blessed. To my niece, MacKenzie, and my godson, Lucas, I love you and am always proud of you. And no, neither of you can read this one either.

To Lane Clarke, thank you for sitting with me on Zoom one random summer afternoon and talking through my weird idea for a ghostwriter mystery love triangle. Zora wouldn't be here without you. You make me a better writer, you are my family, you are truly the realest, and I simply couldn't ask for more. I love you, sis. Shout-out to Brother G, Pax, and Pickles.

To AJ Oakes, thank you for being an early reader—I am so appreciative of your feedback, your insight, and our friendship!

To Denise Williams, Charish Reid, Catherine Adel West, Jasmine Guillory, Sarah Smith, Allison Ashley, Farah Heron, Lane Clarke, Suzanne Park, Jesse Sutanto, Kai Harris, and Danielle Jackson: thank you for reading my work! I am in such awe of your talents and am honored to get to know (and stan) each of you.

To Becca, Kelly, and Rees Literary Agency—thank you for welcoming me with so much warmth. I am so honored to work with you!

To my Canon crew, Better Than Brunch crew, fellow Holograms, DInk Squad, Yay Squad, 99 Dead, Mer-Peeps, my Shut Up & Write crew, Twitterers, IGers/grammers/tokkers, my Zoom buddies: it takes a village! Thank you for the writing sessions, the Slack talks, the phone calls, the boosts, the interview recs, the inclusion. Thank you for encouraging me, nudging me to keep going, sitting with me, procrastinating with me, crying with me, and just being incredible friends. Andrea Williams, Cass Newbould, Alicia Sparrow, AJ Sass, Naz Kutub, Anna Gracia, Robin Wasely, John Clarence Stewart, Aashna Avachat, Traci-Anne Canada, Gates Palissery, Robin St. Clare, Tee, Kyla Zhao, Pammie Delupio, Terry Benton-Walker, Allie Parker, Regina Black, Harper Glenn, Alex Harper, Ariel Heim, Racquel Henry, Dante Medema, Ines Lozano, Hannah Sawyerr, Stephanie Lau, Clementine Frasier, Bianca, Jen, Hector, Diane, Christopher, Jay, Jana, and so many more, I love y'all!

To my D.C. fam: Ka-Ton, Meesh, Neil, Nicole, Sammy, Angela, Charles, Shelby, Ka-el, Elisha, Jazmine, Lawrence, Zoma, AJ, Rosie—I love and appreciate each of you. To the Buzzsaw: Everett, Amir, Matt, Sayyid, Octavius, John—thank y'all for supporting me and always having my back. Thanks to Trev and Bert for showing up and showing out.

To my law school admissions tramily and my higher ed community—words can't describe my love and gratitude. Tracy, Michelle P, Shani, Camille, Stephanie, Lisa, Annemarie, Mae, Maya, Brenda, Michelle A-S, Jannell, Carol, Traci, Margie, Sarbeth, Shawn, Reggie, Allana, Patty, Kelly, Alicia, Joseph, Alice, Juliet, Thembi, Julianne, Eric, Whitney, Anne, Nova, Miri, Abby, Darius, Finney, Linda, Tyler, Tracy, Katya, Gina, Kristina, Kott, Elizabeth, Nicole, David, Selene, Aaron, and countless others. You've seen me through some of my highest highs and lowest lows, and I wouldn't be who I am today without your example, guidance, support, love, confidence, humor, or company.

Cheers to the communities we build to live lives that we can savor!

<3 TJM